• BOOK 1 •

SKYBORN

SPARROW RISING

Spread your wings in skies of blue

AERIES

FORTRESS

MOSSY
DELL

TOWER

CANYON

BLUEBRIAR

LINDEN

THE
CLAN

FOR LESLIEANN

ISBN 978-1-338-65238-3

10 9 8 7 6 5 4 3 2 1   22 23 24 25 26

Printed in the U.S.A. 40
This edition first printing 2022

Book design by Maeve Norton

· BOOK 1 ·

SKYBORN

SPARROW RISING

JESSICA KHOURY

Scholastic Inc.

CHAPTER ONE
· NOX ·

A bolt of lightning startled the boy awake, and he nearly fell out of the tree in which he'd been sleeping. His hands scrabbled at the branch. He regained balance just as a peal of thunder rattled the Forest of Bluebriar.

Cold rain matted his black hair to his head. Curled up to make himself as small as possible, he looked up at the night sky. Hidden behind the stinging rain and shadows lurked eyes that always hunted. The boy's heart pounded against his ribs; he breathed faster and harder as he peered into the blurry darkness.

Was it just the lightning that had woken him?

Or had some inner sense detected danger?

He had flown for hours, until his wings ached and his vision blurred. His pursuers had been thorough in their search, checking the underbrush, every gulch and hollow log. They couldn't have caught up to him already.

Unless they had a Hawk with them.

The thought made him shudder. The people of the Hawk clan could see for miles, zeroing in on the tiniest details below. A Hawk would certainly speed up their search.

His body tensed; he was torn about whether to stay hidden or to fly for his life. Making the wrong choice could mean death. His eyes probed the darkness. It was thick with clouds, and as bad as the men following him were, there were *worse* things that hunted in such skies. Monstrous things, which would kill him without thought. But the boy had no choice. His pursuers drove him relentlessly, and he was forced to risk it.

Suddenly, the tree began to shake as something heavy landed above him. Leaves rained down, and when the boy looked up, he found himself eye to eye with a grinning Hawk clan brute, his dark, striped wings still half extended.

"Got you, worm!" the man snarled.

The boy threw himself backward.

He toppled from the high branch and fell toward the forest floor, branches scraping him as he tumbled. He struggled to grab hold of something but only got handfuls of leaves.

Then, moments from hitting the ground, the boy unfurled his wings.

Nearly six feet wide, shining with wet, black feathers, his wings caught the air. He lifted so suddenly that his stomach seemed to drop. He heard the Hawk man shout, but the boy was out of reach now, the trees too close together for his pursuers' larger wingspans.

The boy flew dangerously fast through the forest; it was nearly impossible to see the trees in the dark and rain, and he had to zig-zag to avoid colliding into the trunks. Though he couldn't hear them over the storm, he could sense his pursuers forming a pack above the treetops, following him, waiting for a chance to strike. It was only a matter of time.

Desperation drove him faster through the trees, until at last he ran out of forest and burst into open air. Fields rolled below, vast and end-less and terribly devoid of shelter.

The boy gasped, half from exhaustion, half from despair. Without the protection of the trees, he became easy prey. He beat his wings, angling upward, hoping to catch a strong wind that might give him an advantage.

Rain lashed his skin, his every muscle straining for more speed. The wind tossed him, the thunder echoing between his ribs. In the bursts of lightning that splintered the sky, he saw bright golden blooms of sun-flowers in the fields below. But of his pursuers, he saw nothing.

He'd lost them at last.

He began to relax, looking for a good place to land and wait out the storm. He thought he might have seen something in that last flash of lightning, a barn perhaps and some cottages.

He sighed wistfully, hoping for a warm pile of hay he could sink into for the night. His wings shivered in anticipation of rest.

Then he felt the hiss of an arrow by his ear.

He hadn't shaken his hunters at all, and now they were trying to shoot him out of the sky.

Heart pounding, the boy rolled to evade the bolts. A spike of light-ning cracked nearby, making his hair stand on end and his feathers shiver with static energy.

He chanced one look back—

And felt an explosion of pain in his left shoulder as an arrow found its mark. His wings folded and he tumbled out of control, head over heels through the storm.

With a scream, the boy plummeted from the sky.

CHAPTER TWO
· ELLIE ·

The sky glowed brilliantly blue the morning of the Goldwing Trials, and everyone from miles around the little town of Linden had come to watch the race.

This far out in the country, most were farmers. They came both on wing and in rumbling carts pulled by sullen donkeys and broad draft horses, making a festive procession down the dirt road that snaked through the sunflower fields. Linden could barely hold them all in its square, where a rope slung between two posts swayed in the breeze, marking the starting point of the race. A space was cleared around it, awaiting the contestants.

Ellidee Meadows stood with a dozen other Sparrow clan orphans and breathed in the crisp morning air. Behind her, Mother Rosemarie fanned herself with a spatula and chatted with the town doctor, occasionally poking any of her charges who fidgeted too much. Ellie had already been prodded thrice, and they'd been here less than half an hour.

"Look at that sky," Mother Rosemarie said. "Blue from east to west. I can hardly believe it, after that storm last night. Did you *hear* the thunder?"

The doctor grunted. "Haven't had a squall like that in months."

"You know, I woke up once and—it was the *strangest* thing—I thought I heard shouting from the sunflower fields, as if someone were calling for help."

"One of yours?" asked the doctor.

"No," said Mother Rosemarie. "Everyone was accounted for this morning. Ellie Meadows, will you *stop* fidgeting?" She poked Ellie again with her spatula.

Ellie practically bounced, her body humming with nervous excitement from her toes to the tips of her red-brown wings, which were folded neatly against her spine. Like the other Sparrows, she wore shades of autumn. Her fawn-colored shirt and leggings were belted with a dark orange sash, and her soft leather boots had grippy soles, perfect for making tricky landings on high places. Her shirt clasped around her neck, then swooped low in the back, leaving her shoulder blades bare so her wings could move freely.

She'd lain awake for hours the night before, listening to the thunder crash. She shared her room at Mother Rosemarie's Home for Lost Sparrows with six girls, and every one of them had snored soundly till dawn, despite the torrents of rain lashing the windows. None of *them* had stayed up all night, worrying that the Trials would be postponed due to the bad weather.

But luck was on her side. Ellie couldn't have asked for a more glorious day than this.

The Trials were held once a year, but she couldn't remember ever seeing so many people turn out for them before. There were at least twenty different clans represented. Many of the younger spectators, kids Ellie's own age, fluttered up to perch on the rooftops of the houses and shops, their wings lazily unfurled behind them. The wind rippled through their feathers with a soft fluttering sound.

The center of the square was filled with taller, more muscular figures—representatives from the high clans of Hawk, Falcon, and Osprey. Warriors and lords and wealthy landowners, it was their children the rest of the town had come to watch.

Clustered around them were the majority of Linden's inhabitants, the low clans of farmers and craftsmen: Grosbeaks, Robins, Jays, Finches, Doves, all distinguishable from one another only by the patterns and shapes of their wings, which ranged from plain gray to bright blue to dark gold. A small group of Cardinal clan members stood out brightest of all with their long apple-red wings, which they continually extended and fluttered vainly; their feathers gleamed from fresh oiling.

But most of the spectators were from Ellie's own clan—the tawny-winged Sparrows. Theirs were all familiar faces to Ellie, because she spent every day with them, out in the sunflower fields, harvesting the seeds that were their livelihood. Ordinarily, after schooling and lunch concluded, Mother Rosemarie would herd the orphans, or *Lost Sparrows*, out of the large house and into the fields their clan had been tending for generations. But they all had today off for the race, and spirits were high.

Glancing back at Mother Rosemarie, Ellie made sure the woman was completely engrossed in her conversation with the town doctor. Thank the sky the woman was sweet on him. Taking advantage of his unwitting distraction, Ellie began edging sideways, away from the other girls.

"What are you up to *now*?" hissed Prina, her freckled wings ruffling indignantly. "You're going to get us all in trouble, as usual."

Ellie grinned, put her finger to her lips, and slipped into the crowd like a minnow darting through a school of trout—small, unnoticed, agile. She kept her wings pulled tight to her back so they wouldn't snag on anything.

Everyone fell silent as the mayor of Linden strode to the starting rope. Davina was from Oriole clan, her wings dark but for a bright stripe of orange along her coverts—the feathers that formed the middle rows of her wings. Her hand clutched a small horn with a bright red tassel.

"Clans of Linden, welcome to today's Trials. As you know, a race like this one is being held in every town and city across the Clandoms on this day. And the top three finishers of each of these Trials will go on to compete against one another in the capital city of Thelantis, in the great Race of Ascension."

The crowd cheered, and Ellie kept moving, trying to get as far from Mother Rosemarie as possible. Her heart drummed in her ears.

"And the top fifty fliers in *that* race," continued Davina, "will be made Goldwing initiates, joining the mighty host of knights who defend our great king and all the Clandoms from the threats above."

Everyone's eyes flickered skyward. Just because there were no clouds didn't necessarily mean the skies were safe. Even Ellie couldn't stop her wings from unfolding a bit, her survival instincts kicking in, urging her to fly to safety.

She knew better than anyone how dangerous that sky could be.

"The time has come," announced Davina, "for those of you twelve years of age, who would prove your bravery: Step forward and speak your names."

The crowd became completely silent, waiting. It took only a moment before the first contestant stepped forward.

"I am Zain of the Hawk clan," said a tall boy with long brown-and-white wings. "I will race."

Ellie grinned. Zain was her oldest friend, and she cheered as he strode to the starting rope, spreading his wings to the roaring approval of the crowd. He was a favorite to place in the top three and advance to the Race of Ascension.

"I am Tauna of the Falcon clan!" rang out a voice, and a dark-skinned girl with black-and-white-striped wings joined Zain. "I will race!"

Three more stepped forward—the Osprey clan twins, Laida and Lowen, and Zain's Hawk cousin Ordo. Davina smiled warmly at them before calling out, "A fine group. Now, will any others put forth their names?"

Everyone began chatting and turning away; there were no more high clan children old enough to enter. The race was ready to begin.

But then Ellie cleared her throat and stepped forward. "I am Ellie of the Sparrow clan!" She had to shout to be heard over the rising noise of the crowd. "And I will race!"

Silence fell again, only this time, it was filled with confusion and disbelief. Every eye in the town settled on Ellie's small frame, as if no one was sure they'd heard her correctly. She swallowed hard but kept her head high.

Then, across the square, came the sharp words she'd been dreading. "Ellidee Meadows! Come back here *at once!*" Mother Rosemarie's face had gone red. The feathers of her wings shivered with fury.

Ellie met the matron's gaze. "I'm afraid I can't do that."

From the back of the crowd, laughter sounded.

It spread quickly. Soon, half the crowd was guffawing. But worse was the silence among the Sparrow clan. Ellie's own people, it seemed, were too mortified to be amused.

Clans were almost as close-knit as families. Embarrass one, embarrass them all. The Sparrow clan chief, a bearded elder named Donhal, shook his head at her, disapproving.

Ellie didn't falter, though her face grew hot and her palms began to sweat. Her wings clamped against her spine.

"Go home, Sparrow!" a Hawk clanner called. "Stupid girl. You'll get hurt!"

She walked straight up to the starting line and took hold of the rope, same as the other contestants. Tauna was the shortest of them, and Ellie only came to the girl's shoulder. Skies, but high clan kids were *tall*.

Zain blinked. "Ellie . . . you're not really going to race, are you?"

Ellie stared at him, wondering if he was joking. "Of course I am. We've been talking about this day since we were five, Zain."

He ran his hand over his spiky dark hair. His eyes darted to the other racers and back to her. "Ellie . . . I thought you were, you know, joking. We were kids."

"We're still kids."

"You know what I mean. Being a Goldwing . . . that's not for . . ."

Not for Sparrows was what he meant.

Ellie's heart fell. None of the others' jeers had gotten to her—at least not too deeply—but Zain's words impaled her like a sharpened stake.

"Not you too," she whispered. "I thought of everyone in this town, *you* at least believed in me."

"I do!" he said. "That is, I think you're a great flier and all, but . . . No Sparrow has ever entered the Trial for a *reason*, Ellie."

Ellie felt like he'd punched her. She saw their entire friendship in a new light now. All those years, the nights she'd sneaked out of the orphan home to build forts with him, the plans they'd made to join the Goldwings together . . . he'd never meant it. Not any of it.

Had they truly been friends at all? Had he ever taken her seriously?

"Just . . . stay out of the way, okay? I don't want you to get hurt." He flicked his wings; like the other high clans, Hawks' wings were long and tapered, perfectly shaped for fast flying. Ellie's Sparrow wings were rounder and stubbier, more suited for short flights. Ellie knew this, but she didn't care.

She said stiffly, "King Garion himself said *anyone* can become a Goldwing, if they're fast and strong enough. That's the whole point of the Race of Ascension. It's not about what clan you're from or how rich or connected you are. It's about how hard you work. You *know* that, Zain."

"Yeah, but . . . Ellie, *why* are you doing this?"

"You know why." She looked him evenly in the eyes.

Zain turned away, his face uneasy. Everyone was still laughing, and Ordo and the Osprey twins glared at Ellie witheringly.

"This is supposed to be a noble test of speed and will," pouted Laida. "And now it's one big *joke*. Go back to your clan, Sparrow. You're a farmer. You don't belong here."

Ellie stared straight ahead. Her jaw ached from being clamped so tightly.

"Enough!" the mayor called out, trying to quiet the crowd. She gave Ellie an exasperated glance but didn't try to dissuade her. Ellie was right about the rules—anyone could enter the Trial. Just because a Sparrow had never raced before didn't mean they *couldn't*.

Across the square, she saw Mother Rosemarie pushing through the crowd, surely intending to drag her back to her clan.

Ellie turned to the mayor. "Please," she whispered. "Start the race."

Mayor Davina had seen Mother Rosemarie too and looked conflicted. On the one wing, Ellie was under Mother Rosemarie's authority, as all Sparrow clan orphans were.

On the other, she knew Mayor Davina was *also* sweet on the town doctor.

"Mayor," Ellie said. "*Please.*"

Ellie had spent her whole life in the sunflower fields, harvesting seeds until her fingers were raw and her cheeks sunburned. It was what her family had done for generations, what her clan was expected to do. It was what her parents had *been* doing, the day they were killed.

No one would ever see Ellie as anything other than a farmer, no matter how much she begged to be taken seriously.

So she would have to do things the hard way.

She would just have to *show* them.

Mother Rosemarie was steps away. She lunged for Ellie.

At that moment, Mayor Davina blew the little horn. At the sound, Ellie exploded off the ground with the other racers in a fury of wings.

Mother Rosemarie's hand closed on empty air.

CHAPTER THREE
· ELLIE ·

The morning wind rippled over Ellie's feathers as her wings pumped. She'd had a good start, her smaller size an advantage over the others when it came to takeoff. They were stronger, but she was lighter.

However, once they reached soaring height, the odds shifted out of her favor. Tauna took the lead, her striped wings soundlessly caressing the air.

The sky was clear in all directions, with no sign of the storm that had rocked Linden the night before. Ellie focused on reaching the first of the five checkpoints they were supposed to pass through before they could cross the finish line. She focused on *why* she needed to reach that line first, the reason she'd spent her whole life preparing for this day, the answer to Zain's question: *Why are you doing this?*

Why race, why risk her clan's wrath, why push herself to heights no Sparrow had ever flown?

Because Ellie knew what dangers waited in the sky above.

She knew how easy it was to lose everything in a moment.

Ellie had been six years old when it happened. She'd just learned how to fly and was always running off to soar over the fields, relishing her newfound wings. But that day, she'd gone too far and hadn't noticed the cloud rolling in.

It didn't *look* threatening, like a storm cloud might. It was simply an errant puff of wool in the sky, drifting lazily and peacefully along. But Ellie knew the things that hid *in* the clouds were far from lazy or peaceful, just as she knew the rigid law: Nobody ever, *ever* flew when the sky was cloudy. This law had been ingrained in Ellie even before the alphabet: *Spread your wings in skies of blue, but skies of gray are death to you.*

But this was just one innocent-looking cloud.

Still, Ellie's parents had come winging toward her as fast as they could fly. Her father caught Ellie, held her close, and together he and her mother turned back for the Sparrows' great barn.

They wouldn't make it.

Instead, they heard a terrible sound, a sound that Ellie would never forget as long as she lived.

The screech of a gargol.

No one knew for sure where the monsters came from, why they attacked without mercy, or even how creatures made entirely of stone could fly at all, but it was known that they often hid in clouds—and if they saw you, they wouldn't hesitate to tear you in half.

That terrible day, the monster had dropped out of the sky before Ellie and her parents, blocking the way to the barn. It had a long rat-like face, a gaping mouth slatted with fangs, grasping talons, gray wings. Every movement of its stone body screeched with the spine-chilling grind of rock against rock. The thing was easily ten times the size of Ellie. In its face gleamed two brilliant blue eyes, hard as diamonds and shining as if lit from within.

Ellie remembered those eyes most of all, bright as stars and jarringly beautiful in such a twisted, ugly beast.

The gargol struck down her mother first, but Ellie didn't see because her father was pressing her face into his chest. When the creature then turned on him, its claws raking down his back and tearing his wings, he still struggled to protect Ellie. But then the creature pulled him away, and he dropped her. She fell, screaming, trying to find her wings but unable.

In the end, though, the monster never laid a talon on her. For out of nowhere, a shining figure in white armor appeared, swooping to intercept the gargol—a Goldwing knight. Ellie gasped as the woman turned the creature aside with one mighty swing of her spear. Her golden hair streamed around her as she yelled, "Get out of here, little Sparrow!"

Ellie found her wings then, but instead of flying away, she watched as the knight battled the gargol. The woman was vastly outsized, but she was swift and dodged the creature's terrible claws. Her armor shone, her spear flashed, and Ellie saw it all. She saw the gargol finally turn and flee. She saw the too-still forms of her parents lying on beds of crushed sunflowers below. She saw the sweat on the Goldwing's brow as the woman gathered her into her arms and carried her back to the barn and the shelter of her clan.

Ellie hadn't died that day. But a part of her had—the part of her that would have been content to pick seeds and spend the evenings in the great barn with her clan, dancing and shelling and hiding, while monsters lurked in the skies above.

That day, Ellie had decided that the next time she faced a gargol, the monster would fear *her*.

Now, six years later, the image of the gargol still burned in her memory. While she usually tried to push it away, today she remembered every stony feature—tooth and talon, claw and maw, those cruel blue eyes. She let her old terror spur her wings, using it to make herself stronger.

This is for you, Mama and Papa.

For every one wing beat of her larger opponents', Ellie had to flap her wings thrice. But she had known this would be the case, so she'd been practicing for years, studying Zain when he flew, strengthening her muscles and endurance so she could keep up with him. She'd volunteered for all the hardest tasks on the farms, hauling heavy pails of seeds and hoeing the soil with a ferocity that had left the other Sparrows rows behind.

Today, there would be no mercy, no allies, no friends. Ellie would have to fight for every inch of sky.

It was a beautiful day to challenge fate.

They shot out over the sunflower fields, each aiming for the same spot: an arch made of sticks in the middle of the western field. Tauna reached it first and dove. A race monitor—a Hawk clan member Ellie didn't know—stood by the arch with a piece of parchment. He marked off their names as each sped through.

Ellie had been practicing the course for as long as she could remember. She knew the route as well as she knew the way from her bed to the front door of the orphanage.

The arches were numbered so that the contestants had to fly in a zigzag, looping back and forth in a test of maneuverability as well as speed. After completing the second arch near the Sparrow clan barn,

Ellie's small form helped her again. She dove through and executed a tight flip that turned her in the other direction, sending her blazing past Zain. She was in second place now. Tauna was far ahead, probably already securing her position as the first-place finisher, but that was all right. Ellie didn't need to be first. She could be second or third and still qualify for the Race of Ascension.

She glanced back once, to see Zain's expression. He looked confused and embarrassed as he fought to catch up. Ellie pressed on, her stomach souring. She'd hoped he might cheer or grin, or do *anything* to show he was still on her side. That was what a true friend would do.

We can win this together, she wished she could tell him. *Just like we'd planned.*

But now she knew Zain had never intended to become a Goldwing *with* her. All along, he'd thought he would leave her behind at that starting line.

Ellie couldn't let him get in her head. She needed every thought to stay in this race. She could do this.

The group sped over the town square again; below, the clans cheered and clapped. Ellie was flying too fast to make out any faces, though she could imagine the fury in Mother Rosemarie's eyes. Oh, Ellie would be in *big* trouble tonight, that was for sure. All the lectures and punishments she'd gotten in the past would pale in comparison.

Zain pulled alongside her, then began to inch ahead. She beat her wings harder, struggling to match him, but fell behind anyway. He gave her one look—rueful, apologetic—before he rushed forward.

Third place. She was still in a good position, if she could hold on to it.

The next arch was set far from town, across the sunflower fields by the forest's edge. The trees of Bluebriar tangled together, ancient oaks and maples and beeches, their leaves rippling in the wind. Tauna reached the arch first, turned, and sped back, the breeze in her wake washing over Ellie, for whom the Falcon girl spared not a glance. Her face was fiercely focused.

Zain reached it next, five wing beats before Ellie, and on any other day, she'd have cheered for the cleanness of his dive, the crispness of his turn. But now she just scowled as he flew past her, and dove with her wings pinned. Slinging herself into a tight bank, she barely made it through the arch without wiping out, the tip of her wing knocking the hat off the race monitor posted there.

Wheeling around, she began the long stretch back to town and the last two arches. But where the land dipped into a small valley of sunflowers, she crossed paths with Ordo. The Hawk boy was panting, his wing beats clumsy as he struggled along.

"YOU!" he snapped. "I am *not* losing this to some nutbrained *Sparrow*!"

By the time Ellie realized what he intended to do, he'd already cut toward her and was reaching for her wing. She gasped and tried to perform an evasive barrel roll, but he'd caught her by surprise. His hand closed on her alula, the delicate joint at the tip of her wing's skeletal structure. With a vicious tug, he wrenched, and Ellie spun out of control. She plummeted toward the ground, too shocked to even scream. Ordo flew on.

Unable to untangle her wings in time, Ellie crashed into the sunflowers, their tough stalks breaking her fall, but still the wind was knocked from her lungs. She skidded across the dirt, rolled, and finally came to a halt, gasping.

Furious, Ellie punched the ground.

Pain lanced through her body, and she knew she'd be covered in bruises tomorrow. But there was no time to nurse wounds. Overhead, the Osprey twins soared toward the second arch, not noticing Ellie on the ground below. Ordo couldn't have chosen a better spot for his attack; in this dip in the land, they'd been hidden from both the town and the race monitor at the last arch. No one had seen him grab her wing, violating the first rule of the race—no physical contact.

But she could still finish. She could still place third, if she gave it everything she had. She was bruised but nothing was broken, and already her breath was returning. She had a lead on Ordo and the twins, but it was disappearing fast.

Ellie crouched, spread her wings, and prepared to push off the ground—when she heard a soft voice call out, *"Help."*

She froze.

Had she imagined it? She must have imagined it. She'd hit her head pretty hard when she'd fallen.

But then she heard it again.

"Help. *Please.*"

Ellie's stomach twisted. She *had* to return to the race or it would all be over. She'd lose and face Mother Rosemarie's wrath all for nothing. Worse, she'd fail her parents. The world would go on as it always had: sparrows farming, high clans protecting, gargols hunting. Everything caught in the same relentless cycle. It would be like their deaths had meant nothing at all, leaving no mark on the world.

Ellie couldn't let that happen. She had to make their sacrifice count. She had to become stronger, faster, better, and make the world safer. For other kids. For her own clan. For her parents' sakes.

She had to become a Goldwing knight.

But then she saw the blood on the ground, and the drag marks, as if some wounded animal had limped through the field. There were feathers too, coal black, scattered along the trail. Someone else had fallen here, and they were hurt far worse than she was. There was an awful lot of blood.

For a moment, Ellie reeled, nearly blacking out. It was all too familiar—the crushed flowers, the blood. She saw them again, her mother and father, crumpled and broken. For all she knew, this could be the very spot in which they had fallen.

Focus, Ellie. Breathe.

"Hello?" she called out.

There was no reply. Whoever it was, they must have passed out or been too weak to answer.

Ellie let out a cry of frustration. "I'm coming! Just . . . just hang on!"

She looked up as Ordo sped overhead. The Ospreys were right behind him, closing in. In moments, they all vanished in the direction of Linden, and Ellie's lead was lost.

There would be no catching up now.

Fighting back tears, Ellie thrashed through the sunflowers, following the trail of blood, upturned dirt, and dark feathers. She could feel the future draining through her fingers like melting snow. She could hear the taunts of the clans, only this time, it sounded like her own voice shouting in her head.

Go home, Sparrow.

Stupid girl.

Too small. Too weak. Too foolish.

Then Ellie parted a thick patch of sunflower stalks, and the words evaporated. The race dropped to the bottom of her mind as she gasped at the sight before her.

A strange boy lay curled on the ground, deathly pale and unconscious, his obsidian-black wings tangled around him. Blood ran from his shoulder, darkening the soil, and in his hand he clenched the broken, bloodied shaft of an arrow.

CHAPTER FOUR
· NOX ·

When the boy opened his eyes, he saw a blur of yellow in every direction.

He blinked a few times, and slowly the world sharpened into focus.

Sunflowers. Thousands of them, swaying gently all around, their bright, sunny petals framing dark centers heavy with seeds. Above them spanned a crisp blue sky.

Gradually, he became aware of the pain in his shoulder, and it made him wish he could pass out again. But something was jabbing him, keeping him awake, sending sharp flashes of red-hot pain through his chest.

He tried to say *stop that*, but it only came out as *"Grrrj."*

"You're awake!" said a voice. Then a face popped into view, a girl with enormous brown eyes and a face covered in freckles. Her hair, spiky brown, had mostly escaped the two stubby pigtails tied below her ears.

Groaning, he tried to sit up.

"Don't," said the girl, gently pressing his sternum so that he was lying flat again. "You're in bad shape. I'm going to get help."

"No," he whispered, grabbing her wrist. "Please . . . no one . . . can know . . ."

"Who *are* you?" she asked. "And who did this to you? Was it gargols?"

"Bandits," he groaned.

The girl's eyes widened. "Mother Rosemarie always said thieves hid out in Bluebriar Forest. I thought she was just trying to scare me away from the place."

The boy's head swam. He shut his eyes again. He remembered the night in flashes—the thunder crashing around him, lightning spiking the air, the wing beats of his pursuers closing in. Then the bright, scarlet burst of pain when the arrow had struck.

"Don't tell," he whispered. "No adults."

"You could die!"

He managed a half-hearted snort. "It's not *that* bad. Anyway . . . I'm on a mission . . ." His mind raced, trying to feel its way through the pain. "Top secret. No one can know . . ."

"Hmm," said the girl, who didn't seem entirely convinced. "Fine, then. I'll go get some proper bandages. Don't go anywhere till I get back."

He laughed hoarsely. He wasn't going anywhere in this much pain.

"I've wrapped your shoulder with my sash," she said. "It'll stop the bleeding for now. The healer's cottage isn't far, and it'll be empty, since . . . everyone's in town. No one will see me."

He nodded and listened as she flew off, cracking his eyes open just enough to see her tawny reddish wings with their freckled primary feathers. *Sparrow clan.* He really was in the middle of nowhere if he'd reached the Sparrow Clandom. They were the most rural of the farming clans, living way out west in the great plains. He'd flown farther than he thought during the storm.

He must have passed out again, because when he next opened his eyes, it was to find the girl applying a poultice to his shoulder. It smelled strongly of honey mixed with garlic. She seemed to know what she was doing. Her tongue poked out of her lips as she concentrated.

"Who are you?" he murmured.

She glanced at his face. "I'm Ellidee. Ellie, for short. You?"

"Uh . . . Nox. Nox Hatcher. Crow clan."

"Well, Nox, the good news is that your wound isn't as bad as it looks. You should mend quickly if you keep it clean."

"You're a healer?" He looked at his shoulder and the tidy bandaging she'd done with her orange sash. The cloth smelled like sunflower seeds and hay.

"Not really," she said. "I just know some basic stuff. I apprenticed for the local healer last summer, because according to *The King's Ladder*—that's my favorite book—every knight in training should know how to . . ." Her voice faded away, and a look so sorrowful came into her eyes that he almost expected her to start crying. But then she tightened her lips and shook her head.

"So you're a knight." Nox lifted an eyebrow.

"I might have been." She glanced at the sky and heaved a sigh. "What's done is done. I should get back to town, before they come looking for me and find you instead. Can you walk?"

"I think so." The poultice she'd used must have had some numbing herb in it, because the edge had dulled from his pain.

"Good. Then go northwest. You're about a fifteen-minute walk from the barn. Hide in the hay behind it, and I'll find you as soon as I can. I'll bring food, water . . ." She glanced at his torn, bloodied tunic. "And a shirt."

"Thanks," he said, studying her curiously. "Not many people would help a stranger like this."

She nodded. Her face still wore a mask of sorrow, as if something bad had recently happened to her. He wondered what it was. That, plus her kindness, almost made him regret the lies he'd just told her.

Almost.

He heard a sudden, distant cheer, as if from a big crowd, and frowned. "What's going on? Where am I, anyway?"

Ellie lowered her gaze. "Linden, the seat of the Sparrow clan. That sound is . . . the Goldwing Trials. They must have finished."

Understanding dawned on Nox. "You were racing. That's how you found me. You quit the race to help some kid you don't even know?"

"Well," she said. "I was sort of *pushed* into it. Doesn't matter anyway. It's done and over and I lost."

"Right, I remember how it works. The top three from each local trial make it to the Race of Ascension in Thelantis."

"Yeah. And you only get to try out once, so . . ." She shrugged. "It was a stupid dream anyway. I'll never make it into the race now."

"What do you mean?" Maybe it was her kindness to him, or maybe it was the effect of the poultice she'd applied to his wound, but Nox was feeling uncharacteristically generous. "You could still enter as a wild card."

She looked up sharply. "What?"

"They always hold open twenty spots in the Race for last-minute contestants. You didn't know that? The first twenty to sign up make it in, regardless of how they did in the Trials, or if they even competed at all. I think they started it years ago, when some important duke's son didn't win his Trial. If he didn't get into the Race, there'd have been a coup or something stupid—hey, ouch!"

"Sorry!" The girl had gripped his arm so tightly it tugged on his wound. She let go, her eyes almost feverish. "Are you serious? I could still get in?"

"If you could get to Thelantis in time, sure. The Race is in . . . three weeks, I guess."

"How do you know all this?"

He shrugged. "I grew up in Thelantis. I've seen a bunch of Races."

"You're *from* Thelantis? Then what are you doing all the way out here?"

"Believe me, I have been asking myself that for days." He grimaced, flicking a curious beetle off his trousers.

"That didn't answer my question."

Nox deflected with a question of his own. "Didn't you say you'd be missed if you didn't get back?"

"Right." She smacked her forehead. "I'll return soon. Meet you behind the barn?"

"Sure," he lied. "I'll be there."

She flew off, and he watched her until she vanished beyond the sunflowers.

Then he turned and began limping in the opposite direction of the barn, south to Bluebriar Forest.

CHAPTER FIVE
· ELLIE ·

Ellie found the town bustling when she arrived. The air was filled with kids swooping and looping on their agile wings, while the adults set out a banquet. The race was over, and the celebratory picnic had begun. The smell of blackberry pie, cherry tarts, and bacon sandwiches made her mouth water. Any other day, she'd be stuffing her face by now.

But she thought of the Crow boy she'd left in the field, and knew she had to hurry back to him. Since Mother Rosemarie kept the larder at the Home for Lost Sparrows locked tight, the only way Ellie could get food for the boy was by grabbing some from the feast. She didn't totally believe his story about a *secret mission*, but Ellie was no snitch. Besides, she owed him this much. He'd shown her she still had a chance—however slim—of entering the Race of Ascension and becoming a Goldwing knight after all.

But it would take an even bigger risk than entering the Trials had been—and more courage, more determination, and probably a bit more stupidity than Ellie was sure she could muster up.

She slunk into the town on foot, careful to avoid Mother Rosemarie or the other Lost Sparrows, who were all complete snitches. Any one of them would turn her in and receive an extra helping of dessert from the matron for their treachery.

Letting her choppy hair hide her face, Ellie shuffled through the crowd. She realized she didn't even know who'd won the Trials. She chanced a look up, spotted Zain in a cluster of his Hawk clan brethren. Judging by the grin on his face and the bottle of fizzy cordial he was raising, he was one of the winners.

"Ellie!" he said, his smile fading slightly. "You made it back. What happened?"

"She spun out at the third arch," Ordo cut in. His hand fell on Ellie's shoulder as if in consolation. She shoved it away, then looked at him more closely. His eyes were red, as if he'd been crying.

"You didn't make it," she muttered, feeling a twinge of savage satisfaction. "One of the Ospreys must have overtaken you."

"They both did," said an older Hawk. He cuffed Ordo on the back of his skull. "Lazy clod. I *told* you to practice more!"

"Shut up," Ordo snarled.

"Ellie," said Zain. "You flew well. I mean, for a minute there, I even thought you might . . ."

"Did you?" She hated how choked her own voice sounded. "I'm happy for you, Zain."

"Thanks!" He put an arm around her in a bone-crunching hug. "I hope I do you proud in the final Race."

Ellie's stomach twisted. "When do you leave?"

"Tomorrow," he said. "It's a three-week journey to Thelantis, and we'll get there just in time. It'll be me, Tauna, and Laida. The mayor is escorting us, and our parents too."

She nodded woodenly. "You might want this, then."

Opening her hand, she revealed his dagger, which she'd pinched from his belt when he'd hugged her.

"Ellie!" he whispered, glancing around quickly to see if anyone else had seen. "You have to stop doing that!"

"You have to stop falling for it." Pinching his knife had been a petty move, really, and didn't make her feel any better.

Another Hawk pulled Zain away to congratulate him with great thumping whacks on his shoulder, and Ordo leaned close to hiss in Ellie's ear. "Listen, Sparrow, you better not tell *anyone* about how you bumped into me and nearly knocked me out of the race."

She bristled. "Fifth place, huh? Even cheating, you still lost."

He snarled, his breath reeking of garlic sausage. "I'm from a high clan, *Ellidee*. There are more things I can do besides becoming a stupid Goldwing. I can join the army or get a cushy job at some fancy castle. But you? You'll never be anything more than a farmer. Enjoy your life of picking flowers." His eyes dropped to her hand, which had clenched at her side in a tight, furious fist. "Oooh, what's this now, are you going to *hit* me?"

"As if you were worth it," she said through her teeth. "A true knight doesn't indulge in petty vengeance."

"You know what else a knight doesn't do? *Give up*." He folded his arms and sneered. "But guess what I saw when I flew back across that field? I saw a little lost Sparrow girl who'd gotten knocked down and stayed there. Admit it. You gave up."

At that moment, clarity burst in Ellie's mind, as powerful as sunlight breaking through a storm cloud. She knew what she had to do. She'd known ever since she'd left the Crow boy in the field, but she'd been too scared to face it straight on and say it aloud, even to herself.

"No, Ordo." Something in her eyes must have cowed him because he took a step back. "I haven't given up."

She *would* go to Thelantis.

She'd fly in the Race of Ascension as a wild card, whatever it took.

Energized by this new purpose, Ellie turned away—only to smack into Mother Rosemarie.

The matron's hands clamped on her shoulders, and she shook Ellie till her teeth clacked.

"You empty-headed, reckless girl! Look at you, covered in scratches and bruises!"

"I'd have won," Ellie snapped back. "If Ordo hadn't cheated—"

"Since when do the high clans ever play fairly?" Mother Rosemarie was white with anger. "It's just further proof of how idiotic this was. If you'd stayed on the ground with us, it never would have happened."

Behind her, Chief Donhal glowered. "You learned a lesson today, Ellie. Sparrows are farmers. That is what we've always been and will always be. It is our clan's legacy."

"I—I'm sorry," she stammered. "I should have told you what I meant to do. But I want to protect people the way that Goldwing knight protected *me*. I want my parents . . ." She felt tears in her eyes but wouldn't let them fall. "I want them to know the world will become a safer place because of what happened to them. I can't just let them have died for nothing. It has to *mean* something, doesn't it?"

"Oh, Ellie," said Mother Rosemarie in a tight voice. For the first time, Ellie felt the matron was really looking at her. "You're truly set on this path?"

Ellie nodded furiously. Was Mother Rosemarie finally beginning to understand? "I want to be a Goldwing. I want it more than anything in the world. Don't we have as much right to learn how to fight the gargols as the high clans do?"

Mother Rosemarie exchanged a look with Donhal. As chief, he was the one who dispensed justice. But Ellie hadn't broken any laws. That was the point. Sure, she'd entered the race without permission, but that was just sneaky, not criminal.

"Very well, then," said Mother Rosemarie. "You leave me no choice."

"No . . . no choice but what?"

"You'll have to go south."

Go south.

The words struck Ellie like a twanging arrow.

"It's for your own good," Chief Donhal added gruffly. "You'll return to us in a few years, once those rough edges of yours have been filed smooth."

Go south could only mean one thing: Ellie would be sent to Moorly House, the place they sent the most troublesome kids in the Clandoms. It was a place she'd heard many rumors about: that they bound the wings of the children held there, that they only saw the sky through barred windows, that it was little more than a prison. And nobody got out until they had grown up and had the souls crushed out of them.

Ellie struggled against Mother Rosemarie's iron grip. She cried out for Mayor Davina, for Chief Donhal. No one helped her. A few of the Sparrows nodded approvingly and whispered the words *"going south"* and *"Moorly House"* and *"for her own good."*

Finally, her eyes met Zain's. His face was white, his eyes wide. He started to take a step toward her, lifting his hand as if he might help. But then one of his uncles gave him a stern look and shook his head. Zain dropped his gaze, unable to even look at Ellie.

She was completely alone.

After exchanging a firm nod with the Sparrow chieftain, sealing the decision, Mother Rosemarie towed Ellie out of Linden and down the half-mile road to the Home for Lost Sparrows.

"I'll write to Moorly tonight," she said, dragging Ellie into the room where she and the other girls slept. "They'll send someone for you within the month. Until then, you're not to leave this room. You'll use this time to contemplate your true place in this world."

After depositing Ellie on her bed, Mother Rosemarie sighed. "I tried with you, Ellie, I truly did. How many times did I tell you not to go chasing moonmoths, fixing your mind on these wild ideas? If something isn't done to tame you, you'll end up just like your poor parents. Next time, it won't be some Hawk clan bully who grabs you, but a *gargol*." She paused, and Ellie thought she detected a glimmer of regret in the matron's eyes. "Ours is a world in which no one truly flies free. You should know that better than anyone."

The door shut behind her, and the outer lock slid into place.

Ellie sat still, her hands in fists. She stared at the door and waited until she heard Mother Rosemarie leave the house. She'd stay in town till evening, with everyone else.

Giving Ellie the time she needed.

She jumped up and ran to the window, prying out the pane of glass that she'd learned to remove years ago, when she'd started sneaking out to meet Zain. All it took was a jimmy with the nail she kept hidden atop the casement, and the pane tilted right into her waiting hands.

Then she turned to grab the already-packed knapsack she'd hidden in her pillowcase. She'd been sleeping on it for months in case she won the Trials but Mother Rosemarie forbade her to advance to the Race of Ascension. Well, things hadn't gone *quite* according to plan, but as it turned out, she still needed to make a quick getaway.

Inside the knapsack were a clay jar filled with nuts, dried apple strips, dry oats, and rounds of hard, flat seedbread. She also had a small pot, flint and steel, a bottle of Sparrow Farms's best wing oil, and a roll of sturdy twine that she was sure would come in handy.

Ellie opened the knapsack to double-check its contents and to add the last three things she'd need: her most treasured possessions. First was her faded copy of *The King's Ladder*, a collection of stories and virtues any would-be knight had to learn before they took the gold-and-white uniform of the Goldwings. Part history book, part training manual, it was ragged with use. It was precious not only for the tales it told but for the warning in the front, written in her mother's flowing hand: *Watch the skies.*

Every time Ellie looked at those words, her eyes began to sting.

The Sparrows had thought her mother was silly for giving Ellie a high clan book about knights instead of the usual Sparrow folk stories and histories, but she believed that some part of her mother had known what Ellie's path would be. That she was meant for something beyond the sunflower fields.

She shut the book and put it in the knapsack.

Next was her dagger in its leather sheath, which had been Zain's until he'd gotten a newer, sharper one. She picked it up, the hilt comfortable and familiar in her palm. It filled her with sadness, reminding her of the new rift that had opened between her and Zain. But still, she was a practical girl, and the knife would be useful. It slipped into the dark orange sash she tied around her waist to replace the one she'd bandaged the Crow boy with.

Then there was the most precious thing of all—her Goldwing patch. It was the size of her hand, cut from yellow leather and embroidered on the edges with gold thread. It had belonged to the knight who had saved Ellie's life, and she'd given it to Ellie later that night, as she'd been weeping for her parents. Now Ellie pressed it to her heart.

Can I become a Goldwing? she'd asked the knight. *I want to help people like you do.*

The woman had smiled sadly, pressed the patch into Ellie's hand, and said, "If you work hard, follow the king's rules, and never give up, you can be anything."

Those words may as well have been carved into Ellie's very bones. They were a promise worth every risk.

She added the patch to her knapsack, then rolled her coverlet and bound it with the same leather cording she used to tie her hair into pigtails. The knapsack went on her back, the rolled coverlet atop it. Then she climbed through the open window, looking up out of habit at the casement above. On the pale wood was a faint dark smudge, soot almost entirely washed away by last night's rain.

Ellie hesitated, then ducked back inside and went to the hearth at the far end of the room. She ran two fingers along the inside of the chimney, pulling them away covered in black soot. Leaning out of the window again, she traced the mark with a practiced hand: a fresh black outline shaped like an open flame.

There was an ashmark drawn over each window and door on the house, as there was on every building in Linden, including the barns, sheds, and shops. And though Ellie had never been outside her town, she knew no matter how far she roamed, she would find the same mark. The ashmark was protection, a ward against gargols, and marking this particular window had been Ellie's responsibility for years. She supposed one of the other Sparrows would have to look after it now.

Her final chore accomplished, Ellie crouched on the windowsill and spread her wings. The whole world stretched before her: yellow sunflower fields, the dark green forest beyond them, and the great blue sky above.

"Sorry, Mother Rosemarie," she muttered. "But a true knight never gives up."

CHAPTER SIX
· ELLIE ·

Ellie searched high and low around the barn but found no
sign of the Crow boy. The place was silent except for the buzz
of crickets and the low rustle of the wind in the sunflowers. Barrels of
seeds waited to be shelled, and the presses that crushed the seeds and
extracted their oils sat silent. Everyone was still in town for the picnic.

Finally, Ellie flew back to the spot where she'd first found the boy,
wondering if she'd imagined the whole thing. But there was still dried
blood on the ground and an indentation in the dirt where he'd lain.

"Aha," she muttered, catching sight of bent sunflower stalks where
someone had pushed through them—heading south. *Away* from the
barn. "Either you're really bad at directions, Crow boy, or you're running away on purpose. Well, we'll see about that."

Ellie followed his tracks from the air. For a girl who'd spent her
whole life in these fields, it was easy enough to see the trail he'd
left—stalks bent the wrong way, blossoms that had the dew shaken
off them. And anyway, he was heading more or less in a straight line.
Which told her he wasn't lost at all; he'd never intended to meet her
at the barn.

She'd thought he couldn't get far with his injury. But when his trail
led her straight into Bluebriar Forest, she felt a moment of panic. If
she couldn't find him, her journey would be over before it had begun.

She had only a vague idea of where Thelantis was—somewhere in the east. Without the Crow boy to guide her, she'd probably wander in circles until her clan caught up with her. Besides, he kind of owed her, not just for the help she'd given him but for wrecking her chance at winning the Trial.

"No," she said, glaring at the trees. "I'm not giving up. And I'm *not* going to get locked up in Moorly House either."

She flitted over the fencing the people of Linden had stretched along the forest's edge and stepped into the trees.

This was the farthest Ellie had ever gone from her home.

She knew there would be a road nearby, leading to the nearest town of Mossy Dell. Mother Rosemarie had gone there once to collect a recently orphaned Sparrow boy.

Forests were dangerous places, because the trees blocked the sky and you couldn't see clouds moving in until it was too late. Gargols weren't put off by the thick canopy. They'd dive right down to the forest floor in search of prey.

Ellie tried not to think about this as she fluttered over fallen logs, rocks, and ravines choked with briars. The forest sounded different than the fields she'd grown up in. Instead of wind in the grass, she heard the chirping of insects and frogs. Glossy ferns sparkled with dew, draping over banks of emerald moss. She stopped to stare at a log covered in a line of orange mushrooms, and at a perfect spider-web strung between two trees, its fat, leggy maker crouched patiently at its center. Beams of sunlight touched the ground here and there, and motes of dust and loose green leaves drifted lazily in the glow.

And to think, this whole other world had been just a five-minute flight away. She'd grown up seeing Bluebriar Forest on the horizon every day, but it had seemed as far as the ocean until now.

She was so busy staring and wondering that she almost forgot she was supposed to be looking for the injured Crow boy. When she stumbled suddenly onto a dirt road snaking through the trees, its edges banked in moss and ferns, she looked for footprints.

But as it turned out, she didn't have to find him at all.

He found *her*, dropping out of a tree with a knife in his hand. He crouched there, eyes narrow, his face white with pain she could tell he fought to hide.

"You! Why are you following me?" he asked. "Did you tell anyone you saw me?"

She scowled at his knife. "I said I would bring you something to eat, so I did. You must be a special kind of stupid, jumping out of trees with a bare blade. Are you *trying* to get impaled? Again?"

He frowned, sheathed his knife, and stepped back. "I'm not hungry."

"Really?" She lifted one skeptical eyebrow and unslung her knapsack. She took out a round of her seedbread and waved it at Nox. He shrugged and looked away, but when she tossed it at him, he caught it and sniffed before taking a bite.

"There." He talked as he chewed. "Food delivered. Promise kept. You can go *home* now."

"Right," she said slowly. "Actually, about that . . . I was thinking, I helped you, so maybe you could help me."

He groaned. "I knew it. I *knew* being nice would come back to smack me in the face. I should never have told you about the wild card thing."

"You're still hurt," she pointed out. "Someone has to change your bandages, watch for infection. You can barely walk as it is."

"I've survived worse than this on my own."

"I brought you a shirt too." She pulled out a charcoal-colored tunic she'd grabbed on her way out of the house, from the bin where Mother Rosemarie kept clothes ready in case a new orphan turned up. It was probably too large for him, but it was clean and untorn, which was far more than could be said for his current shirt. His clothes, consisting of a loose linen shirt, leather vest, and pants tucked into shin-high boots, were all as black as his wings and hair, but the sash he wore for a belt was bloodred.

He didn't even look at the shirt. "Go home, Sparrow. I travel alone."

He turned and walked down the road.

Ellie shouldered her knapsack and followed.

"Stop following me!"

"I'm not. I just happen to be going in the same direction."

He turned, his arms folded across his chest and his black wings unfurled, as if to block her way, and she saw the pinch of pain around his eyes at the movement.

"I'm not even going straight to Thelantis," he said. "I have a stop to make on the way. A . . . an errand. For a powerful lord back home."

"Great! I can help with that too. As long as it doesn't take *too* much time, of course."

He started shaking his head, but Ellie plunged on.

"*Perseverance,*" she declared. "It's the tenth step on the King's Ladder, one of the virtues a knight must embody. And if there's one thing you should know about me on this journey we're taking together—"

"There *is* no journey!" he protested. "We are not together!"

Ellie continued as if he hadn't spoken. "—it's that I *am* going to be a Goldwing knight, and that means sticking to the steps of the King's Ladder no matter what."

Nox gave a long, loud groan.

Ellie folded her arms, unshakable.

"Ugh . . ." His voice faded, and his head cocked to the side as he studied her. His eyes were black as coals. "What about your parents? I can't have some half-crazed Sparrows come looking for you and find me too."

"I don't have any. Do you?"

He deflected with a shrug. "Aunts, uncles?"

"No one will come looking, I swear." The Sparrow clan would search the fields and perhaps go as far as Mossy Dell, but not for two or three days, when they were sure she'd really, truly run away. And she'd be far gone by then. Mother Rosemarie had plenty of other kids to watch; she couldn't very well go flitting across the Clandoms in search of one runaway.

"Yeah?" He looked doubtful. "What lie did you tell them? That you were going to visit a friend?"

Her wings bristled in offense. "I never lie. Honesty is the third step in the King's Ladder, you know."

"*Right.*" Nox looked supremely skeptical. He took the tunic from her. "Well, maybe you could be useful. Help me with my errand, and you can come with me to Thelantis."

She opened her mouth, but he cut her off.

"There are rules," he said. "First of all, *I'm* in charge, Elma."

"*Ellie.*"

"Whatever. It's dangerous out here, and you're . . ." He made a vague gesture at her small stature. "How far from your farm have you even been, anyway? Mossy Dell?"

Ellie gave a weak smile.

"Great skies," breathed Nox. "Not even *that* far? You're practically a fledgling!"

Bristling, Ellie shot back, "I saved your life!"

He rolled his eyes. "Second rule: Stay quiet and out of my way. This is a serious errand I'm on, and I don't need some country kid screwing it up."

But Ellie only half listened. Her heart soared with adrenaline and terror and excitement. This was happening. Really, truly *happening*. She was setting off on an adventure, like one of the heroes in her book. Even more important, the day she'd seen her parents buried in the clan cemetery, she'd made a promise: to make their deaths count. To make them proud.

And now she was finally keeping it.

"Are you coming or not?" Nox called.

Ellie drew in a long breath, then began walking.

CHAPTER SEVEN
· NOX ·

They reached Mossy Dell a few hours before nightfall. Nox was relieved, not just because it meant a chance to rest his throbbing shoulder but because it meant a break from the Sparrow girl.

She had spewed an endless stream of questions as they walked. *Have you ever seen the ocean? How many people live in Thelantis? Have you ever seen the king or queen? Are they as beautiful as they look in their portraits?*

All Nox had given her in reply had been sullen grunts, until she'd finally given up. He'd never appreciated silence quite so much. But even when she wasn't talking, the Sparrow was constantly moving, bounding, fluttering into the air, squealing when she saw a flower or a chipmunk or a dewy spiderweb.

Honestly, he was starting to have second thoughts about letting her come along.

But he did need an extra pair of hands, and this job was important enough to endure *five* chatty Sparrow girls if he had to.

"Is this Mossy Dell?" she asked as the town came into view. "Is there a tavern here? Adventurers *always* go to taverns. Will there be stew? Adventurers always eat—"

"*Enough!*" groaned Nox. "For the love of all things feathered, *stop asking questions.*"

The road followed a high ridge, with Mossy Dell huddled in the glade below. Stone steps set into the bank led down to the houses and shops, which clustered together between massive oaks. Buildings encircled the trunks and spread on wooden platforms between the enormous branches. Ladders and rickety stairs zigzagged through the canopy, but most of the people simply flew from place to place. The sound of their fluttering wings filled the air. At the back of Mossy Dell, a bright waterfall tumbled down a rocky bluff into a bubbling stream that wound through the houses. Lanterns of multicolored glass were strung between the trees.

"How pretty it must look at night," said the Sparrow girl. "All those lanterns lit, like stars on strings . . ."

Nox started down the steps, careful not to slip on the moist stones. "Are you coming or not, Elfie?"

"Is your errand in Mossy Dell?" she asked.

"No, but I'm meeting my crew—uh, I mean, my *companions*—here. They'll be waiting somewhere nearby." He added wryly, "Probably wherever the food is cheapest." *Or least guarded*, he thought.

"Companions? Whatever happened to *I travel alone*?" She dropped her voice to a mocking growl.

He ignored that. "C'mon. Let's circle through the trees. The fewer people who see us, the better."

"Why?"

"We're kids, on our own, no parents. What would the people in *your* town do if we just strolled through?"

"Drag us straight to the mayor or Mother Rosemarie *for our own good*," she sighed.

The residents of Mossy Dell were busy today, chatting, trading, arguing, or simply sprawling on branches, wings spread to catch the sunlight. Nox saw Orioles, Jays, Robins, and a few red-winged children who had to be Cardinal clan. These last were engaged in a game of chase, flying at reckless speeds, their wings crimson blurs. Mossy Dell was, he recalled, the clan seat of the Cardinals, just as Linden was for Sparrow clan and Thelantis for Eagle clan.

Nox navigated around the edge of the town, through thick patches of fern and ivy. To his begrudging surprise, the Sparrow girl moved as silently as he did, following his steps and avoiding dry leaves. They crept behind houses and massive tree trunks, small, overgrown gardens fenced in by sticks, a smithy, a stable, an apothecary, then the largest building in the town—a two-story inn. Its roof was completely covered in moss, the walls shrouded in ivy. The wooden boards looked rotted from the perpetual dampness of the forest.

"Are your friends in there?" she asked.

"They're not *friends*," he said. "More like colleagues. And I doubt it. They won't want to be seen either. But judging by the smell of the blackberry pie coming out of this place, they've got to be close. Gussie can't resist blackberry."

He pushed through the undergrowth, heading toward the waterfall. Here, ferns arced over their heads and white stones jutted from the ground, frilly with moss and pale lichen. Finally, Nox stopped in front of a particularly thick tangle of briars and said, "Hmm." He ran his finger over a dark red substance slimed over a prickly vine.

"Blood?" the Sparrow girl whispered.

He popped the finger into his mouth, grinning at her look of disgust. "Blackberry. Told you."

"That bush is moving," Ellie said, pointing at a nearby laurel. "Is it your—*oof!*"

Something small, furry, and angry came flying out of the bush to land on the Sparrow girl's face. It chittered and scrabbled over her head while she gasped and tried to grab it. *To her credit*, Nox thought, *she didn't scream.*

"Twig," he said calmly as the creature burrowed into the girl's shirt. "Call off your attack rat, will you?"

A whistle sounded from inside the bush, and at once, the creature leaped back into the leaves, leaving the Sparrow covered in scratches. She breathed hard, glaring at Nox.

"What was *that*?"

"Well," came an indignant voice from inside the bush, "Lirri is *not* a rat, she's a pronged marten, and I'd appreciate it if you'd start calling her that, Nox."

Nox pushed aside the briars and leaves to reveal a pair of kids tucked inside the thicket, a half-eaten blackberry pie between them. They looked like they'd been camped out there for a while. Their knapsacks were half unpacked, clothes and boxes and bundles spilling out, and between them sat a large wooden box bound with leather straps.

"Sparrow girl," he said, "meet my crew. The muddy one is Twig, and the grouchy one is Gussie—or *Agustina*, if you want to get on her bad side. I'm kidding, of course. All her sides are bad sides. Crew, this is Elbow."

"*Ellie*," the Sparrow said through her teeth. "My name is Ellie Meadows. Pleased to meet you both."

Twig was a short boy with an explosion of tangled orange hair and a perpetual sunburn on his pale skin. Born to parents of two different clans, he had one brown Mockingbird wing beside one Crane white. He was also the dirtiest person Nox had ever known. It was impossible to tell what marks on his face were freckles and which were mud. Leaves stuck out of his hair. His shirt was so grubby and torn up it hardly passed for clothing anymore.

A long, furry creature was draped over his shoulder, watching them all with open disdain. Lirri looked part squirrel, part ferret. She had two small white horns on her head and could pack more raw fury in her tiny body than a starving bear.

Twig waved at the Sparrow girl. "Hi!"

"Grouchy?" echoed the other kid, glaring at Nox. "You'd be grouchy too if you'd been stuck in a shrub with this walking mud pie for two days. Where have you *been*, Nox? What happened to your shoulder? And what's with the Sparrow?"

Gussie was tall, strongly built, and sported two puffs of curls just a shade darker than her acorn-brown skin, bound in precise buns over each ear. Against her spine were folded the long striped wings of the Falcon clan. Her clothing bulged with many added pockets, each one filled with cogs, wires, nails, and other pieces she salvaged from trash, gutters, broken-down wagons. When she moved, all her scavenged parts jingled slightly, like a jester's bells.

"I got held up," Nox said. "I was chased by those *bandits* who attacked us." He gave each of them a hard look, and saw them catch his hidden meaning. "They nicked me with an arrow, so I brought the Sparrow to help with the *errand*."

"Right," said Twig, nodding slowly. "Bandits. Errand. Good thinking."

"And good timing," said Gussie. "If I had to spend one more night in this bush with this orange-haired health hazard, I swear I'd have dragged him under that waterfall and scrubbed him down with his own ferret. You know he hasn't bathed since we left Thelantis?"

"Hey!" Twig objected, patting the furry little head on his shoulder. "First of all, *pronged marten*. Second of all, I haven't taken a bath in three *years*, just so's we've all got the facts straight." This last he pronounced with all the pride of a Hawk warrior declaring he'd set a weight-lifting record. "I got three-year-old dirt in places you don't even—"

"Stop!" Gussie cried, clapping her hands over her ears. "Ugh, Nox, he's positively feral!"

"What's a pronged marten?" asked the Sparrow. "I've never heard of one."

"They're extremely rare," said Twig, feeding an acorn to the creature. "Extremely cute. And extremely dangerous."

"You don't have to tell me," muttered Ellie, putting a hand to the scratches on her neck.

"What is she, anyway?" asked Gussie, eyeing the Sparrow girl suspiciously. "A scrubdown? Sniffup? Shinybob?"

Ellie blinked. "Are those real words?"

"She's a fighter," Nox said. "And she's going to help with our little *errand*."

"Well," she said, "more knight in training than fighter."

"Hmm, so she's a knockfist," said the Falcon girl, looking unconvinced. "Shame, we could've used a scrubdown, but I guess you'll do."

"Enough talking," said Nox. "Let's move. We have a very narrow window of opportunity and a lot more road to cover by tomorrow night, especially now that we're going to have to walk the whole way." He looked down ruefully at his bandaged shoulder.

"What *is* this errand, anyway?" asked Ellie. "And why do you need three people for it?"

"It's a delivery," said Nox, tapping the box beside Gussie with the toe of his boot. "And the place we're taking this box to is only accessible by air."

"It takes three people to lift Old Bricky Brickface here," said Twig, scowling at the box.

"What's inside?" Ellie asked.

"Bricks, you'd think," Twig moaned.

Nox shrugged. "We don't know what's in it. Not our business. But if we make the drop in time, we'll get a nice payment back in Thelantis."

"From this lord you work for?"

Twig snorted, and Nox jabbed his shin with his foot. "Yes, from the lord."

"Okay." Ellie shrugged. "Sounds easy. I'm in."

"Exactly," said Nox, with a curling grin. "*Easy.*"

CHAPTER EIGHT
· ELLIE ·

They left Mossy Dell without ever visiting the tavern, to Ellie's disappointment. But Nox pushed them at such a relentless pace that nobody even had breath for talking. The Crow boy had a map of Bluebriar Forest and all its little roads and led them deeper into the woods with the ruthless command of a soldier. By evening, Ellie was panting.

"It's nearly dark," Gussie pointed out, breathing even harder than Ellie was. "Nox, we have to take a break."

He frowned but gave in. "Fine. Let's make camp. Nellie, why don't you scout for a spot? Off the road, someplace hidden."

She was now sure that he was messing her name up on purpose, just to bug her. "Me?"

"You've got the shortest wingspan. You can fly through the trees easier than Gussie or Twig."

She nodded, feeling pleased to be entrusted with such a responsibility, and spread her wings. Flying through the trees was tricky work, but nothing she hadn't trained herself for. Of course, she'd only practiced this sort of flying using fence posts. The principles were the same, though, and she tacked this way and that, maneuvering in a swooping zigzag. Ellie drifted through the trees, through dappled patches of sunlight as delicate as lace.

When she spotted a likely campsite, she returned to the others to lead them to it. It was a clear bank beside a small stream, covered in fallen leaves and hillocks of fuzzy moss. Nox looked around, deemed it suitable, and then sank weakly to his knees, his hand on his injured shoulder.

"Let me have a look," said Ellie.

While she applied more poultice to his wound, Twig and Gussie assembled firewood, though Twig returned with more creatures than sticks. By the time they'd collected a pile of wood, each of his pockets had become home to a different animal—mouse, cricket, chipmunk, lizard, snake, and hedgehog. He was a walking menagerie.

"Where did you find them all?" Ellie asked, watching him pat the hedgehog's little nose.

"It's more like . . . they find *me*," he said. Lirri, curled around his neck like a handkerchief, glared jealously at the hedgehog.

"Twig, scout around," Nox said. "I don't want anyone sneaking up on us. You know, bandits and such."

"Oh yeah, wouldn't want to run into any *bandits*," Twig said, clutching his chest.

"Just *go*," said Nox through his teeth, and it seemed some unspoken words passed between them that Ellie couldn't make out.

"Fine, fine, you got it, boss." With a sloppy salute, Twig leaped into the air. His bicolored wings made almost no noise at all.

Once he was out of sight, Ellie leaned toward Gussie and asked, "What's with all the animals?"

Gussie had two little cogs in her hands and was idly locking their teeth together like puzzle pieces.

"If it slithers, crawls, scurries, or climbs," she explained, "then

Twig falls in love with it and it falls in love with Twig. We had to stop twice on the way here, once so he could free a penned-up dog, and then so he could loose a donkey some farmer had been starving. He's part Mockingbird, and you know how their clan is with languages—they pick them them up easy as I read a book."

She chewed her lip a moment, then added, "His parents sold him to a circus when he was little. His knack for learning languages somehow makes it easy for him to communicate with animals, so the circus made him train bears and pigs and things for shows. At least, until he could no longer stand how cruelly they treated them and he set all the animals free. They whipped him badly for it. He's got scars still, but he doesn't like to show them."

"His parents *sold* him?" Ellie said, horrified. "Why?"

"It happens to piebalds," said Gussie quietly. "People are superstitious about them—say they're bad omens who attract gargols and stuff like that. So they get rid of the children as quick as they can. Not that *I*, as a student of science, believe in any of that nonsense."

Ellie shuddered as, above, a strong wind rattled the treetops. Twig returned, landing lightly and assuring them the road was clear; they hadn't been followed by any would-be robbers. She averted her eyes, not wanting him to know they'd been discussing his past.

"Gussie," Nox said, eyeing the windy branches worriedly, "how's the weather?"

"Just a minute, I'll check." She rummaged in her satchel, then pulled out a round glass tube set in a bronze case. Inside the glass sloshed a dark blue liquid.

"What is that thing?" asked Ellie.

"I call it a *predicterator*," said Gussie. "Or maybe *storm glass*. I haven't decided yet." She peered at the glass tube. "It's clear, Nox. We're good."

"Can't you just fly up and take a look?" asked Ellie. The trees obscured most of the sky, but just a few seconds' flying would take one above their highest branches.

"The glass shows the weather to come, not just the weather that is," Gussie explained as she packed it away again.

"Really? But that's—amazing! I've never seen such a thing before."

"Of course you haven't." Gussie grinned, a bit shyly. "I invented it."

"You're an inventor? But you're . . ." Ellie glanced at Gussie's wings.

"What?" Gussie's tone hardened a little. "I'm from Falcon clan, is that it? So I'm meant to be a brick-headed brawler and nothing else, just punching and stabbing my way through life?"

Ellie winced. She of all people knew one's clan didn't—or *shouldn't*—determine one's fate.

"No," she said quietly. "I don't think that at all."

Her stomach growled. The conversation lulled, and she dug in her knapsack for food. First, she had to take out her copy of *The King's Ladder*, which she carefully set on a stone so it wouldn't get dirty.

Gussie glanced at the book and gave a short laugh. "You're really going to fly all the way to Thelantis with ten pounds of silly bedtime stories?"

Ellie's ears began to burn. "They're *true* stories, and anyway, anyone who wants to be a Goldwing knight must first study the Ladder."

"The what?" said Twig.

"The King's Ladder. It's like the list of qualities a person has to learn in order to become a knight. There are twelve stories about historical knights, each one representing one of the twelve virtues that make up the Ladder's steps. You know, honor, courage, discipline, stuff like that." She opened the book to a page creased from use. "It says right here: *Anyone who climbs each rung in the Ladder will prove worthy of the Goldwing's cloak.*"

"Huh," said Nox. "Why would you need a ladder when you have wings?"

Ellie blinked. "That's not the point. It's not *literal*."

Gussie lit the fire with a clever little contraption that sparked flame when she clicked a button.

"Did you invent that too?" asked Ellie, eager to change the subject. Her mother had given her *The King's Ladder*, had read its stories to her, and she didn't like them making fun of it.

Gussie nodded. "I call it a flinter."

"Can I see?"

Gussie handed it over and Ellie clicked the button, delighted when a little flame sprang out of the metal case. "This is ingenious!"

"Careful with that," said Nox, eyeing the device. "You'll set the forest on fire."

"*Pff.* I'll have you know I was the chief bonfire lighter at *every* Sparrow clan solstice festival for the last three years." Ellie picked up a branch bristling with dried, dead leaves and held the flinter to it, then whooped as it caught flame. "I know how to handle a flame."

But when she swung the burning branch in Nox's direction, he shouted and lunged away as if it were a striking snake.

Ellie started to laugh, then stopped herself.

His terror was *real*. He was panting hard, the color drained from his face. For a moment, no one spoke.

"Are you all right?" asked Ellie, dropping the branch into the campfire.

"It's fine," Nox rasped. "I just . . . it nearly burned me, is all. But I'm fine."

Ellie could practically still hear Nox's terrified shout echoing through the trees. It reminded her of her own screams in the nights right after her parents had died. She'd suffered from terrible nightmares, always waking with a bloodcurdling shout that had brought Mother Rosemarie running. So Ellie knew the sound of pure fear when she heard it.

Nox, she realized, was deathly afraid of fire.

Why? Had he been burned badly before? Had his house burned down? What had happened?

But she wasn't about to ask. Instead, she pretended she hadn't noticed anything unusual and sat down.

"It's getting dark," said Nox stiffly. "We should take turns keeping watch."

They set up a schedule, and Ellie drew first duty. She flew up and found a perch on a tall oak tree, which gave her a view of both the sky and the forest floor. Below, the others fell asleep wrapped in the downy warmth of their own wings. Twig and Gussie lay on either side of the fire, near the hot coals, while Nox settled down a short distance away. Ellie watched him and wondered what *his* story was. Were his parents dead or alive? How had he come to work for a lord?

As night fell and the stars came out, Ellie unfolded her wings and enclosed herself in them, her long primary feathers brushing the tops of her feet. Her stomach was a tumbling beehive, nerves and excitement tangled together. This was the first night she'd ever spent outside. Every noise was strange, every star brighter and closer than before. By now, the rest of her clan would know she'd left. How long would it take before they realized she'd flown off, or would they assume a gargol had gotten her?

But as Ellie stared up at the stars, she found her thoughts wandering further, like fireflies that had escaped their jar. She saw the faces of her parents as clearly as she saw the stars above her, and a surge of uncertainty coursed through her.

Am I doing the right thing? she asked them. *Are you proud of me?*

Shivering, Ellie closed her wings tighter around herself, drew her feet beneath the curtain of her feathers.

I will make *you proud*, she promised. *Just watch and see.*

When the moon had completed a third of its circuit in the sky, she woke Gussie for her turn, then curled up by the warm remains of the fire. For a few minutes, she found it impossible to shut her eyes.

She traced her finger in the dirt beside her head, outlining an ashmark but getting no comfort from it. She'd never heard of an ashmark protecting against gargols without walls to keep them out.

The day had been one of the longest in her life. Her wings were warmer and softer than any blanket, and with one crooked under her head and the other draped over her body, she was as comfortable as she could possibly be. And so it didn't take long at all for her to fall asleep, and to dream of a thousand would-be knights racing through stormy skies, all intent on knocking Ellie from the air, back down to the ground where they thought she belonged.

CHAPTER NINE
· ELLIE ·

"You didn't tell me you were delivering this box to a *castle*," said Ellie.

"Not a castle," Nox pointed out. "More like . . . a fortress."

The enormous building sat atop a high, stony cliff, with the great Aeries Mountains at its back. Its walls were made of large stone bricks, with a turreted tower rearing upward. Sure enough, there was no path leading up to it. The only way up was by wing.

Ellie and her new companions stood at the edge of the forest, steps away from the sheer cliff face. She, Twig, and Gussie were dressed in page uniforms Nox had pulled from his knapsack—blue coats with shiny brass buttons and matching pants with white stripes down the seams. On her head, Ellie wore a blue cap with a pair of flight goggles attached. She itched all over.

"No guards," commented Gussie, studying the fortress.

"Yeah," said Nox, pressing a hand to his injured shoulder and wincing.

"Who lives up there?" asked Ellie.

"It's under the command of a General Torsten," said Nox.

"They call him the *Stoneslayer*," whispered Twig. "He killed a gargol."

"Something few living people have ever done," added Gussie.

"Really!" Ellie gasped. "Is he a Goldwing?"

Nox shrugged. "Who cares? Time to use those warrior muscles, Sparrow."

"You'll have to stay here," Twig said to Lirri, handing the marten to Nox. "Sorry, but I just couldn't get a uniform in your size."

Lirri chattered her teeth indignantly, then burrowed into Nox's pocket.

"I'll keep an eye on her," the Crow boy assured Twig.

Together, Ellie, Twig, and Gussie lifted off the ground, hauling the box between them. They heaved and fluttered their wings and groaned, slowly making their way up the cliff's face. Ellie had to keep reminding herself of the seventh step in the King's Ladder— *strength*—the whole way up. She tried to see every ache in her arm and wing muscles as another chance to prove herself, but it got harder the higher they flew.

"What . . ." gasped out Twig, "are you . . . muttering about . . . Sparrow?"

"Nothing," she returned. She hadn't realized she'd been chanting the word aloud.

Finally, they made it to the large front door of the fortress, accessible by a wide stone portico, and set the box down with gasps of relief. Ellie took in the massive structure, with its many turrets and crenellations. Large ashmarks were drawn in soot over the doors and windows.

The lone Hawk clan guard posted at the front entrance frowned. He didn't look much older than Zain. In fact, he could easily have been one of Zain's innumerable cousins. He was dressed in the dark blue uniform of a soldier, complete with a spear and a knee-length cape with slits cut for his wings. "What's this? Who're you kids?"

"We have orders to deliver this *directly* to General Torsten," said Gussie, patting the box. "It's from Lord Bandersly, in Thelantis."

The guard frowned. "I'm not sure . . ."

"Look," said Gussie. "You don't get paid enough to decide whether or not a delivery from *Lord Bandersly*, the war minister of all the Clandoms, is important enough to let us in."

The guard shrugged. "Whatever. I'll fetch the general. Bring it inside."

He opened the door and hustled in, leaving them to haul their cargo.

"Rude," muttered Gussie. "He could've at least given us a cart or something."

"Lord Bandersly's the guy you work for?" asked Ellie, while they dragged the box through the doorway. Inside was a square room of stone, with banners hung on the walls depicting the crest of the Eagle king—laurels around crossed white feathers tipped in black.

Gussie and Twig exchanged a brief, unreadable look, then Twig said, "Absolutely."

"Lord Bandersly's the head of the king's military council," said Gussie. "There's not a man in the army, not even the Stoneslayer, who'd ignore a delivery from him."

"And we're wearing his house's costumes," said Twig, polishing one of his buttons.

"Livery," Gussie corrected him.

Moments later, a man in a gray uniform with lots of medals pinned to it came into the room, his brow furrowed. He was speaking to a soldier behind him. "Keep searching, then. That little miscreant couldn't have got far with an arrow in his shoul—what's this now?"

He barely glanced at Ellie, Twig, or Gussie but peered dubiously at the box.

"General Torsten?" asked Gussie.

"Yes, but I wasn't expecting a delivery," he said. "Who are you kids?"

"I'm sure you'll see what all this is about," said Gussie. "Just allow me to open—"

"Wait," said the general. "I don't like this. Stop!"

But Gussie, ignoring him, sprang forward and unclasped the box. The lid flew open with a bang, and suddenly, the air filled with an acrid green smoke that stank like skunk spray. Ellie gasped and stepped back, just as Twig reached up and pulled her flight goggles down and over her eyes. Gussie's were already in place.

Ellie pressed herself against the wall, holding her breath instinctively. The smell was nauseatingly strong, but it seemed to be more than just a bad odor in the air. She made out the dim shapes of the general and his soldiers, all howling and pressing their hands to their eyes.

"Go, Twig!" Gussie cried. "Ellie, split off! Find an exit and get out—meet up back at the campsite!"

She shoved Ellie toward a doorway. Bewildered and disoriented, Ellie stumbled through it. When she looked back, Twig and Gussie had both vanished.

What in the skies?

What was happening?

She realized the smoke, which was apparently burning the eyes of the soldiers, couldn't affect her through her goggles. Ellie stumbled back to help, but when she laid a hand on one, the man grabbed her wrist and held her fast.

"I got one, General!" he cried, still coughing from the smoke. His eyes were pressed shut, the skin around them red. "They must be spies!"

"Spies!" Ellie gasped. "No, I—"

The soldier shook her by her shoulder. "You'll hang for this, you little rat!"

That shocked Ellie into motion. She twisted away, ramming her elbow into the soldier's ribs. He yelped and released her, and she sprinted out of the cloud of smoke and to the nearest window, as Gussie had told her. Whatever had just happened, it was clear to Ellie that she'd better get as far away from this place as possible.

She threw herself out of the window and, spreading her wings, tore back to the forest.

Nox wasn't where she'd left him. Ellie saw no sign of Gussie or Twig either. Ripping off the flight goggles, she winged into the trees, seething.

They'd lied to her.

She wasn't sure why, or what their true purpose had been, but something was definitely *off* about her new so-called companions. And she was sure the general had been talking about Nox when he'd come into the room. Who else could the "young miscreant" be, with an arrow in his shoulder?

"Nox!" she called. "Twig!"

No one answered. She landed clumsily on the broad branch of an oak to catch her breath and cough the rest of the smoke from her lungs. Her face burned with anger and confusion.

Were they spies? She couldn't imagine who they'd work for. It wasn't as if the Clandoms were at war with anyone.

But they'd been prepared for the smoke, with their goggles and their escape plans. Clearly there was something deeper and far more nefarious going on, and now they'd dragged Ellie into their crime.

What Ellie really wanted right now was an explanation. Who were these three kids, what had they involved her in, and *why*?

Remembering Gussie's last words to her, Ellie set her jaw and flew to track down their campsite.

She arrived to find it empty. In a fury, she set about kicking rocks and clumps of moss, sure they'd intentionally left her high and dry. Used and then dumped, like the country naïf she was. Ellie was just about to take off again, for only the sky knew where, when she heard the crackle of footsteps on dry leaves.

Nox stepped out of the trees, and behind him walked Gussie, carrying her goggles.

"Oh, look!" Gussie said, lifting an eyebrow at the sight of Ellie. "She didn't fly away after all."

"We thought you'd be halfway home by now," Nox said, grinning.

Ellie rushed forward in a blur of wings, shoving Nox against the nearest tree and pinning him to it with an arm across his throat.

"Yow!" Nox cried. "Watch the shoulder, you crazy Sparrow!"

Lirri scrabbled out of his pocket and screeched at Ellie, her fur bristling.

"What," Ellie ground out, *"was that?"*

His eyes shone with maddening smugness. "You were brilliant. Really, we could never have delivered our little *package* without you."

"Tell me what's going on or I swear—"

"What?" he said. "What'll you do? Look, if I'd told you what our real errand was, you'd never have gone along with it, Miss *I Never Lie.*"

"You're right about that! What was that poison smoke? Did we—" She paused to swallow. Hard. "Did we—those soldiers, are they—?"

"Oh, they're fine," said Gussie. "It was just a little mix I concocted to sting the eyes. Well, Twig helped. He's probably the only person in the Clandoms who can bottle skunk spray without *getting* sprayed. That, combined with my special hot-pepper serum and spring-operated explosive device, makes for one nasty eye burn. But they'll be perfectly all right by nightfall, if they wash their eyes out thoroughly."

Ellie gaped at her. "*Why?* And why would you lie to me, bring me into it?"

"Because I need this job to succeed," Nox said, in a tone as hard as granite. "I need it more than anything in the world, and there was no way we could pull it off without a third person to help carry the box."

"Pull *what* off? What job?" Ellie, exasperated, considered slamming him against the tree again.

But just then, Twig emerged from the forest, flushed and grinning. "We got it!" he whooped, and he tossed something at Nox. Lirri sprang onto his shoulder and licked his ear.

Nox held up the thing Twig had thrown. It was a small blue gem set in an iron band with a long, thin chain attached.

Ellie stared.

Something about it pulled at her mind, like a dream she'd forgotten. The way it had flashed when Twig had tossed it through the air . . .

Nox laughed. "Properly done, crew! We got it!"

The three of them exchanged high fives and congratulated one another for their cleverness while Ellie looked on in disbelief.

"You're *thieves*," she realized aloud. "You're nothing but a band of common burglars."

"Common?" retorted Nox. "Excuse me, but after pulling off a job like that, we are anything but *common*."

"That's the truth," added Twig. "You should have seen Nox three nights ago!"

"The fortress was *crawling* with soldiers," explained Gussie. "So this lunatic flies in, pinches one of their swords *right* out of its sheath, and flies off again—with practically the entire garrison on his tail!"

"Shame about the sword," sighed Nox. "I had to dump it in order to outfly them. And even still, they got me with an arrow."

"And to think they're still out there, searching for you," laughed Gussie. "Wait till they find out it was all just a trick to lure away the guards! The Talon's going to *love* this."

"The Talon?" asked Ellie.

"Our boss," Gussie explained. "The Talon. The Lord of Thieves. The Scourge of Thelantis."

"Told you we work for a lord," said Nox, smirking.

"That's it!" said Ellie. "You are all truly horrible. I'm leaving."

She started to turn away, intending to get as far from them as possible. Her stomach churned with guilt and fury.

But then Gussie said, "Clouds!"

They all looked up as the patches of sky visible through the trees began to grow dark. Ellie cursed inwardly.

"There's some old abandoned building to the east," said Gussie. "I saw it on my way back."

Nox nodded and hung the gemstone around his neck. It dropped out of sight under his shirt. "Let's go. Quickly. We'll have to be off

· 62 ·

again as soon as the sky clears. These woods'll be crawling with soldiers soon."

They tramped away, three in a line, while Ellie stood on the mossy bank and wavered. She felt a fool for being taken in by them, and her face still burned with anger.

But the sky was clouding over. Soon, gargols would be hunting.

So she clenched her fists, swallowed hard, and followed.

CHAPTER TEN
· NOX ·

Nox was exhausted, his shoulder burned, and he suspected he was mildly feverish, but he clenched his teeth and said nothing as Gussie led them down a slippery ravine. They half ran, half slid through thickets of glistening ferns and sharp briars as the sky darkened with quick-moving clouds. It was barely past noon, he reckoned, but soon it was so dark it felt like late evening.

By the time they reached the building Gussie had spotted, rain had begun to fall, dripping from leaf to leaf until it reached the forest floor. A droplet slipped down the back of Nox's neck, and he shivered.

"What is this place?" Twig wondered, running his hand over a stone wall.

"It's some kind of tower," said Gussie. "Fallen on its side."

Now that she said it, Nox could see the shape of the tower—curved walls of ancient, crumbling stone. It lay on its side along the bottom of the ravine, almost entirely buried. Trees, moss, and ferns had taken root over it, until only a few surfaces were visible at all. The stones were dappled with silver-and-green lichen. It must have been there for hundreds of years.

He glanced at the Sparrow girl, who hadn't said a word, but he could tell she was intrigued by the old ruin. When she caught him looking, she wrinkled her nose and turned away, her shoulders tense.

Nox rolled his eyes. "See a way in?"

"There's an opening," said Gussie. "Looks like an old window."

Nox went first, easing himself into the dark, damp interior of the fallen tower, suppressing a cry of pain when the movement jerked his wound. He dropped to land on the opposite wall—now the floor.

The others followed, with Ellie last in, after taking a moment to draw an ashmark over the casement. She used a piece of charred wood she must have salvaged from the remains of last night's fire. Nox admitted to himself, somewhat begrudgingly, that even the Talon would approve of the girl's attention to detail.

With barely any light filtering in, they were left to shiver in the dark until Gussie got her flinter out and lit the small lantern she kept tied to her knapsack.

"Whoa," said Twig as light washed over the walls. "This thing is *huge*."

They stood in a long, empty cylinder of stone, like the belly of a giant snake. Up and down its length, trees had dug their roots through, breaking apart the walls. Sheets of moss hung from the ceiling-wall, dripping with moisture. Mushrooms grew everywhere, in every shape, size, and color. Twig happily began picking them.

"Best hiding place ever, Gus!" he exclaimed, chewing the mushrooms raw.

"It'll keep the rain off anyway," said Gussie.

"Don't you wonder what this place is?" asked the Sparrow girl. "Or how old it is? I never heard of a city being here, or anything that would explain this tower."

Gussie tilted her head, eyes narrowing with interest. "Not to mention the style of architecture . . . it's not like anything I've seen or read

about before. This type of stone isn't even found in the Clandoms."
She brushed her hand over the wall, pulling away some of the moss
clinging to the stone. "Hey, come look at this."

Gussie held up the lantern to the cleared wall. Set into the stone
was a faded mosaic made of hundreds of tiny colored tiles and pieces
of glass.

"It's just some old picture." Twig shrugged, chewing a mouthful of
mushroom that Nox desperately hoped was not poisonous. Usually,
Lirri sniffed the mushrooms first and deemed them safe for eating,
but there had been that *one* time . . . He shuddered, remembering
the wretched time all three of them had spent puking in the bushes,
just two days into their trip from Thelantis. He still wasn't convinced
Lirri hadn't done it on purpose. Sometimes the little horned creature
could be more spiteful than any highborn.

Nox squinted at the mural, unsure what Gussie was so excited
about. "It shows people flying around with dopey smiles. So?"

"Look again," said Gussie. "Tell me if there's something strange
about it."

"There are clouds," said Ellie softly.

They all turned to look at her, her eyes wide and reverent as she
studied the old mural.

"They're flying in the clouds," she said again. "And they're happy."

Gussie nodded, pressing her hand against the tiles. Nox saw it now.
The people in the mosaic soared carelessly amid towering cumulus
clouds, piles of them.

"It's just a picture," he said, wondering why it made him so uneasy.
"It's not supposed to be real. Like the stories in your book, Sparrow.
It's meant to show a happy lie instead of an ugly reality."

She scowled at the jab but didn't rise to the bait. She joined Gussie, running her fingers over the tiles. "This place is so old . . . Could it be from a time *before* the gargols?"

"There was no time before the gargols," Nox said with a snort.

"You don't know that. Haven't you heard the story? A thousand years ago, Aron the Fool pierced the moon with his spear, thinking to steal it out of the sky—only to release the monsters that had been sleeping inside it. Those were the gargols, which means there *was* a before, and we once flew freely." Ellie's voice rose, betraying her excitement. "And if we could do it then, why not—"

"That's not how the story goes at all," interrupted Twig. "The gargols had *always* been up there, but they ignored us so long as we left them alone. Then Aron tried to steal their magic, so they got angry and from then on, they killed anyone they saw."

Gussie shook her head. "The way the Falcons tell it, the gargols were once a clan like any other, and Aron was their chief. But when he led them on a flight that took them too near the sun, its fires burned so hot it turned them to stone. They attack us now out of jealousy, because we represent everything they lost." Cocking her head, she added, "Grant you, the story doesn't quite add up with actual *science.*"

"Exactly!" snorted Nox. There were as many legends about the gargols as there were clans, each one dumber than the last. "There's no such thing as magic, and anyway, those old stories are just made up to scare little kids who don't know better. The gargols are no different from any other animal."

"They're made of *stone*," said Ellie. "And yet they can fly. That's not normal."

Nox groaned loudly and flopped down by the fire. "Sparrow girl, you make my head hurt."

"I'm just saying," she grouched. "It's not an impossible idea that the world could change. It gives me *hope*."

"Hope?" he replied. "Can you eat hope? Can you wrap it around yourself to stay warm, or hide under it when the sky is full of gargols? Hope is empty. Hope is waiting for other people to solve your problems instead of doing it yourself." Those were the Talon's words; it was one of many hard lessons he'd taught Nox over the years.

"Oh, stop fighting," groaned Gussie. "Twig, Ellie, get firewood, will you?"

Giving Nox a dirty look, Ellie fluttered after Twig, deeper into the tower where sticks and logs had slid inside and piled up over the years. When they had a proper stack, Nox began breaking them up and piling them for Gussie to light. While keeping a safe distance away, of course.

The flames leaped up hungrily. Nox averted his eyes, shifting farther away until he couldn't feel the fire's heat on his skin.

He knew Ellie had seen the panic in his eyes last night, and he hated that she knew . . . she'd camped with them, and he hated that she knew his weakness. It was bad enough that Gussie and Twig knew. It had been years since he'd struck a match, held a candle, lit a lantern. And no matter how he tried to overcome it, the fear that spiked in his chest when he got near an open flame never got smaller. Fire, it turned out, was simply too good at carrying memories. And if he looked at one too long, the flames would carry him straight back into the past, to a house full of screams, to his mother's tearstained face.

He suppressed a shudder and tossed the last stick into the pile.

Twig had speared some mushrooms and was roasting them with wild garlic and onion bulbs he'd dug up earlier in the day. The smell was making Nox's mouth water.

"This weather is going to last a while," Gussie said, tapping her storm glass. The liquid in the glass swirled angrily, as if she'd bottled a piece of the storm itself. "Probably through morning."

Everyone groaned.

"I guess you're stuck with us a while longer," Nox said to Ellie.

She had taken out her Goldwing book and was staring at it so intently, Nox half expected her heated glare to set the pages ablaze.

"Silent treatment, huh?" he asked. "Suits me just fine."

He leaned back as much as the cramped space would allow and shut his eyes, his lips never losing their permanent smirk.

Even the Sparrow girl's constant glowering couldn't dampen his mood. He'd stolen the unstealable; he'd finished the job no one else in the Talon's crew would dare attempt. The pure satisfaction of the heist was almost a reward in and of itself—but he couldn't forget about the real prize, the payment that waited in Thelantis once he handed the gemstone to the Talon.

The prize that would change his life.

But deep down, he felt a twinge of guilt. Ellidee Meadows hadn't just bailed him out on his all-important mission, helping Gussie and Twig carry the box to the fortress. She had also saved his life. He was indebted to her. And what had he repaid her with but lies, using her in a heist she hadn't agreed to?

But guilt wasn't a burden Nox could afford to bear. There were plenty of times when doing the *right thing* would have gotten him imprisoned or even killed. If the Sparrow girl couldn't stop looking down her nose long enough to see *why* he did what he did, well, he wouldn't go out of his way to explain it to her.

"Do you think they'll look for us in this storm?" asked Gussie.

"Depends how bad they want this back," Nox said, holding up the blue gemstone.

It sparkled like no stone he'd ever seen—and he'd pulled off more than a few jewel heists. It looked almost like a sapphire but was a lighter shade of blue, and its facets each flashed white when he turned it. In a way, it was like a bit of . . . well, crystallized summer sky. The heavy iron band seemed an odd setting for such a prized stone. He wondered why it wasn't encased in silver or gold. Or for that matter, why it wasn't gleaming atop the Eagle King Garion's crown. Not that Nox was any sort of expert on crowns, but this gem seemed like it might be exactly the sort of thing a fancy royal would want on their big fancy head.

"Well," burst out Ellie, "I hope it's worth it, whatever that thing is. I hope it's worth lying, cheating, and *attacking* our own soldiers."

"Hey, easy!" Nox raised a hand in defense. "We didn't attack anybody. And stop acting so high and mighty. If you were starving to death, you'd steal bread from a baker without thinking twice."

"Wouldn't."

"Would."

"I would not. I would ask politely, and the baker would just *give* me some bread. Good people help other people."

"See, there it is," said Nox, spreading his hands. "The difference between you and me. You think this baker would just hand some over because you asked nicely, while I *know* for a fact he wouldn't. People don't work that way. At least, not where I'm from."

"Do you really think other people's bad behavior excuses your own?"

Nox threw his hands in the air. "Of course it does! Exactly! Thank you for finally understanding!"

The Sparrow girl was just like all the people back in Thelantis who'd sneered at him, shaken their heads, and called him *street scum* because his clothes were torn and his feathers a bit tattered. He thought of the innkeepers who'd taken one look at him, then refused to rent him a room though he had the coin to pay. The shopkeeps who called the city watch when he walked in, even when he had no plans of stealing anything. The guards who scowled at him when he simply strolled down the street, then muttered that he'd best keep his hands in his own pockets. He'd been only a fledgling then, and hadn't stolen a single coin off anyone . . . yet.

It was like the Talon had told him years ago, when he'd taken Nox under his wing: When the world treats you like a criminal, what else can you be?

Not that he would say all that to Ellie. It would seem like he was making excuses or, worse, apologies. And he wasn't about to make either.

So he only added, "When you live on the streets, you gotta look out for yourself. We can't all live in some rosy-cozy country clan like you Sparrows."

"My life has *not* been rosy-cozy," Ellie growled. "You don't know anything about me. And you're wrong, anyway. If you're on your own, that's your choice. Why didn't you just go live with the other Crows? That's why we have clans—to take care of one another so no one has to be alone."

Nox's face went cold as the mood in the tower shifted. Twig coughed, while Gussie shook her head at Ellie in warning.

The Sparrow girl glanced at each of them uncertainly. "Uh . . . Why are you all looking at me like that? What did I say?"

"The Crows are a shattered clan," said Gussie quietly. "They can't do anything to help Nox, or any other Crow kid."

"Shattered?" Ellie echoed. "What's that mean?"

Nox sighed heavily. "You really are from the back of nowhere, huh?"

He turned away, wings ruffled, while Gussie explained softly, "A clan can be shattered if they do something really terrible, like start a rebellion against the Eagle king or queen, or like when the Magpies burned down an entire Robin village over a land dispute."

"They did that?" gasped Ellie.

Gussie nodded. "It was over a hundred years ago, and the Magpies still haven't been given their clanhood back. When a clan is shattered, the king takes away everything that held them together—their chief, their clan seat, their crest and motto and lands. And they aren't allowed to own businesses or run organizations, like the orphan home you ran away from. They can't become Goldwings or officers, or enter universities, or hold any important jobs. It's the reason so many Magpies are beggars or cutthroats, and why so many Crows are thieves, bandits, or mercenaries."

"What did the Crows do to get shattered?" Ellie whispered.

"Well, there's a stupid rumor—"

"Stupid is the right word for it." Nox spoke up, his voice hollow. "The rumors are ridiculous, made up to give people reasons to hate us. The truth is, no one knows. We've been shattered longer than any other clan, over three hundred years. The reason why is either a secret only the Eagles know, or it's lost to history."

Whatever his ancestors had done to earn the wrath of the Eagle clan, he wondered if it had been worth the punishment that now clung to every Crow. Most clans passed down land, riches, and wisdom to their descendants. All Crows got was scorn and empty pockets.

"So there you have it," Nox said, giving a mocking bow. "That's why I steal. For someone like me, there's no other choice. When the rules are designed to break you, you have to break rules."

Ellie stared at him, and he hated the pity in her eyes. Nox's blood simmered. Almost more than anything in the world, he hated being pitied.

So what if the Crows were shattered? So what if he didn't have the protection and support of a clan around him? From what he'd seen of clans, they were more trouble than they were help. Why else would Ellie have run away from hers? Why else would Twig have been abandoned as a baby just because his wings were two different colors? Even Gussie was on her own, despite the fact that her clan was one of the richest and most powerful in the world.

Nox didn't need some judgmental clan controlling him. He was better off alone, or with other outcasts like the Talon who treated him fairly no matter his roots.

"Look," he said, "I told you I'd get you to Thelantis, and I will. That is, if you'll even stoop to still travel with the likes of us—what did you call us? Common burglars? Fine. But I don't need lectures along the way." *And I don't need your pity*, he thought, but he bit his tongue.

Ellie tightened her jaw, her face conflicted.

"What makes you want to help me?" she demanded. "You know when I become a Goldwing, it'll be my job to catch people like you."

"*If* you become a Goldwing."

Ellie's face turned pink, and he could practically hear the angry replies gathering in her throat.

"It's not that I think you'll lose the Race of Ascension," he said quickly. "Actually, I've seen you fly, and I think you stand a pretty fair shot."

She glared at him.

Nox knew he was wading into danger, but he wanted to see *her* squirm for a change. She wasn't the only one who could stir up a fight. "The problem, Sparrow, is that they'll never *let* you join the Goldwings, no matter how good you are."

The moment Ellie's eyes began to wilt, he regretted how harshly he'd said it. But that didn't mean he believed it any less. Maybe it was time someone told her the truth.

"And I suppose," she returned bitterly, "that next you'll tell me your *Lord of Thieves* is the only truly honorable man in Thelantis."

"Actually, his word is worth ten Goldwings', and that's a fact. Sure, he's a thief, but the Talon's a straight talker. He's famous for keeping his promises, both the good and bad. You might be scared featherless of him, but you can *trust* him."

If there was one thing Nox had learned of his leader, it was that. Besides, he'd never seen a *Goldwing* take the orphans and outcasts of Thelantis into their care the way the Talon did. So what if he asked for a few nicked coins in exchange? Nox owed the man everything, and the Talon had never played him dirty.

"Look, I get it," he said. "You're a country kid who grew up on stories of the heroic Goldwings defending the Clandoms from monsters in the sky." He nodded at her book, still open on her lap. "But trust me, they don't want some low clan girl showing up their pedigreed kids in the Goldwing Academy. Even if you come in first place, they'll find some way to disqualify you."

"But the rules say—"

"Will you two cut it out?" said Gussie.

"C'mon, Gus," said Nox. "Back me up here. You're a Falcon; you know how it is. Tell her that—"

"I'm not getting in the middle of this."

Gussie pulled out her bag of bits and ends to begin tinkering, which was a sure sign she wouldn't say anything more. Ellie, her wings bristling, went to sit by the mural of the happy people in their happy clouds, staring up at impossible pictures, dreaming impossible dreams. Twig, who was practically allergic to awkward conversations, had curled up to play with Lirri, ignoring everyone else. So Nox was left on his own to wonder why, after he'd spent his whole life learning to shrug off people's bad opinions of him, some country Sparrow girl could so easily get under his skin.

CHAPTER ELEVEN
· ELLIE ·

To Ellie's dismay, the storm continued through the night, just as Gussie's predicterator had, well, predicted. Twig was the only one to fall properly asleep, drool trickling from his mouth and three field mice curled between his collar and his neck. Lirri, his little horned weasel thing, perched atop his head and watched Ellie with unblinking eyes.

"How does Twig *sleep* through that?" asked Ellie, flinching as another peal of thunder rocked the forest. The tower echoed with the rumbling sound.

"Storms, rain, clouds—he doesn't mind them a bit," said Gussie. "But the minute you put him in a crowd of people, he can barely function."

Nox was pretending to sleep, but Ellie caught him with his eyes open more than once. He stared into the charcoals of the fire, his dark wings drawn up to his chin.

Ellie couldn't stop thinking about the shattered Crow clan. She'd never heard of such a thing before, not in stories or even in the gossip among the Sparrows. Perhaps it was too awful a thing to be spoken of, a secret everyone knew but didn't share. After all, one's clan was more than just family. The clan was home. The clan was safety. The clan was *life*. That was why she still dreamed of earning the Sparrows' approval once she became a Goldwing. To live without a clan was like living without any limbs or senses, completely alone and cut off.

She couldn't help but think of Nox a little differently now. Sure, he was the stubbornest, smuggest jerk she'd ever met, and she almost wished she'd just left him in that sunflower field.

But at the same time . . . could she really blame him for becoming a criminal when he didn't have the kind of safety she did after losing her parents? Who was she to think she'd have ended up any different from him if Mother Rosemarie hadn't been there to take care of her? If the other Sparrows hadn't sheltered, protected, and loved her?

It was all so confusing. She'd barely been gone from home two days, and already her head was turned inside out.

When the storm finally cleared and the four of them crawled out of the tower, irritable and exhausted, Ellie realized she'd made up her mind.

"I will go with you to Thelantis," she declared, the first thing she'd said to Nox since their argument the night before. "You owe me that much anyway. And when we get there, you'll see how wrong you are. The Goldwings *will* make me one of them, so long as I win the race."

He grinned. "And if I'm right, who knows? Maybe you'll join my crew instead."

"Ha!" Ellie laughed. "Keep dreaming, Crow."

"If you two are done," said Gussie dryly, "we should get moving. We're not that far from the fortress, and those guards will be searching high and low for us."

Nox's shoulder was starting to improve, so they moved at a faster pace than they had the day before. Ellie volunteered to scout ahead, so she wouldn't have to talk to him.

She liked stretching her wings and the challenge of flying over the twisting road, adjusting at the last moment to avoid crashing into a tree or a high bank. It was good training for the race to come.

The Goldwings would see how strong and fast she was.

They would admit her into their academy when she placed high enough in the race.

They would do it because it had been a Goldwing herself who'd told Ellie, *You can be anything*.

But for all that she believed these things, she still couldn't get Nox's words out of her head. They made her itch with anger. Why, after she'd been able to rise above every other doubtful comment made by everyone back home, did *his* words seem to burrow into her heart?

Well, she hadn't spent her whole life working toward this race just to have it all undone now by the cruel words of some thief.

Ellie flew almost without thinking, her body reacting instinctively to the bends and rises in the road. She wasn't paying much attention to anything outside her own thoughts, so she barely had time to hide when she caught a glimpse of travelers on the road ahead.

Flaring her wings, Ellie changed direction, shooting upward into the treetops. In the canopy, she was almost invisible, and she could flit from branch to branch with barely a whisper. In this way, she crept up on the travelers, taking care to stick to the shadows so her own would not ripple over the ground, alerting them to her presence.

In moments, the murmur of their voices hardened into individual words and speakers. She recognized them even before she saw their faces. There was no mistaking Zain's booming laugh.

Ellie's stomach twisted.

There he was, her former best friend, striding along with all the confidence and swagger he'd always had. On either side of him walked Tauna and Laida. Their parents strode ahead, with Mayor Davina, who held the halter of a pack donkey. Of course they wouldn't be flying, not with the donkey to tow along, carrying camping gear and bags full of supplies.

When Laida complained of a stone in her shoe, the company stopped while she unlaced her boot. Ellie took the chance to crouch on a high hickory branch, her tawny wings blending into the dappled treetops.

"And then," Zain was saying, "I grabbed that snake by its tail and swung it around like this!" He twirled, arm outstretched and fist clenched, as if gripping an imaginary serpent. "Everyone was screaming, but *no one* was screaming louder than me. When I let go, that snake must've sailed a mile! It's probably *still* soaring!"

"You're such an idiot!" Tauna said, laughing as she playfully punched Zain's shoulder.

That punch landed right in Ellie's gut. She'd been there that day, when they'd found the snake curled up on the town well. But she noticed Zain didn't mention that.

It was like he'd completely forgotten she existed . . . or was too ashamed of her to even say her name, not to his cool new high clan friends.

"Eat up, kids!" Zain's father said, tossing each of them an apple. "Got to keep up your strength for the big race."

"Last one to the core loses the Race of Ascension," taunted Tauna, and all three began tearing into their apples with huge, wolfish bites.

"Nonsense," sniffed Mayor Davina. "There's no reason all three of you shouldn't make it. You're the best of Linden, and the strongest contestants we've put forward in years."

Zain won the apple-eating contest, and triumphantly hurled the core into the bushes. Then, putting his arms around Tauna's and Laida's shoulders, he said, "We'll make you proud, Mayor, just wait and see. We're the Invincible Three, and this time three weeks from now, we'll each have a Goldwing patch!"

The Invincible Three. They already had a team name for themselves. They were acting like they'd been friends for years, when Ellie knew for a fact that Zain had thought Tauna was a snob. He barely even *knew* Laida. But apparently, their triumph two days ago had bonded them faster and more deeply than an entire childhood of adventures and fort building and racing over the fields had done for him and Ellie.

And why shouldn't it? she supposed. They were high clan kids. They belonged to a world she'd never been part of. Their parents were all here, shining with pride. The sun itself shone for them.

It could have been me down there.

Ellie couldn't stop the poisonous thought from sidling through her mind.

It had nearly been her, hadn't it? If not for Ordo's cowardly attack, if not for Nox calling for help in the sunflowers, Ellie would have won. *She* would have been one of the Invincible Three.

Instead, she was on her own.

But it didn't have to stay that way. If she placed well in the Race of Ascension, she would finally stand side by side with these high clan kids as an equal. No longer a Sparrow who relied on others to protect her, but a warrior *others* called upon for protection.

We'll be the Fearless Four, she thought. *And Zain will be my friend again.*

"Let's keep moving," said Mayor Davina. "We need to reach the next village by evening."

"You all go on," said Zain. "I'll catch up. Just gotta . . . step behind a tree real quick."

The group of Lindeners resumed walking, while Zain scurried urgently into the bushes.

Sighing, Ellie figured she'd better fly back and alert Nox and the others about the travelers. The last thing she wanted was an accidental meeting between the thieves and the Lindeners.

She started to turn back—only to see a shape hurtling toward her in a blur of wings, a bare blade flashing in the attacker's hand.

CHAPTER TWELVE
· ELLIE ·

With a gasp, Ellie drew her own dagger, raising it in the nick of time to block the driving blade. The impact knocked her backward against the trunk of the tree, the attacker's knife pressed against her own. Their sharp edges were just a hair's breadth from her throat.

"Zain!" she shouted. "Stop!

The Hawk boy's eyes widened, and then he hastily pulled back, lowering his knife. "Ellie? *Ellie Meadows?*"

"What, three days passed and you've already forgotten what I look like, you featherbrain?"

"I heard someone spying on us," he said. "I thought you might be a thief."

Ellie winced at the word. "And if I had been, you'd have just cut my throat?"

"What? No! Ellie, everyone back home is looking for you. Last I heard, Mother Rosemarie was vowing to clip your wings the moment she found you."

She sighed, slumping against the tree. "All the more reason not to go back."

"What are you doing out here, Ellie?"

"I'm going to Thelantis, same as you. I found out they have this wild card option where . . ." She stopped as she saw his expression change. Not to surprise, as she'd expected—but to resignation. His eyes shut and he shook his head slowly.

"You already knew about the wild card draw, didn't you?" said Ellie quietly. "You knew I still had a chance, and you didn't tell me. I had to hear it from—" She stopped herself just in time. "I thought we were friends, Zain. What happened?"

If their positions had been reversed and it had been Ellie who'd won the Linden Trial, she'd have told Zain in a *heartbeat* about the wild card option. She'd have urged him to take it, so that they could win together. Become Goldwings together.

Ellie felt like a fool for ever having trusted him.

"We *are* friends," said Zain. "That's why I'm telling you to go *home*. Go now, before this gets any worse. Before Mother Rosemarie decides to ground you permanently, or worse—some gargol grabs you."

"I'm not going back," she said.

"You—argh!" He raised his hands, as if he wanted to shake her. "You're a *Sparrow*, Ellie! Why can't you just let us stronger clans protect you?"

"Because they didn't protect my parents!" Ellie shouted.

Her words echoed through the forest, pushing outward like a shock wave. She clenched the tree trunk until the bark broke away in dark flakes.

Zain lowered his eyes. "I know. I'm sorry. But—"

"Do you think I want to be a Goldwing because I want to play dress-up in some armor? Well, you're wrong. I want to be a Goldwing because there won't always *be* some knight who randomly happens by at the right time. If my parents had known how to fight, maybe they'd still be alive. I'm so *angry*, Zain, that we have to live in a world that always tells us *hide, run, be afraid*. I'm sick of it—aren't you? Why does it have to be like this? Why do *they* get to rule *us*?" She jabbed a finger at the sky, at every gargol who'd ever poked his stony snout from a cloud. "When do we get to fight back, Zain? When?"

"It's just the way things are," he said in a small, uncertain voice. "You're so stubborn, Ellie. The world won't change just because you want it to."

"No," she agreed. "Nothing will change, you're right about that. Nothing will change until we *make* it change."

"You're only going to get yourself grounded or killed."

"I'm *going* to Thelantis, to become a Goldwing. To *fight back*."

Zain shook his head. He looked so full of concern that she softened slightly. How could she make him see what she saw? How did she open his eyes to a world where *nobody* had to live in fear because *anybody* could become a warrior? Zain had always had trouble seeing what wasn't there, while it was Ellie who built castles out of air. Whenever they'd built a fort out of sunflower stalks, she'd been the one with the designs in her head. She'd realized that a haystack could become a mountain to climb, a pair of rakes could become polished steel swords, a grain sack was a sweeping Goldwing cape.

But this was a vision he couldn't see, no matter how she described it.

"If I win the Race of Ascension," she said, "and become a Goldwing initiate, will you still say I don't belong?"

"Of course not," he said. "We're friends, Ellie. We always will be. If you become a Goldwing, we'll be friends *and* we'll be knights-at-arms. But—"

"Good," said Ellie. "Remember you said that, Zain, three weeks from now."

"Ellie, please, just—"

"And if you *are* my friend, don't tell the others what I'm doing. I can't risk the mayor or your parents trying to stop me. Swear it, Zain."

"All right, all right." He gave her a crooked, weary smile. "I guess some things never change. You're always talking me into things I know I'll regret."

"You won't regret this. Promise."

"Hmm." He looked entirely unconvinced. "Well, I need to catch up to the others. Just . . . be careful, will you?"

He swooped away, his wing beats stirring the leaves. Landing neatly on the road below, he turned to give her a wave that seemed half friendly, half resigned.

"Oh, and Zain?"

"Yeah?"

"If you're going to become a Goldwing, you might want to do a better job looking after your weapons."

She flicked her wrist, throwing the dagger she'd stolen from his belt. It flipped through the air and buried itself in the ground in front of his feet, handle quivering. Zain yelped and jumped back.

"Still falling for that, huh?" She shook her head. "See you in Thelantis."

With a downstroke of her wings, she fluttered into the treetops, leaving him standing open mouthed on the road, his dagger still quivering in the dirt.

CHAPTER THIRTEEN
· NOX ·

That night, Twig took first watch, perched high in a fir tree. But down on the ground, Nox couldn't sleep. He gingerly tossed another log onto the fire and then scurried back as the flames leaped up.

They'd camped in the lee of a large boulder that lurched out of the ground. The fir tree sprouted atop the rock, its massive roots wrapped around it like a kraken gripping a ship's prow in its tentacles. Beneath the boulder, Gussie and Ellie curled in the warmth of their wings, sound asleep.

Nox held the blue gem in his hand, turning it slowly so that it caught the firelight. This little rock was the key to changing his life. It was the opportunity he'd been looking for, for years, and he was having difficulty believing it had finally come. But first, he had to make it back to Thelantis, back to the Talon, to deliver the stone and claim his reward.

If you do this, Nox, my boy, the Talon had said that night, *if you steal this unstealable thing and bring it back to me, I will give you whatever you desire. Coin, promotions, the life of any who've wronged you. A seat in my inner circle if you want . . .*

Anything at all? Nox had replied.

If you bring me the Stoneslayer's gem, lad, you've only to name your prize and it's yours.

And so Nox had. He'd given voice to the one desire he had above all others, the one so impossible he'd never spoken it aloud until that moment. The Talon had been shocked, but he thought it over, and finally, they'd touched wingtips on it—an unbreakable bargain struck.

Nox's feathers shivered, thinking of all he had to gain when he made it home. Of how his life would change forever.

But there was a lot of ground between here and there . . . and a lot of people who'd cut off his wings just to steal this rock.

He sighed and lay back on the cushion of his feathers, knowing he needed to force himself to sleep. He rolled over, trying to get comfortable.

Only to find a pair of eyes glowing at him.

Nox sucked in a breath, frozen to the spot, his wings twitching with the instinct to fly. The two lights gleaming in the underbrush were pale silvery blue, like stars. Was it a wolf? A bear?

But as he stared, more lights began to glow. They winked on all around the campsite, along the tree branches overhead and across the underside of their rock shelter. Nox gasped.

He whirled at the sound of fluttering wings and saw Twig landing on silent feet, his finger pressed to his lips. The glowing beads of light were so numerous and bright now that they shone on his face like moonlight.

"What are they?" whispered Nox.

Twig nudged Gussie with his foot. The girl woke with a groan. "My watch already?"

"*Shhh,*" warned Twig.

Beside Gussie, Ellie woke at once and exhaled softly in wonder. "What in the sky are those?"

Twig smiled. "Moonmoths. Or their chrysalises anyway. They must be hatching."

"Moonmoths are real?" asked Ellie. "I thought they were just a figure of speech. You know: *Don't go chasing moonmoths*."

Nox had heard that phrase plenty of times. It meant don't go chasing foolish hopes, pretty promises that were more likely to lead you off a cliff than to your destination.

"They're extremely rare," said Gussie. "By the sky, I've never heard of so many in one place! This is a major scientific discov—"

"*Shh!*" said Twig again, scowling at her. "Stop talking and just *look*."

Nox pushed himself on tiptoe to peer closer at one of the chrysalises. It hung by a delicate silken thread, suspended from the bark like a curled-up rose petal with veins of gold. It shone like a tiny, extraordinary lamp. He could just make out the dark form of the moth's body inside.

He pulled back as a crack suddenly shot over the casing and several thin, spindly legs pried their way free, pulling the rest of the moth through. The body was dark blue and furry, the black eyes large, glinting with intelligence. Wings the width of Nox's hand glowed silvery blue, the same color as the full moon. Unlike his feathered wings, the moth's were leaflike and thin, each membrane so fine it seemed a wonder they didn't tear from the smallest movement. Long tails shot out from their lower curves, the ends slightly feathery. The moth shook itself, glittering dust raining down as it did.

"Incredible," breathed Ellie, raising her hand to catch the dust on her palm. It glowed faintly on her skin before fading.

"Hmm," said Nox, trying to look bored. "They're all right."

"All right?" said Gussie, rolling her eyes. She reached for a chrysalis. "Don't pretend like you're not fascinated, Nox. This will be an amazing specimen for—*ouch!*"

Twig slapped her hand. *"Hands. Off."* He placed himself between her and the chrysalises, arms crossed, jaw jutting.

"There's hundreds of them!" Gussie protested. "I just want one to study. D'you know what the Entomological Society will pay for one? Nox, back me up. *You* appreciate a payday, at least."

Nox watched a newly hatched moonmoth struggle to free itself from its chrysalis, spindly legs grappling with the membrane. Carefully, he reached up and slipped one finger inside, pulling it open so the creature could escape. "Leave them, Gus," he said softly.

"Fine, fine," sighed Gussie. "Such a scientific waste, though."

These creatures looked too . . . *sacred* to be bottled or pinned down. Not that he'd ever say a thing like that aloud. It sounded foolish. Dreamy. More like something the Sparrow girl would say.

He glanced at Ellie and caught her staring at him with an amused expression, as if she could read his thoughts. Face warm, he scowled and looked away.

All around, with a sound that reminded Nox of a hand sifting through a basket of seashells, chrysalises were cracking open, moonmoths wriggling out and unfurling their fresh, damp wings. The forest shivered with gleaming new life. Paper-thin wings tested the air, silver dust sprinkling the loam.

The four kids stood utterly silent. Nox had never seen anything so beautiful or strange as this little glen filled with living stars.

A few brave moths took to the air first, fluttering about like dancing candle flames. As if emboldened by their siblings' first flights, more soon followed, and then the air was full of them. A torrent of moonmoths fluttered all around the trees. One landed on Nox's arm, its delicate legs tickling his skin. When it lifted away, the movement was effortless.

Nearly all the moths had emerged now. In a swirl of bright wings, the creatures began to gather in the air, forming a spiraling cloud of light that twisted upward. Higher and higher the moths flew, the great column of them rising into the treetops.

Ellie, as if caught in a trance, spread her wings and took flight in pursuit, closely followed by Twig.

"Hey! Come back!" Nox said. But they only flew higher, as if they couldn't even hear him. "What are you—Gussie, you too?"

The Falcon girl launched upward, wings flapping lazily as she followed the cloud of moths, a hazy look in her eyes.

Nox felt the strange, alluring tug of the moths, as if they were whispering, *Follow, follow* . . . But he resisted. This was ridiculous. The whole thing was starting to make him uneasy.

But *someone* had to make sure those idiots didn't fly off into the night.

So despite the wrench of pain it sent splintering from his still-healing wound, Nox took off after the others. His dark wings stroked the air with barely a rustle.

They rose through the forest canopy amid the flurry of moths, in a fine rain of silver dust. It was like some mystical ceremony, one that made Nox's stomach twist with apprehension even as its weird beauty drew him onward and upward.

It was *magical*, which might have been another way of saying *wonderful* to anyone else. But to Nox, the word was dangerous. Foolish. Impossible. It was the kind of word he avoided. He didn't like things he couldn't understand, riddles that had more secrets than answers, pieces that didn't belong in the practical puzzle of reality.

Ellie, to his lack of surprise, followed the moths right through the trees into the open sky above the forest. Her wings stirred the tree-tops, lifting her higher, aiming for the stars.

Until Nox grabbed her hand and pulled her back.

He, Gussie, and Twig stood on the highest, slim branch of an oak, heads above the trees, but Ellie struggled against him, trying to pull free, completely entranced.

"Wake up, Sparrow," Nox said firmly. "Don't go chasing moon-moths, remember?"

Ellie blinked. Slowly, she sank down, to stand beside him on the branch. "But . . . where are they going?"

The moths soared upward, nearly blending into the stars. The farther away they got, the more they looked like a faint silver cloud drifting across the night sky. And still even Nox's wings twitched, longing to follow them, though he resisted the urge. So the whole *don't go chasing moonmoths* thing wasn't just a turn of phrase, he reckoned. How easy it would be to simply trail after them into that dark, danger-ous sky, forgetting every care, every worry, every painful memory . . . up until the moment a gargol sank its claws into you.

"No one knows where they go," said Gussie. "That's the big mys-tery of moonmoths, and it's why they're so rare. You'll only ever see a live one when it emerges from its chrysalis. Once they fly off into the night, they're never seen again. Those who tried to follow them ended up, well . . ."

She didn't have to finish that sentence.

Nox peered into the dark but found only stars. The glowing creatures may as well have melted into the sky like smoke.

For several minutes, no one spoke. Twig's cheeks were damp with tears he didn't seem to know were there.

"Well," said Nox at last. "That was fun. Back to bed."

"Your shoulder!" Ellie said. "You flew all the way up here—"

"It's fine." He shrugged, then immediately regretted the movement as a spasm of pain shot across his chest. "Mostly, anyway."

He waited until Gussie and Ellie had flown down, just to be sure neither would turn around and try to chase the moths again. Then he turned to Twig.

"Want me to finish your watch?"

"No. I couldn't sleep now anyway. Not after that."

"Just don't go after them, okay? A gargol would snap you like a, well, *twig*, skinny as you are."

Back on the ground, Nox found Gussie already fast asleep, spread haphazardly across the leaves.

"Wow," he said. "She was tired."

"Mmmtired," said Ellie. "Mmmhmm."

"What?" Nox turned around to see the Sparrow girl yawning, her hand fumbling for a tree to support herself. Her eyes were half lidded, her freckled wings dragging on the ground.

"Jusssleeepy . . . Nox . . ."

She collapsed beside Gussie and began to snore, one hand flung wide, the other over her face.

Nox stared. He slapped a hand to his neck, feeling the bite of a mosquito, then knelt beside Ellie's and Gussie's prone forms.

"Are you two messing with me?" he asked. "Because thasssnot . . . thasss . . ."

His tongue thickened in his mouth. His thoughts began to swim. A wave of sleepiness overwhelmed him and he swayed. The world tilted around him, his head slamming into the ground and his wings going limp, unfurled on the leaves. Nox had the wits to raise the hand he'd slapped the mosquito with.

Only it wasn't a mosquito on his fingers. It was a tiny, feathered dart.

Nox dropped it with a vague feeling of horror, then yawned.

"Oh . . . *thasssnot* . . . *so good* . . ." he sighed, and then he fell deeply, terribly asleep.

"We're missing one."

"The general said bring back three—and we got three."

Ellie worked her tongue, her mouth gritty and dry. The voices above her sounded wobbly, and she *really* had to pee. Also, there was something hard jabbing into her back, but she was only distantly aware of it. A soft, relaxed feeling spread through her, as if she were floating in a calm pond.

"But the little orange-headed one—"

"I swear, Tholomew, if you bring it up one more time, I'll knock you so hard your nose'll never pop rightways out again. It'd be an improvement on your overall look, anyway."

"Well, now you're just being *mean*, Bratton. And I did see an orange-headed one when they dropped that skunk bomb on us. Went blazing past me like a fire demon, he did."

One of the voices got louder, as if the speaker were walking toward her. "I am *not* tramping all's over this forest for some fire demon." Something prodded Ellie's hip—a boot, she reckoned. "Why're the brats still out? How much gumroot did you dose 'em with, you axe-brained lump?"

Gumroot. She remembered the herb from her studies with the Linden healer. It was powerful stuff. Its leaf was an effective pain reliever, while the root could be sleep-inducing in concentrated amounts. The guards—she still wasn't sure how many there were—must have sneaked up on the campsite while they were in the treetops, and drugged the kids with darts when they'd landed.

But Twig had gotten away. Who else could be the *orange-haired fire demon* the soldier meant?

Not that he could be much help against full-grown soldiers. No, there was nothing for it now but to be hauled away and thrown in prison forever. Stealing was one thing; stealing from a top-ranking general and bombing his fortress with pepper-and-skunk spray no doubt carried a life sentence.

Before she could stop herself, Ellie groaned in dismay, catching the guards' attention.

"Here we go!" said the one who'd prodded her. "Rise and shine and sing for us, you thieving little pustules."

No point in faking it anymore. She pried open her eyes one at a time and blinked at the soldiers.

There were two of them. The nearer one, a Falcon with a full beard tied in double braids, grinned at her with crooked yellow teeth. The other one she at first mistook for two people as her eyes adjusted to the light, but no, he was just one man, so broad and tall he took up the space of two. He looked sulky, and was toying with the flinter from Gussie's pack, trying to figure out how it worked. His sharply patterned wings marked him as a member of the Harrier clan. They were still at the campsite beneath the big rock.

"Where is it, Sparrow?" the Falcon asked. "The quicker you talk, the less we clip."

Confused, Ellie started to ask what he meant but then she saw them: the pair of scissors in his hand.

"N-no!" she managed to gasp, trying to wriggle away as he reached for her wing. But her hands and legs were bound, and she bumped into the sharp thing behind her—Gussie's elbow, it turned out. The other girl was still unconscious, bound behind Ellie. Nox lay above her, and as she struggled to pull her wings out of the soldier's reach, she saw one of Nox's dark eyes open and fix on her.

"Be still!" ordered the soldier. "You'll not be flying for a while anyway, where you're going. Don't make it harder than it has to be."

"Don't touch me!" Ellie snarled. She kicked with her bound feet, swiping the soldier's ankles. He fell with a shout, and the scissors sailed from his grip—impaling the soil just inches from Ellie's nose.

While the sulky one burst into laughter, the one Ellie had kicked sprang up again and seized her left wing, forcefully expanding it and grabbing his shears.

"You'll regret that!" he seethed. He held the blades open, high around Ellie's primary feathers. Her blood curdled. A slight clip could hamper her flight, slowing Ellie and making her clumsy in the air. A high clip would ground her entirely. It'd be *years* before she could fly again. Clipped feathers didn't grow back. You had to either pull them out—which was extremely painful—or wait till they molted. Then the new feathers could grow in, but that took months and months.

A test of courage proves the knight's heart, she recited desperately to herself. It was one of her favorite lines from *The King's Ladder*. But if this was a test, she felt she was failing it badly. She didn't feel courageous at all—only terrified.

"Please!" she cried at last. "Don't! *He* has it! The Crow boy—he's got the gemstone!"

Now Nox's other eye opened, and he gave her a disappointed shake of his head.

"Really?" he muttered. "Less than a minute and you crack?"

Ellie glared back. She wasn't about to sacrifice her *wings* so some thief could get away with his crime.

But instead of letting go of her to search Nox, the soldier only raised the scissors a few inches higher on her wing. "We already searched the three of you. We know you haven't got the skystone on you, so where *is* it?"

"I don't know!" Ellie said, tears swimming in her eyes. "Honestly!"

"We sold it," Nox said as calmly as if they were all sitting around the fire sharing a pot of tea.

The soldier's grip on the scissors relaxed a bit, and Ellie released a sob of relief.

"Sold it?" the man echoed.

"Yes," said Nox. "To a traveler on the road. A high clanner and his mates, couple of Hawks, Falcons, and an Oriole."

Oh skies, thought Ellie. Nox was telling the soldier about Zain! He described them exactly the way Ellie had when she'd told him about the group on the road yesterday. She could picture it in horrifying detail—the soldiers chasing down her fellow Lindeners, questioning them, mentioning a certain Sparrow girl . . .

She opened her mouth to tell them Nox was lying . . . then stopped.

His lie, after all, had kept the soldier from clipping her wings, at least for now.

"They saw us with it," said Nox. With a grunt of effort, he pushed himself onto his knees, shaking leaves and dirt from his dark wings.

"And, well, I don't have to tell *you* what high clans are like. You type want the shiniest of everything. So I sold it to them, cheaper than I'd have liked, but then there's not much room for negotiation when some Hawk clan lout's got you pinned against a tree."

The soldier narrowed his eyes and let go of Ellie's wing. She pulled it in quickly, tucking it behind her back. Gussie had begun to rouse behind her, moaning and looking around in confusion.

"Well, now," said the soldier, "I dunno if you're lying or not, but I reckon it'd be a good idea to keep you close till we find out. So, c'mon, boy. Wing out." He snipped the scissors in the air, grinning nastily at Nox, who glared back and kept his wings pinned securely to his back. He was making a show of not being afraid, but Ellie saw his face pale.

"Aw, Bratton," said the other soldier. The Harrier man still stood on the far side of the camp, scratching his rump. "Do you have to be such a beast about it all? They're just kids."

"Shut up, Tholomew!" snarled Bratton. "If we find that stone, it's a promotion for the both of us."

"All promotions mean is more work," complained Tholomew.

"Easy for you to say! You usually guard the war room. Do you know what door *I* have to guard? The latrine, that's what! Do you have any idea, Tholomew, what kinds of things I have to *smell*, every day, hours on end, all so's . . . what? Nobody steals the dung bucket? Do you know the bounteous variety of odors a body can emit? Because I do." Bratton tapped his skull. "I know 'em all, got 'em all catalogued up in my noggin whether I like it or not. I'm sick of it! I deserve a promotion, and that's the truth!"

"Oh, fine, then. But I want no part of it. I could have been an artist, you know," moaned Tholomew. "But no, we of the Bonce family are soldiers, said my mum, not scummy *artists*. So here I am, in the middle of nowhere, having to watch you torture kids for fun."

"We've a job to do, you scabby toad!" Bratton jabbed his scissors in the air. "Bring back the thieves and the skystone, that's what the general said. Want me to tell him you were too busy moaning to do your job? Get over here and hold this Crow's wing for me."

Tholomew relented, plodding over with a look of distaste. Ellie and Nox shared a panicked glance.

"Right, then," Tholomew sighed. "Let's just finish this so we can all go home and—"

Crack!

The soldiers froze as the sound echoed through the wood. It sounded like someone had stepped on a stick, but a hundred times louder. No *person* could take a step that big.

"Go look," Bratton ordered Tholomew.

Drawing his sword, Tholomew crept toward the noise. The forest had gone very still, as if it had drawn in its breath and held it. Nothing moved. No leaves stirred.

Then the trees in front of the soldier *exploded*.

CHAPTER FIFTEEN
· NOX ·

A roar ripped through the forest, flattening the air. Chips and chunks of wood shot in all directions. Nox ducked just in time to avoid being impaled by a jagged limb that hurtled at him like an arrow. Two trees had been snapped in half by a massive, fifteen-foot *thing* charging straight at Tholomew. It looked like a mossy hill, only with four trunk-like legs and a whole lot of yellow fangs.

Nox stared, his mouth dry.

"What *is* that thing?" Ellie cried out.

"Mossbear!" said Gussie. "This is very, very bad!"

The thing was shaped like a bear, but it was covered in layers of moss, grass, and vines. Nox had heard of them, late at night in the taverns of Thelantis, when hunters came in from the wilderness to swap stories. He'd always thought tales of mossbears were exaggerated.

He now knew he was wrong. If anything, those hunters had undersold the size and ferocity of the creatures. Mossbears were rare, found only in the deepest recesses of Bluebriar Forest. Six times the size of normal bears, they slept for weeks on end, never moving, and so the forest just grew *over* them as if they were mossy hillocks, hence their name.

Once woken, though, they were the most dangerous animals on four legs.

Tholomew screamed and threw himself aside just in time to avoid being trampled. Bratton cursed and drew his blade.

Nox twisted like a fox in a trap, trying to get free of the ropes around his wrists and ankles. The three of them were helpless, bound, and hobbled on the ground, with a bear the size of a house barreling toward them. But first, it seemed intent on crushing the fallen soldier.

"Tholomew!" Bratton called out. "*Fly*, you idiot—you've got wings, remember?"

Tholomew blinked, as if he *had* forgotten just that, then hastily scrambled to his feet and spread his wings, launching into the air a moment before the bear's massive paws slammed into the ground where he'd been cowering. Bratton also took flight, and the bear rose up on his hind legs and began swatting at the airborne soldiers. The men couldn't get close enough with their swords to strike.

Nox managed to pull his legs through his arms, putting his hands in front so he could chew the ropes with his teeth, but there was no time.

Because at that moment, the bear's head turned toward the helpless kids on the ground. Its nose quivered as it sniffed the air, and a huge glob of snot dribbled from one large nostril.

"*Oh skies,*" gasped Ellie. "It sees us."

Nox twisted and kicked, trying to crawl away. But then he heard a rustle behind him, and turned with dread, expecting to see another mossbear.

Instead, he saw something way weirder—a flood of squirrels poured from the trees, scampering toward them.

Gussie saw them too. "What the . . . ?"

Nox gasped as the squirrels swarmed around and over him, tiny paws gripping his clothing and hair. He heard Ellie yelp as she too was overtaken by the teeming, furry mass.

Then, suddenly, Nox's hands broke apart, the ropes falling away.

The squirrels had chewed right through them.

He laughed as the little animals set to work on his bound ankles, their sharp teeth separating the tough rope fibers in seconds. He now knew exactly who was orchestrating this strange escape plan.

"It's all right!" he said to Ellie and Gussie, who were still struggling to bat the squirrels away. "Let them help."

As if angered by his shout, the bear let out another deafening roar.

Nox sprang up, then helped Gussie to her feet. Ellie stood shakily, brushing away the remnants of the chewed rope. As quickly as they'd come, the squirrels vanished, skittering back into the trees.

They had to get away *fast*, but first, Nox needed to retrieve the gem—or *skystone*. Thanks to the soldiers, he now knew what it was called.

He was glad he'd thought to hide it when they made camp. *Loot's always safer stowed than towed*, the Talon had taught him.

Nox dove beneath the big boulder and began digging in the soil.

"What are you *doing*?" Ellie called.

"Get your stuff and let's go!" he replied.

Ellie grabbed Gussie's bag and tossed it to her, then reached for her own knapsack. She launched into the air—just as the bear broke into a charge.

"Nox!" Ellie screamed.

The bear was coming for him at the speed of a tornado. Its thundering steps shook the ground, making the trees shiver and a torrent of leaves shimmer down.

"Got it!" Nox said, his hand finally closing on the muddy gemstone. Then he turned and saw nothing but a wall of moss-covered fur and a wide, gaping jaw lined with fangs. The breath from its throat smacked into him like a wet, rotten wind as it roared.

Nox shut his eyes and waited for it to bite off his head. There wasn't even time to scream.

Instead, abruptly, the bear fell silent.

He peeled one eye open, his entire body clenched like a fist. The mossbear still loomed over Nox, but now it sat back on its rear end, eyes widening, ears flicking forward. It let out a short, friendly chuff.

"Twig," he sighed. "Cutting it close, don't you think?"

The boy had appeared from nowhere, and now stood next to the bear, grinning.

"Sorry," he said. "I had to say bye to the squirrels first. By the way, say hello to Mossbutt." He reached out and scratched the bear's chin.

Nox, his insides still wobbling, stared at the snotty, salivating mountain of fangs and fur in front of him. "What did I tell you about adopting things that could tear you in half?"

"How about things that just *saved your skin*?" returned Twig. "Anyway, Mossbutt would never hurt me. We've bonded." To prove it, he scratched the bear behind his ear, and the great beast practically purred.

"TWIG! NOX!" Gussie cried. "Shut up and *fly*! We've got other problems!"

She was right. The bear might have transformed into a tail-wagging puppy, but the soldiers had realized their prisoners were now free.

"Don't let them get away!" screamed Bratton. "Cut them down if you have to!"

Nox grabbed Twig and jumped into the air, spreading his wings.

"Bye, Mossbutt!" Twig called sadly, waving at the bear.

"*Fly*, you lunatic!" Nox said, pushing the kid along.

They winged through the trees with the soldiers in pursuit. There was no time for careful zigzagging; Nox crashed his way through limbs and leaves.

It was Ellie who took the lead, finding their path through the trees, calling to watch out for low branches. The girl could *fly*, and even Nox had to admire it. She turned on a hair, pivoting in midair, then slipped sideways and over and under branches so quickly it made his head spin.

But despite her brilliant flying, Bratton and Tholomew gained on them, their wings somehow navigating the trees with more precision than Nox had thought their larger bodies could possibly have.

Then, all at once, they burst out of the trees. The ground dropped away into a deep forest canyon, a roaring river churning through it. Nox's head reeled at the sudden change in altitude, but Ellie did not hesitate. She pinned her wings to her back and dove.

He gasped, expecting to see her smash into the river. With her wings clamped to her spine, she was diving headfirst toward the rocky river.

"Ellie!" he called. "Stop!"

Just before she reached the water, she flared her wings and pulled up, skimming over the surface. White water plunged over rocks and crashed against the canyon walls, the spray washing over the Sparrow girl. Beads of water slid over her oiled wings and fell away.

"C'mon!" she shouted.

"She's nuts!" Gussie said.

"She's also right," Nox replied. "The canyon is our best chance to shake those thugs."

Nox sucked in a breath, then dove, with Gussie and Twig close behind. They pulled up just short of the river, close enough that they could have stretched out a hand and dragged a finger through the water.

"It worked!" Ellie shouted, rolling to point above them.

Sure enough, Nox spotted the two silhouettes of the soldiers, high above the canyon. They'd lost sight of the kids. The river was camouflaging their escape.

When the canyon walls closed in, forming a passage no wider than a doorway, they had to slip though single file, tilting perpendicular to the ground.

Finally, they came to a place where the river spilled onto a wide, shallow bed of black pebbles. Here the water burbled calmly, and sleek spotted fish idled in the deeper pools along its edges. It was a bright, pleasant spot. Nox hoped they could pause to catch their breaths.

But, to his horror, the river below began to darken beneath a spreading shadow. The air cooled, causing Nox's skin to prickle with goose bumps. Even before he rolled to look at the sky, he knew what he would see.

A massive thunderhead slunk across the sun, swallowing it whole. Its flat belly seemed to nearly touch the treetops, while its swollen trunk towered into the atmosphere, bulbous and bloated. Lightning shivered in its depths, sending out a tidal wave of thunder.

It was the sort of cloud that was practically *guaranteed* to be teeming with gargols.

"Hide!" yelled Gussie.

Nox looked around frantically, his heart clashing against his rib cage, the rumble of thunder vibrating in his chest.

"There!" he shouted, and he angled desperately for a narrow crevice in the canyon wall. Little more than a slit in the stone, it was just tall enough for them to crawl in on their bellies, wings pressed flat. Nox waited till the others were all inside before he followed, barely pulling himself into the crevice before the sky tore open and rain lashed the ground.

The river, which had been babbling over the pebbles, now thrashed, turning to white froth. Thunder rebounded off the canyon walls. In minutes, the river began to rise, boiling rapids forming just below the four kids.

Then a pair of boots landed on the smooth rock bank before them, inches away.

"They're here somewhere!" It was unmistakably the voice of Bratton, the crueler of the two soldiers. Nox scrunched backward, his wings tightening. He could still hear the snip of Bratton's scissors.

"We need to find cover!" came Tholomew's reply. "That cloud—"

"Finish the job and quit whining!" snarled Bratton. "I'll tear the wings off those brats when I get my hands on them!"

Nox exchanged a look with Ellie. He grinned, as if this were all some kind of game and he was winning. When he'd given Nox charge of his own crew, the Talon had taught him that once the leader panicked, everyone panicked. It was his job to help them stay coolheaded, or they were done for.

But Bratton was only steps away. All he'd have to do to find them was . . .

Exactly what he did next.

Turn around.

The soldier dropped to one knee and bent his head down—locking eyes with Nox.

"HA!" he roared. "Got you! Be afraid, scum, because Uncle Bratton's gonna have some fun with—"

"SCREEEEEEEEEE . . . !"

Nox's heart shriveled as the strange cry rang out of the storm, interrupting the soldier. Nails dragging over slate, trees splintering in two, the keening of a lost, frightened child—the scream was all these things and much, much worse.

The sound was darkness.

The sound was despair.

It was a sound he'd heard before, distantly, outside the walls of Thelantis, but never this close. Never so loud it was like a physical force, a rod of sound driving through his skull.

It was the scream of a gargol.

CHAPTER SIXTEEN
· ELLIE ·

The gargol's screech impaled Ellie like a spear, sliding deep into her mind until it struck the memory of her parents.

Falling from the sky.

Broken before they hit the ground.

That scream cracked her open, pain splintering outward as sharp and fresh as if no time at all had passed, as if she were a fledgling again, screaming and helpless and terrified.

Ellie wasn't sure if she grabbed Nox's hand or if he grabbed hers, but suddenly she was aware of her fingers squeezing his.

Bratton looked shaken by the sound, but he didn't flee. Instead, he dove toward them, drawing a dagger. Ellie reached for her own knife, but before she could pull it from her belt, Bratton grabbed Nox by his hair and dragged him into the open.

"Give me the skystone!" Bratton hissed. "I know you have it. Hand it over *now*, boy, or I'll cut your wings off one by one!"

Unbelievably, Nox smiled. "All right, all right, you win."

He opened his hand—and there on his palm sat a smooth black pebble, just like the ones scattered in the river below.

"You think you're funny?" Bratton snarled. Then he froze, his eyes settling on the chain around Nox's neck.

"Ha!" He tugged it, yanking the skystone out of Nox's shirt, but

Nox twisted, knocking the man's dagger away and seizing the chain himself.

They tugged back and forth, while Ellie watched the sky anxiously.

"There's a gargol up there somewhere!" she cried. "Stop it, Nox, *stop it*! Just let it go!"

There wasn't a jewel in the Clandoms worth dying for. But Nox and Bratton struggled on, the chain of the necklace stretched taut between them and the skystone dangling at its center.

"*Let . . . go!*" Bratton roared, and he heaved on the chain.

The iron band that held the skystone broke. Nox's hand lashed out to catch the gem—but it never fell.

Instead, impossibly, it began to *float*.

From under the protection of the rock, Ellie craned her neck to watch as the bright blue gem lifted into the air as lightly as a soap bubble. Its facets flashed even in the gray light of the storm, as if lit from within.

"What the . . ." Bratton blinked, stunned just long enough that Nox had time to snatch the stone out of the air.

The soldier's face twisted with anger. He grabbed at the thief, but at that moment, Ellie sprang out and slashed her dagger, splitting his trousers and cutting his shin. Bratton howled and reeled backward.

Ellie grabbed Nox. "Back under the rock! *Now!*"

Above them, another gargol screech rent the air. This time, it was louder.

Closer.

"*Hurry, Nox!*" Ellie yelled.

The Crow boy slid under the rock as Bratton leaped up and charged. Ellie gasped and scrambled into the crevice. Nox and Gussie grabbed her arms to pull her in.

"Sparrow scum!" the soldier roared. "I'll gut you—"

His shout cut off as Bratton *vanished*.

One moment his legs were there, the next they were gone, snatched up into the sky—right out of his boots, which remained planted on the rock. The soldier screamed, his terrified voice raw with pain until, abruptly, it ended. Rain drummed steadily in the silence that followed.

Ellie couldn't breathe. She stared at the spot where he'd been, her body stiff with terror.

A second later, Bratton hit the river with a large splash. He sank, then resurfaced downstream, floating facedown, a dark stream of blood in his wake.

The river carried him away, leaving only his boots behind.

"Holy skies," Nox breathed.

Ellie held tight to his hand, her very heart standing still.

Then came a grinding, crunching sound. She looked up . . . to see three stone claws curling around the lip of rock above them, digging into the stone until small chunks of it broke away and rained down.

Ellie *heard* the gargol, inches away, but could see only those three deadly claws. She heard the groan and grind of its stone body, the heavy, labored breaths. It inhaled as if its lungs were filled with rocks—great, dry, wheezing gasps.

Her eyes slid to Nox, their gazes connecting. He looked back at her, his dark freckles stark against his pale face.

The gargol released another ear-shattering screech, its claws digging deeper into the rock, and then it launched away. Still Ellie could not see it, but the heavy beat of its wings was unmistakable, great *whump-whump*s of air.

Then it was gone.

For several long minutes, no one spoke. Embarrassed, Ellie pulled her hand from Nox's. His palm was as sweaty as her own. She stared at Bratton's abandoned boots and the careful stitches along the toes where he—or someone who'd loved him—must have patched up holes. Behind her terror came a wave of shame and anger, in a thick, ugly tangle that clotted her lungs. She hated cowering like this. She hated feeling so scared she couldn't *breathe*.

"Sparrow, are you . . ." Nox faltered.

"I'm fine," Ellie snapped. "Better than poor Bratton, anyway."

"*Poor* Bratton?" echoed Nox. "You realize that was the same slimeball who was about to clip your wings and cut my throat?"

"Nobody deserves that," Ellie whispered, still gazing at the empty boots. "Nobody."

"Excuse me," said Gussie, her voice strained. "But did I lose it for a minute there, or did that skystone *float*?"

Nox raised his hand, then slowly opened it finger by finger. The four of them stared as, freed from Nox's grasp, the skystone lifted gently from his palm and began once more to rise. The thief grabbed hold of it, then released it again. Still it bobbed up, like an apple underwater, rising for the surface.

Ellie *had* seen a rock like that before, she was sure of it. She stared hard at the skystone, trying to remember what it reminded her of.

Ellie started to reach for it, but Nox got it first, giving her a narrow look. "Only *I* touch it."

"It's lighter than air," whispered Gussie. "But how? That's impossible. Rocks don't float."

"Magic," breathed Ellie.

"Oh, c'mon. There's no such thing as magic." Nox pressed the stone back into the iron band, clicking it into place. The metal weighed it down and made it hang from the chain like an ordinary rock again. "Anyway, it doesn't matter if it can float, sing, or play cards. It's worth a fortune, and I intend to cash it in."

"Of course you do," grumbled Ellie.

As a distraction, she tried to puzzle out how the stone worked and why it felt so familiar. Not that she thought she'd forget something like a magic rock. Still, she just couldn't shake the feeling . . .

But her mind wouldn't concentrate, instead slipping back to Bratton's choked scream as the gargol had seized him, and the monster's stony claws inches above her head.

She squeezed her eyes shut. Her chest pinched, ribs pressing her heart. Flashes of memory spasmed in her mind—gargol claws, her parents' screams, the burst of white armor and steel that was the Goldwing knight. Sunflowers, sunflowers spread as far as the eye could see, beaming their sunny yellow gazes as if everything were all right. As if nothing had happened. As if none of it mattered.

No.

She wouldn't let the past swallow her up. She wouldn't become like that Sparrow kid Mother Rosemarie had brought from Mossy Dell, after he'd lost his parents to gargols. That kid had worn his grief like a shroud, never speaking, never looking anyone in the eye, never laughing or smiling or playing. He'd just sat there, as if the gargol had snatched out his soul and left the shell of his body behind. Only when someone made a loud, sudden noise did he stir, falling into a fit of shrieks and diving beneath beds or tables. A boy ruled by fear. *Consumed* by it.

That wouldn't happen to Ellie.

She could control her fear. Push it back. Banish it, by force of will. She *would not* be afraid. She would be a Goldwing, and soon, when she faced another gargol, she would face it head-on. All she had to do was reach Thelantis, win that sky-blasted race, and finally, finally put on her knight's armor.

No more hiding.

No more fear.

CHAPTER SEVENTEEN
· ELLIE ·

Ellie was first to crawl out the next morning, beneath a sky so clear it was if the storm had never happened. The river must have risen higher in the night, because it had swept away Bratton's boots, but now it burbled peacefully.

It wasn't yet dawn, the sky just barely pink. The others were still sleeping. Twig's collection of animals was like a living, breathing fur coat. Squirrels, hedgehogs, mice, and some animals Ellie didn't even have names for clung to him, with Lirri in the place of honor against his cheek. Gussie lay with her head on her arm, drooling, her other hand curled protectively around her bag of parts. Nox's wings wrapped around him, so all Ellie could see of him was a bundle of black feathers and hair.

By the river's edge, Ellie spread her feet wide and drew a deep breath. She'd gotten distracted from her morning routine since leaving Linden, but the gargol attack had reminded her what was at stake. She had to be prepared for the race.

She set down *The King's Ladder* on the driest rock she could find, open to the pages depicting the twelve steps. A routine of stretches and fighting poses, there was one set of moves for each of the twelve virtues the book taught. They were meant to help knights in training remember the lessons by practicing them both mentally and physically. Performing the steps had become her morning ritual, but she hadn't done it since leaving home three days ago.

The fluid moves took her from one form to the next in a smooth flow of motion. Legs wide, arms high, legs crossed, body bent, slow, precise turns and twists and reaches. She whispered the name of each step as she performed it: *"Humility, courage, honesty."*

The smooth stone bank provided solid footing, and her bare feet pressed against the stone for stability. Her wings worked too, spreading, folding, synchronized with her other limbs for balance.

"Loyalty, generosity, obedience."

High above, the canyon walls blocked much of the sky, but the golden glow that burned along their edges told her the sun was now rising.

Ellie moved into the sparring portion of the routine. *Strength, discipline, sacrifice.* She punched, ducked, rolled, kicked, envisioning her opponent. This morning, her imagination conjured up Zain. *Perseverance, responsibility, honor.* She could almost hear his laughter as she jabbed a fist at his eye. Sometimes, he'd joined her in the routine, and whenever she'd actually managed to land a blow, he'd insisted he *let* her do it. She hadn't realized it, but even then he didn't truly believe in her. How could she have been so blind?

Careful, her conscience warned her. *You're starting to sound like you agree with that thief.*

No. She gritted her teeth. Just because she'd been wrong about Zain, that didn't mean she was wrong about the Goldwings.

"Your hips are too stiff," said a voice.

Surprised, Ellie lost her balance mid-kick and toppled over with a yelp. She landed on her rear in the river shallows, the smooth black pebbles much sharper than they appeared.

"Gussie! You can't just sneak up on me like that."

The Falcon girl stood a few strides up the bank, arms folded as if she'd been there a while.

Ellie hauled herself up, wringing water from her tunic. "I know what I'm doing," she said.

"If you did, then you'd know the energy you put in a punch *starts* in your feet and travels through your hips. Stiffen the hips, you block the energy. You've got to loosen up a little."

Ellie tilted her head, looking at Gussie more closely. "I thought you didn't do warrior stuff."

"Not anymore." Gussie shrugged. "Doesn't mean I wasn't trained for it since before I could walk. Sparring was considered more important than actual literacy in my family."

Ellie clapped her hands together, elated. "Will you teach me? Please, oh *please*—"

Gussie waved a hand. "No. Like you said, I don't do that stuff anymore. It's stupid, all the punching and kicking and solving problems with brute force. The only thing fighting ever produces is more fighting."

"Well, it might stop a gargol," muttered Ellie. "It might have saved my parents."

She resumed her routine, hurling punches at the air, her jaw tight. She worked for another minute in silence, ignoring Gussie. Then, when she spun to flick another punch at the air behind her, her fist met Gussie's outstretched palm.

Breathing hard, Ellie froze, matching gazes with the Falcon girl.

"The only person you're going to hurt punching like that," said Gussie, "is yourself. And me, because it's so painful to watch."

Ellie stepped back. "You can make fun of me. I don't care. I've heard it from plenty of people already." Squaring her feet, she resumed her punches. "I've heard it all." *Punch.* "Too small." *Punch.* "Too weak." *Punch.* "Too Sparrow." *Punch.* "Well, turns out I'm also too stubborn."

She kicked, punched again, and spun—to find Gussie swinging for her face.

"Like *this*," Gussie said. Ellie gasped and clumsily dodged, shocked at the power rocketing through Gussie's arm.

"See?" said Gussie. "Drive through the hip."

Ellie eyed her, wondering at the Falcon's sudden change of heart. "Show me again."

They sparred up and down the water's edge, then in the shallows of the river. Braced against the current, bare feet struggling for footing on the pebbled riverbed, the girls exchanged punches and kicks. Gussie showed Ellie moves she'd never seen and taught her how to adjust her stance and attacks to compensate for her smaller stature.

"You're half the size of most high clanners," said Gussie. "And half as strong."

When Ellie began to scowl, Gussie added, "What you think of as weaknesses are actually strengths. You've just got to use them right. You're quicker, you can be smarter, and your small size makes you a smaller mark. They won't expect that. They're used to swinging at higher targets. You'll put them off balance, and that's when you'll find your opening."

Nox and Twig had woken while the girls were sparring. Nox sat on a rock upstream, trying and failing to spear a fish with a sharp stick he'd fashioned. Twig explored the water, lifting rocks and poking at things that wriggled in the mud. He'd rolled up his trousers and left his shirt on the bank. It was the first time Ellie had seen his back and the ropey scars where the circus master had whipped him for releasing all the animals. She turned away, feeling sick and angry, but not wanting him to notice she'd seen.

"So why'd you help me?" she asked Gussie. "What happened to *fighting is stupid*?"

"Trust me, it is," Gussie said dryly. "But I guess . . . I know what it's like, to be told you shouldn't be who you are. To have your own clan disapprove of you."

Ellie waited, wondering if the girl would finally open up about her past. Her curiosity buzzed but she bit her tongue, knowing that if she pried, Gussie was more likely to shut down than talk.

Gussie picked up a black pebble and squeezed it. "I can see how badly you want to ask, Sparrow. So go on. Get it over with."

Ellie burst out, "Where's your family?"

"In Vestra, where they've been for generations."

Vestra. The ancestral clan seat of the Falcons. All Ellie knew of the place was that it sat atop harsh cliffs overlooking the sea, and that it was famous for producing some of the toughest warriors in the Clandoms.

"They have very firm ideas about what Falcons are and are not supposed to be," Gussie continued, rolling the pebble in her palm. "And *scholar* is definitely in the *unacceptable* column. So when I announced I wouldn't attend the Vestra Warrior Academy like every other kid in my clan . . . well, let's say that was one awkward family dinner."

"They wanted to make you into something you're not," Ellie said softly. "I know what that feels like."

Gussie tilted her head. "Yeah. I guess you do."

"So you ran away like I did?"

She gave a short, acidic laugh. "I didn't even have a chance to. They kicked me out, then and there."

"They . . . what?" Ellie's eyes went round.

"It's called a *farflight*," sighed Gussie. "When a kid from a high clan refuses the family business, they get sent out to 'wander the wilderness until they find their inner warrior.'" Her voice turned mocking. "Most kids on a farflight return in a few days, their wills broken. But a lot of them either take up quiet lives far away, or . . . don't survive at all."

Ellie looked at the river, not wanting Gussie to see the horror in her expression.

And she'd thought the Sparrows had been tough on *her*.

What kind of people threw out their own child just because they wanted something different in life?

"Not all Falcons are like that," Gussie added. "Many of the families who live outside Vestra aren't so . . . traditional. But I guess I drew the unlucky card."

"No," Ellie said harshly. "It's your family who are the unlucky ones. Clearly they couldn't see how smart you are. I bet one day, when you're a famous inventor, they'll *beg* you to come back."

Gussie snorted. "And I'll tell *them* to go on a flappin' farflight."

But by the look in her eyes, Ellie guessed the Falcon girl was secretly hoping for that exact thing. Ellie certainly was. The only thing sweeter than imagining herself as a Goldwing knight was imagining celebrating her victory with her Sparrow kin.

Why was the love that was supposed to be free the hardest kind to earn?

"I take it you didn't give in," Ellie said. "You went to Thelantis with or without their blessing."

"Kind of like a stubborn Sparrow I recently met," Gussie said, with a rare smile. "Yeah. I went to Thelantis to enroll at a university, but none would take me without my parents' permission. I'd have to wait till I was sixteen before I could enter on my own. I thought I'd find work in the city till then, but my first night there, some goons tried to rob me."

"Nox?" Ellie growled, shooting a dagger look at the Crow boy.

"No, it was a gang of Jay clanners. They wanted to kidnap me for ransom or some stupid thing—it's a real misconception that all high clan kids come from rich families, you know. I mean, *I* do, but it's not like my family would've . . ." She tossed her hand, as if batting away a fly. "Anyway, they start to grab me, and next thing I know, there's some maniac across the street yelling curses at the guys. They got mad and go beat him up instead, and I took off." Gussie rubbed her thumb over the pebble, looking lost in the memory. "That maniac was Nox. He made himself a distraction so the Jays would leave me alone. And he got two black eyes and a broken rib for it."

Ellie looked upriver, to where Nox had given up on spearfishing and was instead packing his knapsack, preparing for the day's journey. "He really did that? Without even knowing you?"

Gussie nodded. "He's annoying and bossy and half the time you think he's going to get you killed. But at least you know if anyone dies, he'll make sure he goes first. I guess that's why when he offered to let me join his crew, I said yes. There are other monsters besides gargols in Thelantis. You've gotta have someone watching your back."

Upstream, Nox had taken the skystone out of his shirt. He was tightening the iron band around it, so it wouldn't float away again.

"Nox lost his parents, didn't he?" she murmured.

Nodding, Gussie said, "He won't talk about it. All I know is his father's dead and his mother's in prison. But because they're a shattered clan, the Crows can't take care of their orphans like other clans do. So according to the *rules*, a kid like Nox would've just ended up in some workhouse disguised as an orphanage, hardly better than a slave."

"When the rules are designed to break you," Ellie whispered, "you have to break the rules."

Nox's motto. At first, Ellie had thought it sounded like an excuse to do what he wanted, and to ignore the laws everyone else lived by.

But maybe there was more to it than that, and the world wasn't as simple as Ellie had thought.

"Hey!" Nox shouted, landing silently behind Ellie and making her jump nearly out of her skin. "Since when do you two sit around gossiping?"

"None of your business," said Ellie.

"Why? Were you talking about *me*?" He gave her a cocky grin.

"*Yawn*," said Ellie. "These rocks would be a more interesting subject."

He clapped a hand to his heart, as if wounded. "Well, say goodbye to your precious rocks, Sparrow, because we've wasted enough time. Twig, put that down and let's go!"

Upriver, Twig made a face at Nox and gave the crayfish he was holding to Lirri. The vicious little creature bit the head off in one crunch, then shoved the rest down her throat.

Ellie sighed and stood up, shaking out her wings. She was not looking forward to another long day of fleeing justice.

"Hey, what's that?" Gussie said, pointing.

A lump of cloth was floating in the water, spinning in an eddy.

"Someone's garbage," said Nox, shrugging. "Leave it."

Ellie fluttered to the eddy and plucked the thing out of the water. It dripped all over her shirt. "It's a *doll*."

It had a clay body clothed in a carefully stitched little dress, complete with an apron and bonnet and wilted felt wings. The expression painted on its face looked startled, the lips a perfect O and the blue eyes wide.

"Creepy," said Nox. "Now throw it back and let's go."

"Wait." Ellie brushed away the mud and leaves from the doll's face. "Someone scratched a word on her forehead."

Nox grimaced. "Okay, *double creepy*. You'll probably have seven years' back luck just for touching that thing."

"What's it say?" asked Gussie.

Ellie stared at the one-word message, her heart starting to beat faster. Then she looked up at the others and said, "'*Help*.'"

CHAPTER EIGHTEEN
· NOX ·

"It could have been in this river for years," Nox pointed out. He was starting to feel anxious. The longer they stuck around, the more likely the soldiers would catch up to them. They didn't have time for distractions. "Or the storm may have washed that thing for miles."

"Or," said Ellie, "they could be nearby, desperate for help. Maybe hurt or sick."

"You do realize we're already behind schedule?" Nox said. "If you don't reach Thelantis in three weeks, you'll miss your only chance at the Race of Ascension. And if I recall, the last time you answered someone's cry for help, it *cost* you a race."

"And if *I* recall, that someone was *you*, and I saved your life," she snapped back.

He shrugged. "Look, it's your future you want to throw away."

"He's right, you know," said Gussie. "This person could be really far upriver, or the message could be days old. Maybe someone else found them or . . ."

Or maybe it was too late, was what she didn't say.

"One hour," said Ellie. "We can scout upriver for one hour and if we don't find anyone, we turn back."

"I'm in," said Twig eagerly. Probably just because he wanted to look for more crayfish or something.

Nox pinched the bridge of his nose. "We're not heroes, Twig. We're not responsible for whoever this person is."

"I agree," said Gussie, shouldering her knapsack, its many filled pockets jangling. "We should keep moving. This is not our problem and turning back now would be counterproductive. Upriver, if you haven't noticed, happens to be the direction of the fortress we just robbed, and thus the soldiers hunting us."

"Good," said Nox. "We're decided then."

"*I've* decided I'm going to help," said Ellie. "Come or don't come. But what right do I have to be a Goldwing if I won't help a person in need? It's like Sir Garesh the Red says in *The King's Ladder*: A heart without honor is no heart at all."

"Honor!" scoffed Nox as Ellie shot into the air. "Well, you know what the Talon says? He says honor makes for a fine funeral shroud and little else."

"Go!" she said. "I'll catch up to you later."

"Fine!" Nox shouted as she flew away. "Go be honorable and dead! Meanwhile, I'll be smart and . . ." He sighed. "She can't hear me, can she?"

"Nope," said Twig. "She's gone."

Ellie had taken off through the canyon without even looking back.

"She's insane," said Nox. "I mean, you both agree, right? She's completely, totally—"

"I'm going with her," said Twig, and he took off with a flutter.

Nox growled in frustration and looked at Gussie.

"You're right," Gussie said. "She's crazy. But . . . I kind of like her. Besides, aren't you a *little* curious who dropped the doll?"

He groaned as the Falcon girl took flight, and then all three of them were gone.

Lunatics, the lot of them.

Nox remembered the day the Talon had made him watch as the Goldwings hanged a thief from a rival gang. Nox asked how the man had been caught.

"His girl walked into a sting, got herself nabbed selling stolen pearls to undercover guards. She was lost the moment she stepped through the door, but this fool ran in anyway, thinking to save her." The Talon had shaken his head in disappointment. "We look after our own, Nox, but you can't look after anyone if you've walked into a noose. You want to survive this world? Listen to your wings, not your heart. Your wings will always tell you when it's time to fly."

Well, his wings didn't like any of this one bit.

Nox growled and kicked at pebbles, determined not to let Ellie drag him into danger. They'd be back soon anyway, after finding nothing and nobody in need of saving. He cursed the Sparrow girl and her stupid hero complex, and her storybook with all its ridiculous platitudes. *A heart without honor*, indeed. Well, at least at the end of the day, *his* heart would still be beating.

But after five minutes of sitting on a rock, he stood up and yelled, "Fine! Have it your way! But only because I'm bored and I wanna see your face when you realize what a mistake this is!"

He planted one foot on the rock he'd been sitting on and bounded up, wings spreading.

Remembering the bend in the river, Nox took a shortcut over the treetops, through a sky tossed by strong winds. The forest below shook and roared like ocean surf.

He gritted his teeth and swooped back down to the river, just as Ellie, Twig, and Gussie rounded the bend.

"Ha!" Ellie said, slowing to hover in front of him. "Don't try to talk me out of this, Nox."

"As if I could," he sighed. "I'm here to hold you to your promise—*one hour* of searching, no more."

Ellie grinned, then flew past him. "Try to keep up!"

At least his shoulder was a lot better; it still twinged painfully, but he could fly without feeling like every wing beat would kill him. And he wasn't about to ask for a break to rest, not when his pride depended on it. He kept pace with Ellie as she flew farther upriver.

After another forty minutes, Nox fluttered to the front of the group and flared his wings, stopping them. "Time's up. There's nobody out here."

Ellie shook her head. "But—"

"Sparrow, we had a deal."

"Nox—"

"I'm not budging on this. We have a schedule of our own, you know, and—"

"Nox, *look*," Gussie interrupted.

He turned to see what she was pointing at.

A little girl lay on a rock in the middle of the river, curled up so that she was hard to see at first. Rapids churned all around her.

"She's trapped," whispered Ellie, swooping past Nox.

They landed on the rock, startling the girl lying there. She couldn't have been more than six years old, her reddish-brown skin shivering uncontrollably and her black hair hanging in wet ropes.

"Who—who are you?" she said, scrambling back. "Are you here to help?"

"Yes," said Ellie gently, kneeling beside her. "We got your message. Why are you on this rock? Why don't you just—"

Nox saw it the same moment Ellie did: the reason the girl hadn't flown to safety.

Her wings were gnarled and twisted as old tree branches, the few feathers clinging to them ragged and useless. The delicate skin stretching over her wing joints, which should have been covered in protective down, was dry and scaly.

Ellie, who'd reached for the girl, now withdrew her hand as if from a snake. Nox sighed and lowered his gaze. He'd seen this kind of thing before.

"What . . . what happened?" the Sparrow asked, her voice a rasp. "How'd you end up here?"

"My mother," the girl said. "There was a rockslide and we fell. She—she's stuck up there."

She pointed upriver, where a heap of boulders piled into the river and up the bank. Nox could just make out a bundle of clothes in the mess. His stomach dropped.

"What's your name, kid?" he asked.

"M-Mally," she stammered. Her lips were nearly blue.

"Let's get you warm. Then we'll see about your mother. Oh, and I think someone's been missing you." He took the doll from Ellie and handed it to the girl, who hugged it tight.

"Sam," she whispered, kissing the doll's cheek. "I *knew* you'd bring help!"

Stepping around Ellie, who was still staring at the girl's withered wings, Nox scooped Mally up. She was light as a sack of seed, and at once she nestled into his warmth.

"Nox," whispered Ellie. "What if she's contagious?"

"She's not," said Gussie sadly. "It's wingrot. Not contagious, but very dangerous. Half the people who contract it don't—"

"*Gus,*" Nox said sharply. "Why don't you go check on the mother?"

Gussie blinked, then winced. "Right. Sorry. C'mon, Twig."

They fluttered toward the rockslide, and Nox drew a deep breath, preparing to launch himself into the air over the rapids.

Then Ellie laid a hand on his arm. "Let me help," she said. "You're not in much better shape than she is."

Nox relented because his shoulder was starting to throb.

"Together," he said, and Ellie nodded.

He held Mally's shoulders and Ellie took her legs, and together they flew over the deadly rapids to the shore, landing on a muddy bank.

"Stay with her," said Ellie. "I'll help Twig and Gussie."

He nodded, unable to speak, as his pain was starting to make his vision blur. He sat beside Mally and tried to keep his breaths even.

"Thank you," Mally whispered. "I thought I was gonna die on that rock."

"What were you and your mother doing out here?"

"We were going to Stillcreek. There's a doctor there my mom thinks might . . . might help me." Her broken wings twitched, and he noticed her face flinch with pain.

"Yeah," he said, his heart wrenching. "Maybe he can."

But he knew the truth. There was no cure for wingrot. It was a new disease, and a fast-working one, destroying a person's wings within days. He'd known a few people in his home neighborhood of Knock Street who'd caught it. They'd all been driven out of the city, because even though the disease wasn't contagious, people still feared what they didn't understand. A whole new village called Rottown had sprung up outside Thelantis's gates, full of the afflicted. Some survived and returned, but their wings were always so mangled it was obvious they would never fly again.

Most never returned at all.

"Look," he said to Mally. "Here they come with your mother."

Ellie, Gussie, and Twig landed, supporting a Dove clan woman between them. Her soft gray wings were healthy and unharmed, but she had a nasty bruise on her leg. She landed gingerly, and Twig grabbed a stick for her to lean on.

"Mama!" Mally cried, jumping up to hug her mother. "Are you okay?"

"Yes, love. My leg was pinned under a rock, but these brave young people helped. Are you hurt?"

Mally shook her head and cried as she squeezed her mother.

"I'm Shayn," the woman said, nodding to Nox. "Thank you for coming to our aid. You are brave young heroes, and we're in your debt."

"Yeah, sure," he mumbled. He was used to being cursed at and chased away, not praised. This whole thing was starting to feel really embarrassing.

"It was Nox's idea to come, the minute we found Mally's doll. Wasn't it, Nox?" Ellie shot him a wicked smile.

He scowled back. "Glad we could help."

"Let me return the favor," said Shayn. "There's an inn west of here. We planned to spend the night there. I can pay for your bed and supper. Please. I have means."

"Thanks," said Nox, "but we really—"

"Would *love* to," Gussie quickly inserted. "Warm, dry bed? Hot supper? *Absolutely*." She glared at Nox.

"Relax," Ellie said, nudging him with her elbow. "We deserve a little break, don't we? You heard the nice lady. We're *heroes*."

She laughed, patting Mally on the head as Nox hung his head and groaned. He knew when he was defeated.

CHAPTER NINETEEN
· ELLIE ·

After a few hours of walking with Mally and her mother—the time mostly filled by Twig showing off his pets to the delighted little girl—they came to a crossroads, five paths meeting at the largest tree Ellie had ever seen. It was easily as wide as the Home for Lost Sparrows, its bark so tough and gnarled she doubted there was an axe in all the Clandoms that could dent it.

Driven into the ground at the bottom of the tree were three signs:

GRANNY TAM'S BATHS! BEDS! AND BREAKFAST!

LOOK UP

MORE UP

Ellie tilted her head back until she nearly lost her balance, then finally spotted the building huddled in the large branches. The inn didn't look like it had been built in the tree so much as *dropped* from a very great height to crash higgledy-piggledy into the canopy. Rooms, porches, and staircases leaned at disastrous angles, as if at any moment they'd break away and plummet to the ground. Multiple chimney stacks belched gray smoke into the leaves, and a string of laundry dangled between two branches. Strangest of all were the four large pods hanging like massive fruits from the branches. Yet it all held together somehow, and the smell wafting out its windows was undeniably—

"*Bacon,*" sighed Gussie. "And potatoes."

They flew up cautiously to scout the place. Mally and her mother took a rickety staircase that wound up and around the trunk.

No soldiers waited to ambush them inside, and no posters with their faces on them had been pasted to the walls. Ellie's nerves unclenched a little.

The inn's main room consisted of a dining hall—the floor slanting downhill—and a kitchen. An old woman sat between them, behind a wooden counter, smoking a pipe. She had one eye covered with a patch, leathery skin as dark as sunflower seeds, and gray hair bundled in a gravity-defying pile atop her head.

"Well, well. *Hello,* tadpoles," she crooned, smiling around her pipe. A cloud of curiously familiar, sweet-smelling smoke hovered in the air above her, and Ellie suddenly realized it was the same scent she often sniffed in Mother Rosemarie's private rooms back at the Home for Lost Sparrows. "What can I do for you?"

"If you please, I'll take a room for my daughter and me, and these four as well," said Shayn, laying down coin.

"Lovely," said the old woman, leaning forward to swipe the coins. "Poor dears, how tired you all must be, and traveling in such dreadful weather as we've had! Tsk! You let old Granny Tam take care of you now. I'll heat the baths if you want them."

Twig made a face. "Forget it—"

"We'll *all* have baths," Gussie said sternly, driving an elbow into Twig's ribs.

"Anyone else staying here?" asked Nox, who was still looking around suspiciously.

"Alas, it's been a quiet season," sighed Granny Tam. "Fewer travelers lately, likely due to the rise in . . . Well." She glanced pityingly at

Mally's wings. "There are many sad stories in the wind these days. It's a strange time, and a cruel one. I reckon I know what kind of help you're seeking, poor dears, and I wish you good fortune."

Shayn put an arm around her daughter. "Thank you."

"Your staff!" said Gussie, pointing to an odd stick leaning on the wall. It had one large crook, like a shepherd's staff, and a shorter hook protruding from the other side. "It's a lockstave, isn't it?"

"Sharp girl," said Granny Tam, considering Gussie more closely.

"I learned about all the ancient fighting methods," Gussie said. "I didn't know anybody used lockstaves anymore, except for . . ." Gussie's eyes widened. "Are you a member of the Restless Order?"

"That I am," said the old woman, her crinkled smile spreading.

"The Restless Order?" asked Ellie.

It was Nox who answered. "They're a group of hermits who live up in the highest mountains, where they worship rocks or something."

"We don't *worship* anything," sniffed Granny Tam. "We spend our time in meditation, attempting to understand the secrets of the natural world in order to settle the restlessness in our souls."

"*Bums who stare at rocks,*" said Nox. "Leastways, that's how I've heard them called. Um . . . not that I, personally, have ever called them that." He cleared his throat.

"Rocks, young man," said Granny Tam, "have quite a lot to say, if you know how to listen."

"And they can see the future," said Twig.

Everyone turned to stare at him.

"Rocks?" asked Ellie.

"No, the Restless," he muttered. "What? There was an Order monk in the circus I was in. He did fortune-telling for a half-copper."

"Oh, good grief," said Gussie. "Nobody can tell the future."

"Strictly speaking," said Granny Tam, winking at her, "you're right, young Falcon. Loosely speaking, however . . . sometimes the future tells *itself*, to the sensitive ear."

Gussie scowled. "If you're in the Order, what're you doing way down here?"

"The thing about mountains is they get cold, and old bones dislike cold." She shrugged. "There are as many rocks down here as up there, and trees, rivers, and plants to boot. We of the Order meditate upon all nature's wonders."

Granny Tam rapped her knuckles on the counter, making them all jump. "Enough talk. Supper needs cooking, bodies need scrubbing"— her one eye fixed on Twig's muddy face—"and the day grows no younger. You're a hungry bunch, I can tell."

No one argued against that.

That night, bellies full of roasted carrots, potatoes, and apple tart, and bodies and hair scrubbed to shining with warm water and goat's milk soap, Ellie and the others followed Granny Tam to their sleeping quarters, one of the large hanging pods made of pale woven reeds.

"You'll have to all share," said the old woman. "The others were damaged in the recent storms. But there's room aplenty."

Anchored to the tree by ropes on all sides, the suspended pod barely moved when they stepped in. A hanging plank walkway afforded access from the main building, so Mally had no trouble reaching it. Ellie was sure to check that the ashmark over the pod's door was freshly drawn.

The interior was cozy, a circular floor piled with straw-stuffed pallets, clean blankets, and cushions. The springy, woven walls breathed in the cooling night air, so there was no need for windows.

As they unpacked, Mally scooped up *The King's Ladder* from Ellie's pile of stuff and cooed over it.

"Pretty! Has it got pictures?"

Ellie grinned. "Mally, did you ever hear the story of Sir Chan the Loyal?"

When the girl shook her head, Ellie took the book and sat beside her.

Shayn smiled and gently brushed Mally's hair while Ellie read to her of the Goldwing knight who'd once led an entire town to safety during a gargol-infested storm.

"The lesson of this story," said Ellie, "is to teach the fourth step in the Ladder of Ascension: *loyalty.* That might be loyalty to friends, to the promises you make, or to the duty you've been given."

Mally traced the illustration of Sir Chan with her fingertip. "He was very brave."

"Yes. He's one of the reasons I want to be a Goldwing too. So I can help people like he did."

The story over, Mally lost interest in the book and wandered over to poke at Gussie's collection of parts. Gussie, panicking, gathered up anything sharp or fragile.

Shayn smiled. "Thank you," she whispered to Nox and Ellie, who stood near her. "For helping us, and for being kind to her. It's been hard since her wings . . . People have avoided us like . . . well, like the plague."

Ellie's heart broke. Gussie had explained Mally's sickness to her on the way to the inn, and she'd spent the whole day shivering at the thought of losing one's wings to an unstoppable, unexplainable disease. She'd never heard of wingrot, but Linden was so small a town it made sense no one there had yet contracted it.

Nox shook his head, his face grim. "I know folks in Thelantis who got wingrot. None of them were contagious. People avoided them too. Never made sense to me."

"I'm no fool," said Shayn. "I know she'll probably never fly again, but I have to try something."

"I know what you mean," said Ellie. "Many people just let things happen, and say that's how it is, and never try to change anything. I have to believe things can get better, if only we stop being afraid to *try*."

"Like a Sparrow becoming a Goldwing?" asked Shayn, lifting an eyebrow.

Ellie looked down. "Maybe. I know it sounds like a silly dream. Impossible, even."

"Never be ashamed for wanting to change the world," said Shayn gently. "As Granny Tam said, we're in a strange, cruel time. This terrible sickness spreads with no cause or cure in sight, and gargols hunt in the night. Our world needs all the silly, brave dreams it can get."

She sounded so much like Ellie's mother at that moment that Ellie nearly flung her arms around the woman. But then Shayn went to make up beds for her and Mally. Ellie, sniffing a bit, pushed back the wave of longing that had risen in her belly.

She nudged Nox with her elbow and grinned. "You know, you can act like you only care about yourself, but you *did* come help us save Mally and her mom. I don't think you're half as selfish as you pretend to be."

"Oh, help!" Nox threw a dramatic hand across his forehead. "The Sparrow's seen right through me to my soft, squishy heart."

"All I'm saying is, maybe I was wrong about you before," she continued in a serious tone. "I mean, you *are* a criminal, but maybe that doesn't mean you're *bad*. And since a knight owns up to her mistakes, I just want to say . . . I'm sorry I misjudged you."

Was it her imagination, or was Nox blushing?

"Wow," he muttered. "Good to know Ellidee Meadows, mighty knight of the Sparrow clan, doesn't think I'm all that bad. What next? A golden statue of me in the center of Thelantis?"

"You *wish*. You'd probably steal your own golden eyeballs."

"You're right I would."

"I know how to admit when I'm wrong," Ellie said. "Humility is the first step in the—"

"Please!" Nox grimaced and stuck his fingers in his ears. "If I have to hear about that stupid ladder one more time, I'm going to *eat* my own eyeballs."

She laughed.

"Anyway," Nox added, removing his fingers, "you're not so bad either. I mean, the whole *noble knight* thing gets old, and I still think you're deluded about how great the Goldwings are, but . . . I do know this, Ellie Meadows." He looked her in the eyes. "You mean what you say, and unlike most people who go on about honor and truth and all that sappy stuff . . . you actually *live* it. So whatever the Goldwings end up doing with you, they won't half deserve you."

He walked away then, to help Gussie spread out the sleeping pallets, and left Ellie blushing right down to her wingtips.

CHAPTER TWENTY
· ELLIE ·

The lantern hanging from the pod's domed roof burned lower as the night darkened. Soon, the chorus of crickets, cicadas, and frogs struck up its gentle, buzzing drone, and sterling moonlight gleamed between the gaps in the woven wall. Ellie and the others began settling into their pallets, yawning.

"Ahhh," Ellie sighed, relishing the cushions. "And to think, we could be sleeping in a hollow log or something right now instead."

"I wonder at your master's poor judgment," said Shayn. "Sending children into the woods on their own, with no means or plan for lodging."

Ellie grimaced. On the road to the inn, Nox had told Shayn they were the apprentices of an herbalist, who'd sent them to gather rare specimens in the forest. Her conscience had flinched at the lie, but she'd bitten her tongue.

Beside Shayn, Mally let out a little whimper.

"Oh no," Shayn murmured. She put her hands on either side of Mally's face. "Is it hurting again, love?"

Mally nodded, her face scrunched in pain. "My back . . ."

"Take some more gumleaf. But only a little, remember, or you'll sleep through tomorrow night." Shayn pulled a bundle of dried leaves from her pocket, and Mally chewed on one. Ellie breathed in the familiar lemony scent of the herb, which many Sparrows back home used to ease muscle pains after a long day in the fields. She also remembered—with less affection—waking up to find herself trussed up by Bratton and Tholomew, after they'd drugged her with the leaf's more potent root.

"Oh!" cried Mally. "What's this?"

She picked something up off the floor, sending blue flecks of light dancing over the pod's walls.

The skystone.

Ellie saw Nox's hand go to his throat and hold up an empty chain; the stone must have slipped off. The iron band around it still weighed it down, or else it might have gone floating around the pod like a dandelion seed.

"That's mine," Nox said quickly. "It's just a cheap glass toy. Give it back, please."

"Can't I just hold it a little longer?" begged Mally.

Everyone else gave Nox withering looks.

"Nox," Ellie whispered, through a wide, tight smile, "if you don't let that sick little girl hold the shiny rock, I'll personally fill your shirt with spiders while you sleep."

Nox gave her a flat look. "Fine. Just don't lose it."

Mally grinned and lay back, holding up the stone so that it sparkled. Ellie was struck again by how strange and beautiful—and oddly familiar—the gem was. She saw by Shayn's narrowed eyes that the woman didn't believe for a minute it was merely cheap glass. Did she suspect the truth, that they'd stolen it? That they were not some herbalist's apprentices?

Soon Mally began yawning and rubbing her eyes as the gumleaf's soporific effects kicked in.

One by one, they scooted into the corners to sleep. Shayn lay with her soft gray wings curled around Mally, providing the warmth her little daughter's own wings could no longer give her. The girl slept soundly, clutching the gemstone to her heart.

"It's just one night," Ellie whispered to Nox, when she caught him staring nervously at Mally. "Then you can steal it all over again, from a little girl no less. Shouldn't be a problem for your cold stone heart, should it?"

Her tone was light, teasing more than accusing. But he frowned and looked away with only a shrug.

Gussie fluttered up to blow out the lantern, and the pod went dark. Ellie yawned and lay down, arranging her wings around herself. The cool night breeze curled through the small gaps in the woven reed wall, and the pod swayed slightly, lulling as a mother's arms.

Everyone else fell asleep quickly. She saw Nox roll fitfully, as if he were stuck in a nightmare. Twig had one hand curled around his hedgehog, the other around Lirri. Gussie slept sitting up, her head propped against the wall, her long Falcon wings folded over her legs.

But just when Ellie's eyes began to slide shut, a glint of light caught her attention. She squinted at the darkness, wondering if it had been the beginning of a dream.

Then it gleamed again—a swelling of blue light from across the pod.

Ellie sat up.

The skystone, clenched in Mally's fist, was *glowing*.

"What in the sky . . . ?" Ellie whispered.

She sat absolutely still, blinking hard as if that might banish the illusion. But the stone only shone brighter, until Mally's small frame was illuminated by its silver-blue light.

A rustle caught Ellie's ear. All of Twig's pets were emerging from the blankets and pockets where they'd been sleeping. They crept nearer to Mally, stopping just outside the pool of light, and sat there still and attentive, watching the girl and the stone.

Slowly, Ellie reached for the nearest sleeper—Nox—and tapped his head until he woke.

"Sparrow?" he groaned. "What . . . ?"

His eyes widened when he saw the light.

"Nox," Ellie whispered. "What's happening? What *is* that stone?"

"I don't know," he replied. "I . . . I don't know. I thought it was just a shiny rock."

Gussie woke then, gasping a little and rousing Twig. They all stared as the light around Mally grew brighter, saturating her skin and hair and delicate eyelashes. Soon, her entire frame was glowing as brightly as the stone itself.

Shayn woke last, with a startled cry. "Mally? What—what's happening?"

She shook the girl, but Mally didn't even flinch. It was as if she were dead, but her chest still rose and fell with deep, even breaths.

"It's the stone," said Ellie. "It started glowing and then . . . Mally did."

"What did you give my daughter?" Shayn cried, trying to pry open Mally's hand. But the girl's fingers were like iron, locked around the stone.

"Wait!" Ellie said. She crawled across the floor to put a hand on Shayn's arm. *"Look."*

The light was now moving through Mally's body, flowing like water, draining from her limbs and face and hair and gathering into a tight, glowing knot between her withered wings.

They watched, speechless, as Mally's crumpled wings began to stretch out. The gnarls and bumps and scales vanished, and the bones grew straight again. Her few feathers unfurled to their full length, the black, dry barbs flushing with new life, turning Dove clan gray. Along the now shining, healthy skin over her wing bones, soft down began to appear—like the early feathers babies grew in their first weeks of life.

"Holy skies," breathed Shayn. "It's . . . healing her."

"Impossible," said Gussie, across the room. "That would be—"

"Magic," said Ellie. She'd said as much yesterday, when they'd learned it could float.

Through all of this, Mally slept, her face peaceful. Never once did her fingers loosen on the skystone.

"This can't happen," Gussie said. She and Twig had crept closer. Only Nox hung back in the shadows, his black eyes wide.

"We're *watching* it happen," said Ellie. "The skystone is healing Mally."

"If it can heal," returned Gussie, "why didn't it heal Nox's shoulder? He's been carrying it for two days. It makes no sense."

"Yeah, and it also floats, remember?" Twig pointed out. "Does that make sense?"

"Did you just say it *floats*?" said Shayn.

"Nox also doesn't have wingrot," Ellie murmured. "Some cures only work on certain diseases."

Still Gussie shook her head. "There's no such thing as magic."

"Sure there is," said Ellie. "What do you think ashmarks are? They're protection against gargols, the reason they don't smash through our doors. What else could that be?"

"Superstition, obviously. Ashmarks make people feel safer, that's all. Gargols don't smash through doors because they're territorial, and if we're inside, they don't see us a threat to their territory. Mystery solved. Magic doesn't exist. Ask Nox! He should know."

"Huh?" Ellie looked at the Crow boy, still hunched against the far wall. "What does she mean?"

"Remember how I said there are rumors about why the Crow clan was shattered hundreds of years ago?" asked Gussie, rolling her eyes. "They say it's because the Crows used to practice dark sorcery. Stupid, of course."

Nox groaned. "It's *beyond* stupid."

"Well, I know what I see with my own eyes," said Ellie. "And that stone is magic."

Did General Stoneslayer know of the skystone's power? Did Nox's boss, the Talon? Was that why they both wanted it so badly?

The stone was weird, sure. It floated, for sky's sake, as Twig had reminded them. But this was weird on an entirely different level.

This was *big*.

Ellie's head drummed with excitement. She wasn't sure why, but she had a feeling something had changed this night. A secret had become known that couldn't be unknown. A door had opened that couldn't be shut.

This stone was way more than just a valuable gem. It was more important than Ellie could have guessed. Not even Nox had known what it could do.

She glanced at the Crow boy and found he was already watching *her*, his dark eyes catching the faintest reflection of the skystone's blue light.

She looked away quickly, unsure why his gaze now struck a nervous chord in her body. Why was he being so quiet about the stone? He'd seemed as surprised as the rest of them, but he'd kept his distance from it the same way he did around fire . . . as if he were *afraid*.

Ellie didn't see what there was to be scared of. If that stone could heal Mally, then it was wonderful. A miracle.

A stone like that . . . could change the world.

CHAPTER TWENTY-ONE
· NOX ·

Nox did not sleep.

After an hour or so, Twig, then Gussie, then Ellie all dropped off, and Shayn last, still sitting with Mally's head in her lap.

But Nox, no matter how he tried, couldn't make himself fall asleep.

Even when he pressed his eyes shut, the skystone's light was still there, eerie and strange and persistent. He turned away, only to see its glow on the reed wall.

There was no escaping it.

Magic.

The word sank into his heart like a serpent's fangs.

He remembered a day, months ago, when he'd seen a lonely, scared Falcon girl get targeted by a gang of Jays. Gussie had been outnumbered and outmatched, and Nox had gotten the Jays' attention long enough for her to fly away. The Jays hadn't let him off lightly, though he'd taken down at least two before they managed to pin him down. Then the leader, a kid who'd dyed his hair as blue as his wings, had spat on Nox and said, *"Oooh, watch out, he'll put a hex on us! Witch boy, witch boy!"*

The rumor about the Crow clan doing dark magic had been just another reason for people to hate and mistrust him. And it *was* stupid, because magic wasn't real. At least, that's what he'd always told himself.

Until he saw that glowing gem heal a little girl of the most feared disease in the Clandoms.

It has to be a trick, he thought, though he knew deep down that was even more impossible than the idea of magic itself.

But one thing was certain: The stone was trouble.

The sooner he handed it over to the Talon, the better. He wanted to be done with endless flying and gargol attacks and, most of all, magic rocks.

By morning, the skystone had stopped glowing, but Nox still sat wide-awake. The sun began stretching curious fingers through the woven walls, casting freckles of light over the people sleeping inside.

Shayn, who'd slumped over, now sat up quickly, blinking. She looked down at Mally and gasped.

"I thought it was a dream. Mally? Mally!"

The little girl woke and smiled. "Mama."

Shayn wept, gathering her up in her arms. "Do you feel all right? Does it hurt?"

"Huh? No. I feel . . . I feel nice."

Mally's wings were healed. There was no denying it, especially with the golden sunlight dappling her feathers. She wouldn't fly for at least a year, since most of her gray feathers had yet to grow back. But the bones were straight and strong, and even the girl's face looked fuller and healthier than it had the day before. Mally had a new chance at life, and she might get it—as long as she kept her mouth shut.

"If you tell anyone," he whispered to Shayn, "they'll never leave her alone. They'll want to figure out how it happened, run tests on her, experiments . . ."

"I know." She pressed the stone into Nox's hand. "I don't know how you came by this, or what you intend to do with it, but you must keep it safe, young Crow. It could be the most important object in the Clandoms." She paused a moment, then said, "I hope *you* know what you're doing with it."

He felt a stab of cold at the words, but nodded. Then he carefully hung the stone around his neck. He was sure to twist the hook on the iron band around the chain, so it wouldn't slip loose again.

"Don't worry," Shayn said. "I won't tell anyone about it, or you, or what happened last night. It would be trouble for us all."

"Thanks." Nox turned to the others, who had pulled Mally away to admire her wings.

"I dreamed I was flying," Mally said, "and when I woke up, it was like my dream came true!"

She didn't know about the stone, Nox realized. Her mother must have plucked it from her hand when she'd woken, and she'd forgotten all about it.

"Good for you, kid," he said, giving her a high five. "Fly circles around everyone back home for me, will you?"

Mally flung her arms around Nox and squeezed tight, startling him.

Awkwardly, he patted her head. "Well, we've got to get flying ourselves."

"And we'll head home," said Shayn. "There's no point in going to Stillcreek now, I suppose."

In minutes, they'd packed everything they had back into the knapsacks, folded Granny Tam's blankets, and were ready to depart.

But when Nox put his hand on the door, it didn't budge.

"What the . . ." He pushed again. Something was barring it from the outside.

"The old lady's staff," said Ellie, peering through the gaps in the reeds. "What did you call it, Gussie? A lockstave? She's used it to jam the door. Why would she do that?"

Nox's blood went cold. Had they been made? Had Granny Tam already sent for the soldiers hunting them? They could very well have scouted all the inns in Bluebriar, describing the thieves and offering a reward for their capture.

It had been a bad idea coming here.

"HEY!" yelled Twig, kicking the door. "Old lady, let us out!"

Gussie threw her shoulder against the door. Because it was made of the same woven material as the rest of the room, it bowed under her, springing back when she pulled away.

"Granny Tam!" called out Shayn. "Granny Tam, can you hear us?"

"Oh, I hear you, dears."

They all went still, listening as Granny Tam's voice crooned through the walls.

"Tsk, tsk, got yourselves stuck, have you?"

Nox used his fingers to pry open a small gap in the worn reeds, allowing him to peer out.

There sat Granny Tam on a branch. She saw Nox looking and waved.

"What are you doing?" said Nox.

"Meditating upon the leaves," said Granny Tam in a strange,

taunting voice. "Listening to the forest's whispers. It's fascinating, my dear boy, the things one hears when one only listens."

"Let us out," he said. *"Now."*

"For example, one might hear the strangest rumors . . ." The old woman grinned, but instead of the warm smile she'd first greeted them with, this one reminded Nox of a snake. "Rumors of a general hoarding treasure, shiny treasure that glints and gleams, special treasure that heals and restores . . ." She chuckled. "Oh, the things one hears. The things one *sees*, shining in the night . . ."

Nox's eyes widened.

"We're made," whispered Nox, cursing himself inwardly. The Talon would have seen the woman's treachery a mile away—it was like Nox had forgotten every lesson the man had taught him. "She knows about the skystone. She saw it healing Mally last night."

"What do you want from us, old woman?" Ellie called through the woven wall.

"The stone, of course," said Granny Tam. "Hand it through the wall, and you'll be free to go. Delay, and you'll meet with the general's soldiers. They've been all up and down the road these days, searching for a band of little thieves. *A Sparrow, a Falcon, a Crow, and a piebald.*"

Nox rubbed his face in frustration while Shayn called, "If you let us out now, I can pay you forty aquilas."

"Fifteen *thousand* aquilas," said Granny Tam. "That's how much General Stoneslayer has offered for the capture of *each* of you, and thirty thousand for the return of his *family heirloom*."

Nox's spirit nearly lifted out of his body. Thirty thousand aquilas was more than the Talon's entire gang made in a year.

"I thought to myself," continued Granny Tam, "why would anybody pay so high a bounty? And what heirloom was worth a life's fortune? Well, now I know."

Nox held his finger to his lips, then motioned to Gussie and Twig with the Talon's secret signal for *back door*. They nodded in understanding. Gussie began rifling through her bag while Twig released Lirri onto the wall, and the little animal began chewing the reeds.

"Oh yes," said Granny Tam. "Now I know. I saw that blue light in the night. I saw it fusing into that girl's broken wings. I saw them made whole."

Shayn pulled Mally closer.

"Now," said Granny Tam. "A stone like that might be worth far, far more than thirty thousand aquilas. Why, a body could charge a thousand a head just to let them hold it."

"You want to exploit people suffering from wingrot?" Ellie burst out. "When they have no other hope? What kind of monster are you?"

"An ambitious one," crooned Granny Tam. "Oh, aye. There are *hundreds* of folk with the disease by now, I've heard. It's turned into a proper plague. And no cure, how tragic. But that stone . . ."

Twig and Gussie weren't making much progress on the wall. Lirri chittered angrily, unable to cut through the reeds. Nox waved at them, urging them to move faster.

"Now hand it through the gap," said Granny Tam, "and I'll let you be on your way, no harm done."

"And if we don't?" said Nox.

"Well . . ." Granny Tam chuckled. "Let's not make this nasty, hmm?"

Mally whimpered. "Mama, I'm scared."

"Shh," whispered Shayn. "We'll be all right, dear." She cast Nox a pleading look.

"C'mon . . ." whispered Nox. "Twig?"

Twig shrugged, Lirri leaping back onto his shoulders. "It's too thick for her."

"Last chance," sang out Granny Tam. "I *will* get it, one way or another."

"What's the worst one old lady can do?" Twig whispered.

"She could hand us over to the Stoneslayer's men," Ellie pointed out.

"And let *them* take the skystone?" Nox shook his head. "She won't risk it. She wants it for herself."

"Give it to her," said Twig, shivering. "I just want to get out of here."

"And then what?" said Nox. "We go home and tell the Talon that we got shaken down by an old lady? No way. Anyhow, I *need* to finish this. I need that stone."

"Nox, what if—" Ellie coughed. "What if we just talked to her, tried to make her see reason—" She coughed harder. "What is that smell?"

"Smoke," intoned Gussie.

"She's lit a fire under us!" gasped Shayn, picking up Mally and pressing her face into her shoulder. "Skies above! These are children in here, you mad old crone!"

Nox's heart nearly stopped. He looked down, kicking aside the mats on the floor, to see a red glow beneath the pod—hungry flames leaping up. Beneath the nest, Granny Tam had hung large bundles of hay and set them aflame.

Panic clawed at his ribs.

"D'you—*cough*—really think she'd burn us alive?" Ellie said, coughing harder.

The smoke was so thick now that Nox had trouble seeing. He gripped the wall, trying to block the dark clouds with his neckerchief held over his nose.

"Probably just wants to—*cough*—knock us out long enough to—*cough*—grab the stone," replied Gussie.

"I'm not waiting that long," said Nox. He turned to Gussie. "Give me your flinter. If it's fire the old crackpot wants, let's give her fire."

"Nox . . ." Looking uncertain, Gussie pulled out the flinter.

He fluttered upward and grabbed the lantern hanging overhead. Then he smashed it against the wall. Slick oil splashed over the reeds.

"Everybody stand back!" Nox shouted, snatching the flinter from Gussie's hand.

"I thought you were terrified of fire!" Ellie protested. "You'll burn your face off!"

"Unlikely," muttered Nox.

He clicked the flinter and set its flame to the oil.

The reed wall caught at once. Fire erupted outward, licking Nox's bare hands and arms. He jumped back as the blaze spread and the reed began to blacken and flake into ash. He'd have to work quickly, before the whole pod caught flame and they burned alive.

"Wait for my signal!" Nox shouted as he stepped toward the flame.

"Nox!" Gussie croaked. "Get away from there!"

"Wait!" he said, his hands grabbing hold of the weakened reeds. He ripped as hard as he could, and the wall began to tear. "Wait . . . wait . . . *now*!"

He stepped back as Gussie and Twig charged forward. Ellie helped Shayn with Mally, and together they rushed for the opening Nox had torn open. There was a gaping hole in the wall now, the flames still spreading outward in a fiery ring.

"Your hands!" Ellie cried.

"Go!" Nox shouted. "Don't worry about me!"

"You first," said Ellie, giving Shayn and Mally a helpful push through the opening. Shayn clutched Mally tight and fluttered free.

"Now's no time to play hero, Sparrow," Nox said, and he shoved her so hard she stumbled, barely managing to spread her wings as she tipped out of the nest and into open air.

He started to follow, but then a mass of cloth and hair and fingernails slammed into him, driving him back into the pod. He landed hard on his back, the wind knocked from his lungs, with Granny Tam pinning him down. She had her staff in hand and pressed it to his throat.

"I meditated upon you too, boy," the old woman hissed. She was terrifyingly strong. "And guess what I saw? Don't you want to know, hmm? I saw your death, Crow. I saw your death in flames and ashes. It's not long away now. Perhaps it is today. Give me the stone, and you might stave off your doom a while yet."

Nox couldn't reply; her staff was pressed against his windpipe, cutting off his air. He struggled, but the smoke in his lungs had weakened him.

Granny Tam began searching his pockets, her eyes wild. "Where is it, where is it?"

Nox's vision began to darken as he struggled to breathe. His eyelids fluttered.

"You don't even know what it *is*, do you?" Granny Tam said. "Where it comes from? Whose magic infuses it?"

Nox's eyes shut.

And then a strong gust of wind swept through the pod, clearing the smoke for just a moment.

Ellie Meadows hovered above them, her wings pushing away the smoke as she dove at Granny Tam.

"Get off him!" Ellie roared, sailing forward.

The old woman let out an *oof!* as Ellie tackled her to the floor.

Nox gasped in a long, choking breath. The Sparrow girl seized Granny Tam's staff and grabbed his shoulder with the hook. She flew out of the burning pod, dragging Nox behind her.

"Your death!" the old woman howled. "I have seen it, boy! You will *burn!*"

Then Nox slid out of the tear in the wall and fell toward the ground. He struggled to open his wings, but his lungs were still empty and his head spun. There was nothing he could do.

Ellie swooped beneath him. Turning onto her back, she hooked her arms beneath his. Nox dangled beneath her, head lolling, unsure which way was up and which way down.

"Saved your skin *twice*," Ellie muttered, trying to rouse him with the jab. But he only groaned.

She spiraled to the ground and landed heavily in the grass at the foot of the great oak tree. Twig and Gussie ran to help Nox, while Shayn and Mally watched the branches for Granny Tam.

"Your hands," said Ellie. "They'll need a burn poultice or . . ."

Nox tried to pull his hands away, but she grabbed them, turned them over in hers.

"Nox . . . there's not a mark on you." She ran her fingers over his palms.

He looked away, still coughing. "Got lucky."

"But . . . I saw . . ." Her brow furrowed.

Nox yanked his hands back. "Did the old woman make it out?"

Shayn shook her head. "She's still up there."

Groaning, Ellie heaved herself to her feet. "I'm going back up."

"Leave her," growled Nox. "She tried to murder us!"

"I can't do that," Ellie said softly. "No matter how wretched she is, I can't leave someone to die."

He coughed and shook his head as the Sparrow launched herself upward. Minutes later, she returned, having dragged Granny Tam out of the pod. Ellie left her unconscious, slumped on the porch of her own inn. The fire was starting to burn out, and the pod was almost entirely gone. Ash fluttered down like snow, landing softly all around them.

"She'll live," Ellie told the others. She looked at Nox. "Will you?"

He nodded, giving her a weak grin. "Might have left a lung behind, but I'll make it."

She glanced at his hands again, but he'd put them deep into his pockets. For a moment, he thought she might say something more, but then she shook her head as if dismissing some thought.

"Then let's fly," Ellie said. "That smoke will bring every soldier for miles around."

For once, Nox completely agreed with her. He wanted to get as far from this wretched inn and its wretched owner as possible. He wanted to wash away the smoke and the acrid words stinging in his ears.

I have seen your death, boy . . . Granny Tam's voice cackled in his head. *You will burn.*

CHAPTER TWENTY-TWO
· ELLIE ·

Ellie was sorry to say goodbye to Shayn and Mally that afternoon. The little girl was so bright and happy, and her mother reminded Ellie almost painfully of her own.

They stood at a crossroads south of Granny Tam's inn, beneath a grove of pine trees that swayed and creaked in the wind. Everyone's faces were still streaked with soot.

"Well, good luck," said Nox.

"Thank you for everything." Shayn took his hand and squeezed it. He looked so uncomfortable at this that Ellie wondered when the last time it was that anybody had behaved motherly toward Nox Hatcher. "You *do* understand what you carry around your neck, don't you?"

Nox grinned. "I understand I'm getting a smashing payday back home."

Shayn didn't smile. "If the skystone could heal Mally, how many hundreds or even thousands of others could it help? There are so many suffering from the same disease, without any hope. To carry hope is a powerful thing, young Crow. Granny Tam would have hoarded it. Will you?"

Nox dropped his gaze and muttered, "Just here to do a job, not save the world."

Shayn sighed, looking conflicted, then added, "I'm only asking you to consider that what you do next could determine the fate of many."

Ellie lowered her gaze. She understood what Shayn was telling them, even if the others refused to.

"I can't tell you what you must do," Shayn said gently. "Only ask that you consider the difference you could make. There are countless children like my Mally who suffer."

"Right. Well, good luck, then. We'd better get going." Nox gave an awkward wave, then fluttered off on the east road. Gussie quickly followed, and Twig called to Lirri. The animal leaped from Mally's shoulder to his. He departed with a sheepish look.

Ellie was last to say goodbye. After she gave Mally a hug and marveled at how quickly the girl's feathers were growing back, Shayn pulled her close.

"These are dark times, brave Sparrow. Sickness is spreading. We are losing our wings. And impossible times call for impossible heroes." She gave Ellie a long, meaningful look. "I wish you the courage to follow your heart, whatever it tells you is right."

Ellie gave a small, uncertain nod.

Shayn took Mally's hand. "Goodbye, Ellie Meadows. Watch the skies."

Ellie's eyes tracked mother and daughter as they walked away down the dusty western road.

Then her gaze turned in the other direction, to the clear blue horizon and Nox's retreating form.

"Watch the skies," she murmured.

They flew for hours, veering off the road and into the woods, still moving generally eastward, but in a random, zigzagging pattern to throw off any pursuers. The advantage of constant flying over walking was that they left no tracks, but it was also exhausting. Even Ellie, after years of endurance training, was starting to ache all over. She knew Nox had to be feeling much worse; his shoulder was nowhere near fully healed.

Finally, in the late afternoon, they came across a river. Ellie thought it might be the same one they'd followed in the canyon yesterday. Here, it tumbled and splashed over boulders, before cascading into a wide, silky waterfall.

They rested on a sandy bank, shedding their bags and gear. Ellie still carried Granny Tam's lockstave, which she leaned against a tree. The weapon might prove useful, and she liked the weight of it in her hands. It had come through the fire unscathed, and she'd found a carving on it she hadn't noticed at first: an ashmark, artfully worked into the wood just below the larger of the two hooks. She didn't feel bad about taking it from Granny Tam, considering the woman had tried to kill Nox with it. As it stated in the *King's Ladder* chapter on responsibility, to bend one's weapon to selfish purpose was to lose the right to bear it forever.

Twig dove into the river, which pooled at the bottom of the falls. Ellie followed, shivering at the chilliness but glad to wash off the smoke clinging to her skin, hair, and clothes.

Soon they were all floating or swimming. Twig ventured beneath the falls to let the water flatten his hair. Gussie stood in the shallows, fluttering her wings to dry them.

After her swim, Ellie sat on the bank and groomed her own wings. With a soft bristle brush, she combed sunflower oil over her feathers. The oil kept the fine barbs from fraying, while protecting them from dirt and dust. It also made them relatively waterproof. It felt good to massage the oil into her aching wings, especially the joints and slender bones that framed them.

Nox, pulling his shirt back on, waded over and stretched out beside her, hands laced behind his head and his dark wings spread to dry in the golden sunlight beaming down. The light brought out the blue-and-emerald undertones in his feathers. Shutting his eyes, he let out a long sigh, then a cough. They were all still feeling the aftereffects of the smoke.

She glanced at his hands, still finding it weird how he'd escaped that burning pod without so much as a singed eyebrow.

"Thanks for getting us out of there," she said. "You might say you were almost *honorable*."

"Whoa, hey!" Nox waved a hand. "I do not need you ruining my reputation like that, Sparrow. Anyway, you're the one who got *my* butt out. That's twice you've saved my life."

"I never thought it'd be this hard just to reach Thelantis. This was supposed to be the easy part."

"It will be," said Nox. "From here on, we'll play it safe. No more stopping at inns, no matter how nice the old ladies inside seem."

Shayn's words ran circles in Ellie's head.

I wish you the courage to follow your heart, whatever it tells you is right.

Those words, and the message she knew Shayn had really been communicating, ate at Ellie relentlessly. She glanced at Nox's chest and the small lump beneath his shirt where the skystone rested.

She stoppered her jar of oil and set it aside. "You know, Granny Tam was a nightmare, but . . . she did kind of have a good idea."

Nox's wings flared slightly. "Which idea? The part where she tried to set us on fire? Or when she nearly throttled me to death?"

"No, no, not that, obviously. I mean, that weird jewel has some kind of power to heal wingrot. And if that's true, doesn't that mean we have a duty to, well, *use* it?"

Nox's hand closed over the skystone. "Use it?"

"To heal people, of course!" Ellie turned to face him. "Look, what good will it do anyone if you just hand it over to your crime lord? Even if he uses it to help people, won't he try to charge them fortunes for it, the way Granny Tam would have? You saw Mally and her mother. They couldn't have paid that in a hundred years."

Nox looked away.

"I'm just saying," Ellie pressed, "I think . . . I think we should give it to the Goldwings. Or even King Garion."

"Ha!" Nox snorted. "Now *that's* the worst idea I ever heard."

"What? Why? He's the king. It's his job to take care of his people. He'll know the best way to make sure everyone who needs it—"

"Here we go again," groaned Nox. "You and your blind trust in people you've never met. I can guarantee you, if you gave King Garion that stone, he'd just imprison you for thieving it in the first place. Then he'd probably lock it up in his treasury—or only use it to heal other high clanners."

"Oh, I didn't realize you knew the *king* so well! Do you meet up once a week for cards or something?"

"You don't get it, Sparrow. I don't have to know him personally to know what he's like. I see his hand at work every day in Thelantis, in the rules he makes, the way his soldiers treat us, the way he makes poor people rot in prison for not paying their debts, while rich high clanners can just buy their way out of any crime. He *doesn't care* about you, about Mally, or anyone but his own kind."

"Then why does he send his Goldwings to defend us from gargols?"

"Haven't you heard of the gratitude tax?"

"Huh?"

Nox dashed his hand through the air. "Every time a Goldwing saves someone, their town has to pay an extra tax in return. They call it a gratitude tax."

"I . . . I never heard of that."

"It's just another way of building up more power and more glory for themselves. Goldwings don't save people out of the goodness of their hearts. They do it for money. They're no better than mercenaries."

"That's a lie!"

"Why would I lie about it?"

"Because you lie about *everything*! The first words you ever spoke to me were lies and it's been nothing but lies ever since!"

"Not *all* of it," he grumbled. "I told you about the wild card thing."

"You can't honestly tell me you think it's better to let that stone sit in some lockbox when it could be saving hundreds of lives?" Ellie gazed at him pleadingly. "I *know* you're not that heartless, Nox! You helped Mally without a second thought. You risked your life to get us out of Granny Tam's. You might do a lot of bad things, but you're not a bad person."

"I wish I could help," he said, rising to his feet and spreading his wings. "But I have no choice, Sparrow. The stone goes to the Talon, and that's the end of it. Like I said, I'm only here to do a job and get my reward."

"Nox, wait!"

"You've got to learn to listen to your wings instead of your heart, Sparrow."

"What's *that* supposed to mean?"

Shaking his head, he flapped his wings and lifted away. "Forget it. You wouldn't understand. I'm going to have a look around, make sure no one's following us."

Ellie sighed and let her face fall into her hands. How could she get through to him? Why was he so *selfish*? She had seen good in him, even selflessness for a moment, but once again he proved that he was nothing more than a thief and a liar who only thought of himself.

Ellie let out a frustrated groan.

"What about *you*?" Ellie called to Gussie, whom she knew was eavesdropping from farther up the bank. The Hawk girl had been staring far too intently at a clump of grass, and Ellie didn't think it was because she'd developed a sudden interest in botany. "Do you side with him after what happened?"

Gussie flicked water from her wingtips. "I don't know what happened. Whether that stone healed Mally or not . . . it needs further study. Look, I want to know more about it too. Once we turn it over to the Talon, I'm going to ask him if he'll let me run some tests on it. Maybe I can figure out how it works."

"And you?" Ellie turned to Twig, floating on the river.

He looked at Gussie, then back at Ellie, and shrugged. "Nox is right. You can't trust grown-ups. You try to do the right thing, they'll just punish you for it." He slipped underwater with a burble.

Gussie gave Ellie a helpless shrug, then lay back and shut her eyes.

Well, they'd be no help. Which left Ellie only one choice, though it made her sick.

This felt like another test. Another moment when the eyes of all the Goldwings who'd come before her were watching to see if she'd prove worthy, if she possessed honor, strength, perseverance . . . the whole of the King's Ladder. Everything she'd ever believed in and hoped to be seemed balanced on that shiny rock around Nox's throat.

If she failed this test, would anything else she did matter? Would she even *deserve* to fly in the Race of Ascension?

I wish you the courage to follow your heart, whatever it tells you is right.

Her heart, unfortunately, was not being shy. It pounded in her ears like a drum giving marching orders. It knew exactly what she needed to do.

She would have to steal the skystone herself.

CHAPTER TWENTY-THREE
· ELLIE ·

For the next two weeks, Ellie worried and plotted. Plans drew together in her mind, then collapsed, as they drew ever nearer to Thelantis.

How was she supposed to steal from thieves?

In the mornings, she woke at dawn and performed the steps of the King's Ladder, sometimes with Gussie offering advice. She watched Nox closely to see if he ever put down the skystone, but he seemed more paranoid than ever, sleeping with his hand clasped around it.

With Nox's wing on the mend, they flew farther each day, camping in caves when they could find them, in enclosed dells when they could not. The weather held and the wind blew from the west, as if to hurry them along. After two weeks of traveling like this, Nox, who had been tracking their course on his map, assured them they'd reach Thelantis in two more days.

That afternoon, Ellie flew higher than she had in a long time, floating on a warm thermal. An invisible pillar of churning hot air, the thermal lifted her like a dandelion seed. She spread her wings and soared, relishing the heat as it ruffled her feathers.

The trees below shrank until the forest spread like a bed of moss beneath her. The river twisted southward, calm yellow water and churning white rapids. To the north, the Aeries Mountains were just visible, the peaks hazy blue on the horizon.

But it was eastward that Ellie looked, and she let out a soft breath as her eyes picked out the glint of white among the green. It took her a moment to understand what she was seeing.

Thelantis.

The great capital of the Clandoms sat between two high ridges that rose like buttresses to support the towering height of Mount Garond, the tallest peak in the northern range, named after the first of the Eagle kings. The mountain was also the site of the Race of Ascension, Elle recalled with a tingle of nervousness. In three days, hundreds of young fliers would race to its top in a bid to become Goldwing knights. Even from this distance, the mountain loomed dauntingly high.

That night, they camped in an abandoned marble quarry that scored the green forest like a scar. There were still signs of the masons who'd once cut and shaped the stone—broken-down wagons, rusty pickaxes and chisels, half-collapsed stick huts. Large cubes of marble were scattered around like the abandoned toys of a giant.

Ellie and Nox salvaged wooden boards from the old huts and laid them crosswise between two marble blocks, creating a shelter beneath. Twig foraged for blackberries that grew on the quarry's edge. Lirri seemed to eat them nearly as quickly as he could pick them.

Ellie volunteered to gather firewood. She wandered far and long, stalling, trying desperately to think of a plan.

She had to make her move tonight.

They were close enough to Thelantis that she could find the rest of the way on her own, and she figured it would be easier to steal the stone and lose the others out here in the wilderness rather than attempt it in the city, where they'd be on their home turf.

Lost in thought, Ellie reached for a slim log perfect for the fire, only to be stopped by a sharp voice:

"Don't touch that!"

She turned to see Twig flying toward her, his hands stained with blackberry juice. He landed and let out a long breath. "You nearly killed yourself."

"Huh?"

He pointed to something lumpy and orange on the log, which she'd taken for lichen. But when she looked closer, she saw it was a spiky caterpillar.

"He's kinda cute," she said.

"He's also kinda extremely venomous," Twig said. "One touch and his barbs would knock you flat."

She cocked her head, peering at him thoughtfully. "How do you know that? Did it . . . *tell you* so?" She still wasn't sure how Twig's affinity for animals worked.

"Of course not," he retorted. "Caterpillars don't talk. No animals do."

"But you understand them so well, I thought . . ."

With a long-suffering sigh, Twig lifted a stick and carefully moved the venomous caterpillar to a nearby bush. "I *do* understand them. But it's not like they're talking to me in animal voices. It's more like . . . I hear them in here." He patted his chest. "I just know what they want, in a language that's not words."

"Like reading their minds?" asked Ellie.

"More like . . . feeling their moods."

After checking the stick for any more deadly surprises, Ellie added it to her bundle. "So that's a Mockingbird clan thing?"

His face went flat. "I don't know. I guess. That's what people tell me anyway. It's the Mockingbird clan's legacy or something."

Ellie winced. She should have remembered that he was abandoned as a baby. He probably didn't know much about his own heritage.

"Funny," she murmured. "The Sparrow chief once told me *farming* was my clan's legacy. That's a lot less interesting than yours." A thought occurred to her then. "Does it work on people? Your . . . inner ear or whatever. Can you understand people the way you do animals?"

He stared into the trees, his hand absently stroking Lirri's head. Ellie wondered if she'd offended him. But then he said softly, "People don't like that. And neither do I."

So it *did* work on people. She was instantly filled with curiosity. Could he see through lies, pick out individual thoughts, or discern a person's true intentions?

That last possibility made her feel queasy. What if he figured out she intended to double-cross them and steal the skystone? Ellie averted her eyes, as if her gaze might give her away. She felt suddenly nervous around Twig, now that she knew there was a deeper, more dangerous side to his odd ability.

"I shouldn't have told you that," Twig said quietly. "You already see me differently, don't you?"

Ellie looked up. "What? No! I mean . . . maybe a little, but not in a bad way."

"I can't read your mind, if that's what you think. Only your feelings, really. Maybe your desires. But even that weirds people out."

She couldn't help but ask, "So what am I feeling?"

Twig swallowed, as if uncertain, but then he shrugged and said, "Are you sure?"

No, thought Ellie. But her curiosity got the better of her, and she nodded.

"Hold still, then. I haven't done this in a long time."

Then his gaze intensified until he looked like a totally different Twig. Instead of the grubby little boy whose thoughts danced as erratically as a butterfly, he became older and sterner. He tilted his head as if he were listening close, while his gaze didn't focus on Ellie at all. Instead he stared just over her shoulder, his attention seeming to be more focused on his ears. Ellie froze, holding her breath, and hoped she hadn't just outed her own treacherous plans in her curiosity.

Then Twig let out a short breath and his gaze cleared.

"You're nervous," he said. "And guilty about something. And you really, *really* want to become a Goldwing knight. Like, I already knew you did, but *whoa*. That's intense."

She held back a gasp, feeling a cold sweat on her neck.

Twig's face crumpled when he saw her expression. "Now you think I'm a freak."

"No!" said Ellie. "You're the one who just saw into *me*. You probably think *I'm* the freak. No wonder you don't like people, when you can hear their true feelings."

He frowned. "Is that what you think? That I don't like people?"

"Well . . . you do seem to keep away if you can help it."

"If I keep my distance," he said, his tone sharp in a way she'd never heard him speak before, "it's not because I don't like people. It's because *they* don't like *me*." He shook his bicolored feathers. "First it's these—my bad-luck wings. But when they learn about my weird ability . . . well, most folks don't like being around someone who can see inside them. Animals don't react that way, though. They don't care how weird you are. If you feed them and love them, they just love you back. It's . . . simpler with them."

Ellie's heart sank. She'd completely misunderstood Twig. All this time, she'd thought he *wanted* to be left alone. But like her, he really wanted to be accepted. Instead, he'd been abandoned as a baby, then mistrusted and disliked ever since, for things he couldn't control. It was completely unfair.

"I'm sorry," she said. "And you don't have to do your . . . *thing* to know that, because it's true. I like you, Twig. I like you because you're a little different. It makes you interesting."

He blinked, his expression skeptical, but then he gave a cautious smile. "Really?"

"Really." Ellie forced a grin, nearly choking on the surge of guilt that clotted her throat. What was she thinking, acting like his friend when she was about to betray him?

"Twig," she said, hoping he didn't hear the tremble in her voice, "what will you do with your share of the payment for the skystone?"

He looked confused at her sudden change of topic. "I'm going to get on a ship and sail to the southern jungles. They have animals called *elephants* there that are as big as a house! Can you imagine? And anyway . . ." His voice lowered. "Someone told me once that two-colored wings are considered lucky in the south. But I mostly want to go for the elephants."

She nodded, her stomach wrenching. "That's a really nice plan. I hope it works out."

"Thanks. Well. I should get back to finding blackberries. Lirri ate everything I picked."

"Right. Of course. And me too. With the firewood, I mean."

As Twig flitted away, Ellie felt her eyes burn with guilty tears. Maybe she'd been wrong about her plan. Maybe she should let Nox and Gussie and Twig collect their rewards for the skystone. She didn't agree with their methods, but they weren't *bad* people.

And then she saw it: a clump of gumleaf growing around the roots of an oak tree.

It was so obvious, the plan so suddenly perfect in her mind, that it was like a sign.

A line from *The King's Ladder* sprang into her thoughts.

When tempted to stray from the honorable path, it is only she who perseveres in the Ladder who proves worthy of knighthood.

Ellie chewed her lip a moment, stomach churning with guilt, then quickly pulled up the whole plant, discarding the milder leaves in favor of the potent roots. Straining to look casual, she flitted back into the quarry where the others were waiting for the firewood. The gumroot burned like hot coals in her pocket.

Nearby, a half-completed sculpture kept vigil over the stone, a man partially emerged from a tall block of marble. He leaned out, one arm outstretched, one wing spread, trapped in an eternal struggle to pull free of the stone. Twig made a crown of leaves, which he placed on the statue's head, laughing. But Ellie felt sad when she looked at him. She imagined he was reaching for the sculptor who'd never completed his work.

"Who do you think he's meant to be?" she asked Gussie.

The Falcon girl popped a blackberry in her mouth. "Some Eagle king, probably." She pointed out the royal crest carved on his breast-plate: crossed feathers in a crown.

"Creepy," said Nox, frowning at the statue.

"These oats are delicious," said Twig, talking with his mouth full. "Thanks, Ellie!"

Ellie gave him a weak smile, anxiously watching as he shoveled more into his mouth. She'd made supper for them, sacrificing the last of her oats and seedbread. Gussie and Nox had already finished their bowls.

She volunteered for first watch and wasn't surprised when the others quickly fell asleep. She'd put enough gumroot into the oats to knock out three full-grown men, she reckoned. There should be no reason for any of them to wake before dawn.

By midnight, the full moon floated above the quarry, and the marble glowed in its light. The Eagle king's statue seemed to be gazing nobly at the moon.

Seated on the base of the statue, Ellie wrapped her arms around her legs and watched not the sky, but the three thieves sleeping on the ground. The fire had all but burned out, the embers still pulsing with orange heat.

She had to make her move. She'd been putting it off for hours, but if she waited much longer, she'd lose her lead . . . and her nerve.

Silently, Ellie dropped to the ground. The marble was a gift—it kept her footsteps quiet, so she could move like a shadow. She tried not to look at their faces, innocent in sleep. Even knowing she was doing the right thing, passing the difficult test laid before her, Ellie was sick with guilt.

Since when did being good feel so . . . *bad*?

The stone would be around Nox's neck. She knew he was a light sleeper and had no idea how well the gumroot would work. She'd have to be quick and silent.

His wings were folded over himself, so she had to push aside his dark feathers. Then, carefully, she took out her knife and slipped its point beneath the thin chain around Nox's neck.

Please, please don't move, she thought desperately. *Or I'll slit your throat by accident.*

But at that moment, Nox's eyes snapped open.

Ellie froze.

He seemed immediately aware of the knife at his neck, and he didn't move. But his eyes glittered like black stars.

"Sparrow," murmured Nox. "I'm surprised it took you this long, to be honest."

"I'm sorry," she whispered. "But I have to do what's right."

She cut the chain in a swift motion and grabbed it; the skystone slithered out of Nox's shirt and into her palm.

Then Ellie jerked back, turning on her heel and spreading her wings in one fluid motion.

"Stop!" Nox cried, his speech slurred from the gumroot. "You won't get far, Sparrow!"

"Neither will you," she replied sadly.

He found that out for himself when he tried to jump up, only to stagger and fall. The gumroot made him groggy and unbalanced. She must have overestimated the amount she'd put into the oats, but at least it was doing *something* to slow him down.

She knew Twig and Gussie had to be waking now, also hazy from the herb. She didn't look back to check. Ellie tore into the sky with all her strength.

She flew high over the treetops. It was incredibly dangerous to fly at night, when there would be little warning of clouds moving in until it was too late, but Ellie would have to risk it.

"Sparrow!" Nox wasn't far behind her. She glanced back and saw him, illuminated by the full moon. Gussie and Twig trailed behind, the Falcon girl already closing in on Nox with her long, tapered wings. But she could tell by the clumsiness of their flying that they were struggling against the effects of the herb.

"Just cut it out!" Gussie yelled. "This is stupid! It's too dark to fly, Ellie!"

Just then, Ellie felt a splash on her cheek. At first, she wondered if she were crying—but then she felt another, and another. Drops of water began peppering her skin.

Rain.

Oh skies!

Ellie pulled up, her wings treading the air as she peered into the dark. Stars scattered over the black, but to the west, they had begun vanishing one by one into shadow. Then the moon too disappeared.

The world went dark.

Sky and ground became indistinguishable from each other.

Ellie's wings shivered as a roll of thunder rattled the air, and below, the trees rustled like a rushing river, wind pulling at their branches.

It was a storm.

A *big* one.

A gust of wind bowled her over, and she tumbled, wings fighting to steady her. She bit off a scream, instead focusing all her energy into flight.

"Dive!" yelled Gussie. "Find cover!"

Ellie pitched for the trees. In the dark, she couldn't see anything, so she crashed through the limbs like a blundering, crazed animal, getting scratched all over.

When she smacked right into a trunk, she nearly blacked out. Lights danced in her eyes. She slid downward, landing hard on her stomach atop a wide branch, the wind pressed from her lungs. Wheezing, Ellie dragged herself onto the branch and straddled it, one hand pressed to the trunk, the other to her chest as she struggled to breathe.

Above, the sky shuddered as the rain began to fall in earnest, great gusts of water that drove like needles. Even under the shelter of the leaves, Ellie was drenched in seconds.

She cursed her luck. For a week they'd had clear skies, but on the one night it really counted, the weather finally broke.

"Sparrow!"

Nox's call rang out between peals of thunder. Ellie flinched.

"She's here somewhere!" Twig called out. "I saw her dive right there!"

She sat with her back against the tree, legs stretched along the branch. She clenched the lockstave in one hand, the skystone in the other, and stared with wide eyes into the rain.

"Turn back," Ellie whispered. "C'mon, Nox. No rock is worth dying for."

Lightning splintered across the sky, and for a blinding second it seemed the entire forest was illuminated. In that moment, she saw the Crow boy, crouched on a branch across from her, his eyes already fixed on her. Then the forest plunged back into darkness. His black wings blended into the night.

Ellie scrambled up, but too late. Nox slammed into her, pressing her against the tree.

"Give it back!" he said.

"I won't."

"Ellie! I *need* it! You don't—"

A scream interrupted Nox, coming from above their heads.

"Gussie," Nox whispered. Then he yelled, *"Gus!"*

He shot upward, and after a moment's hesitation, Ellie flew after him.

They burst through the canopy into the open sky. Rain sharp as glass pricked Ellie's skin as she turned a circle, looking for Gussie.

Then, in a flash of lightning, she saw her: flying clumsily, her wing injured, pursued by not one, not two, but *three* enormous gargols.

Ellie and Nox exchanged one look.

Then they both charged at the monsters in a blur of wings.

CHAPTER TWENTY-FOUR
· ELLIE ·

Lightning pulsed, throwing the scene into a horrible shifting tableau, image after image of gargols and Gussie, like drawings flipping in a sketchbook.

The creatures closed in on the Falcon girl.

One grabbed her.

Gussie screamed again.

Ellie stopped thinking altogether and acted out of pure, reckless instinct. Gripping her lockstave, she took the lead ahead of Nox. A roar sounded in the sky, primal and ferocious, and Ellie realized with a shock that the sound was coming from *her*.

She clashed with the gargol holding Gussie, driving the staff into its stony jaw. Gussie screamed and fell away, tumbling toward the trees.

Ellie couldn't swoop after her. She was entangled now, the gargol's claw clutching her sash, her staff stuck in its teeth. Terror and adrenaline surged through her like a swallow of lightning.

She stared into the monster's face, just inches from her own, and gasped.

Its eyes.

No wonder the skystone had looked familiar to her.

The gargol's eyes looked just like two gleaming skystones.

Or rather . . . the gargol's eyes *were* skystones.

Blinking, realizing she was inches away from death itself, Ellie planted her feet on the gargol's chest and kicked off, pulling her staff with her and feeling her sash rip free.

Flipping through the air, Ellie pinned her wings to her spine, controlling her wild spin and diving downward before opening her wings again—a flight combat trick Zain had taught her.

Then she whirled, heart thumping, searching for Gussie. In the darkness, she had no choice but to wait for another flash of lightning to see anything at all.

It came a second later, a searing burst that stung her eyes. Threads of lightning spiked through the clouds, brightening the sky from horizon to horizon.

In that moment, her eyes wide and unblinking, Ellie saw . . . *something*.

Not Gussie, not gargols, but shapes, enormous and solid against the sky.

A . . . castle?

There, rising from the clouds—turrets and towers and battlements, framed against the black sky and thrown into sharp relief by the hot blaze of lightning. She gaped, time frozen, as her brain struggled to make sense of what she was seeing.

Then, just as quickly, the sky went full dark again, and the image vanished.

Impossible, Ellie thought. Baffled, she stared harder into the night but could make out no sign of the castle in the sky, or whatever it had been.

Then, hearing a shout below, she tilted to see Gussie.

Nox had the Falcon girl in his arms and was fluttering down toward the trees. Twig appeared and helped him. Between them, they were just able to support her weight.

Ellie had other problems. All three gargols were streaking toward her, screeching over the thunder. Their skystone eyes glowed with malevolent magic.

Ellie's heart stopped.

She'd never outfly one gargol, much less three. They would tear her into pieces before she could even scream. In a flash brighter than any bolt of lightning, she saw the broken forms of her parents, sprawled on the crushed sunflowers. She was a fledgling again, help- less and alone in a stormy sky, with death speeding to claim her.

No, she thought.

Not tonight.

Ellie closed her wings and let herself fall.

Wind rushed around her ears as she dropped. There was no time to be afraid, no time for anything but speed, speed, *speed*.

Tilting backward, Ellie wheeled herself into a dive, hands at her sides, wings pinned to her back, legs straight. She pointed herself at the ground, not even breathing, knowing a single second of hesitation could mean her death.

She pierced the canopy like an arrow, leaves and branches whip- ping by, and only when she'd dropped below the largest limbs did she flare her wings open again. The movement jerked her as if she'd hit a wall, but it kept her from slamming into the ground. She flew between the trees, branches scraping her face.

Gasping, Ellie struggled to get her bearings. Above, the canopy cracked and branches rained down. The gargols had followed her.

She could hear them beating their way through the forest. When one of them let out another ear-shattering screech, she knew they weren't far. And from what she'd heard, gargols had excellent night vision.

But of course they did.

Their eyes were magic—the same magic of the skystone. And who knew what else those jewels could do. Shoot fire? See through stone?

"Sparrow!"

Ellie jolted, looking around for Nox.

"Down here!" he cried. "A cave!"

Ellie turned sharply, guided only by his voice.

Then she crashed right into him.

They hit the ground hard and tumbled, entangled and yelling. Nox was the first to collect himself, and he grabbed Ellie and hauled her into the shadows.

The ground turned damp and squelchy beneath her feet. Nox pulled her beneath an outcrop of rock, into a deep recess slick with moss and rivulets of water that trickled from the stone above. Gussie lay there, crying silently into Twig's shoulder, her injured wing limp.

Crashes and furious screeches shook the woods. The four of them huddled together in the mud, breathing hard and watching the darkness outside. Ellie's heart ached from pounding against her ribs. The rock was a poor shelter, and if one of the monsters spotted them, there would be nowhere to run. With barely any effort at all, the gargols could haul them out one by one and disembowel them there in the mud.

Ellie pressed herself as deeply as she could into the wet ground, suppressing sobs of terror, hating the fear she felt. Hating the sky for always turning against them. Hating the world for *being* this way.

Would it ever end? Was this really how she would live her life—constantly looking up in fear, forever marking hiding spots wherever she went?

She did not want to live as prey.

She wanted to fight back. And she *had*. Behind the terror and adrenaline coursing through her hummed a quieter note of triumph. She'd been grabbed by a gargol and she'd fought back. They'd saved Gussie and escaped with their lives.

So far, anyway.

She let her head rest on her hands, forcing herself to breathe more slowly, and gradually her heart calmed. The crashes faded and the forest returned to silence. Over the next few hours, the storm ebbed, spitting out a few grumbling last words before moving on. But the rain continued to fall, soft and steady, pattering on the leaves.

The gargols had gone.

Rising to her elbows, she gave a long, relieved exhale. Somehow, they'd survived.

Then she turned, only to lock gazes with Nox. The Crow boy was glowering at her, his eyes ablaze with dark fury.

CHAPTER TWENTY-FIVE
· NOX ·

Nox hauled himself out of the mud, driven by rage.

He shook water out of his wings, then turned and glared at the Sparrow girl. She lay on the ground, her face smeared with dirt, her hair pulled out of its pigtails to frizz around her head. In the dim moonlight, her face was pale enough to show her freckles.

Ellie stared back, her eyes wide, and whispered, "Is everyone okay?"

Nox reached down and helped Gussie up, too angry to speak.

"Gussie," Ellie stammered. "Your wing . . ."

"Would be *fine* if we were still sleeping in the quarry," Gussie snapped.

"I—I'm sorry," she said. Then she added, "Wait. No. I'm *not* sorry. Not about taking the stone, anyway."

Her hand went to her pocket, and she froze.

"Looking for this?" Nox growled.

Of course, he had already stolen it back. He'd grabbed it the moment he'd pinned her to the tree.

He was angry at her, but also at himself for letting her nearly succeed. Ever since Granny Tam's, he'd known she'd try to steal it. Shayn hadn't helped with her talk of *hope* and *doing what's right*. Ellie slurped that kind of thing down like warm soup, and he was only surprised by how long she'd waited.

In truth, he'd begun to hope he was wrong about her, and that she'd either changed her mind or had never planned to steal it in the first place. He'd let himself get lazy.

He'd let himself *trust* her.

Oh, the laugh the Talon would have if he saw Nox now.

Nox had been played for a fool. And why? Because some country Sparrow had called him a *hero*? Because she'd told him there was good in him, that he could do greater things than steal and lie?

When had he started listening to her?

Worse, when had he begun to *believe* her?

But like everyone else in his life, she'd proven what she really thought of him—that he was selfish scum. That whatever his reasons were for doing what he did, they couldn't possibly be as important as her own.

In the end, she was just like everyone else.

"Tell me, Sparrow," he said, "where does *betrayal* rank on your precious ladder?"

Sighing, Ellie pulled herself up and joined them in the rain. The corner of the moon peeked out just enough to illuminate the forest floor. Ellie faced Nox, her chin high.

"You want to practically throw the skystone away," she said. "I want to save people with it. I won't apologize for that."

Nox stepped forward, his ears buzzing with anger. "Throw it away? Is that what you think? You don't know anything about us. After a few weeks, you just *decide* we're bad guys who want people to suffer and die. And yet you're the one who'd hand this over to the real villains!"

"Why do you hate the Goldwings so much, Nox? Why are you so convinced they're evil?"

"Because they killed my father!"

Rain pattered in the silence that followed.

Nox stared hard into the trees. A sinkhole had opened in his chest, and he felt himself slipping deeper and deeper into it, into the empty black that had always lurked inside him.

"You never told us that," Twig said softly.

"Yeah, well, some things aren't that fun to share," Nox replied.

Ellie lifted a hand. "Nox, I—"

"They killed him in front of me," Nox spat. "Executed him for a crime he *never* committed. They said he started a fire in the building beside ours. There were three families living in there. He went in to save them, but . . . he was too late."

Nox could smell the smoke, hear the screams, his own voice among them. He'd stood in the doorway and called for his father until the smoke choked his lungs and his mother pulled him away.

"When he came out," he continued, his voice acid, "they said *he* had started it. And they hanged him then and there, strung him up for the whole city to see."

For years, he hadn't let himself relive that day, and he was stunned at how clear and detailed the memory still was now that he surrendered to it. A gathering, murmuring crowd; the Goldwings' pennants snapping in the wind; the creak of the gallows steps and his father's last, sad smile. Nox wasn't supposed to watch. His mother had ordered him not to watch.

But he had.

"Then they came for my mother and me." It was like he'd cut a slit in a bag of sand. The story poured out too quickly for him to make it stop, no matter how badly he wanted to. "They put her in prison and I ran. My parents never did anything wrong, not *anything*. But they *killed him*, without a trial, without facts, without any reason other than that he was in the wrong place at the wrong time. And when I was left on my own, it wasn't a Goldwing but the Talon—a *thief*—who took me in, fed me, protected me, taught me how to survive. It was a *thief* who saved me . . . from *them*."

He was breathing hard, his fists clenched so tightly they trembled. Not all the dampness on his face was rain.

Ellie raised a hand as if to touch him but hesitated. "They . . . they couldn't have . . ."

Nox finally looked at her, straight in the eyes. "You think I'm wrong. That because I was a little kid, I didn't understand what was happening? You're like everyone else. Is it because I'm a Crow from the big bad shattered Crow clan?"

"No! I just—maybe there was more to it than—"

"Stop!" he yelled, not because she was wrong . . . but because she was right. There *was* more to the story, but he wasn't ready to admit that, even to himself. That last, miserable secret was too dangerous to be spoken aloud—the real reason they'd hanged his father. The truth about *why* he'd run into that fire.

Nox exploded upward, black wings striking the ground as he launched himself away.

"Nox! Wait!"

He hovered above Ellie, the downdraft from his wings whipping her hair.

"This skystone is my mother's freedom," he said, pulling it out of his shirt. "*That's* the reward the Talon promised if I deliver it. She'll die if I don't get her out. The day they dragged her away, I swore I'd save her. And maybe I'm a thief and a liar and everything else you hate, but I *always* keep my word."

Ellie raised her hands. "If we give the skystone to the king, maybe he'll free your mother!"

Nox groaned loudly. "You still don't see it! They're not who you think they are. The Goldwings, the king—they're only interested in one thing: protecting themselves. Their power. Their place at the top of your stupid ladder. And they'll kick down anyone who dares climb as high as them. They won't give me *beans* for this stone. I'd be lucky if they didn't imprison me too, or kill me the way they did my father."

Turning to his crew, he said, "Gussie, Twig, let's go. Goodbye, Sparrow. I hope you get everything you want. It's what you deserve."

He did not mean it as a compliment.

Gussie and Twig fluttered up after him wordlessly, their faces strained. Nox could tell they wanted to say something but were holding back. It didn't matter. With Gussie limping slightly on her injured wing, they flew off together, leaving Ellie standing alone in the rain.

CHAPTER TWENTY-SIX
· ELLIE ·

When Ellie reached the gates of Thelantis two days later, she knew she must look like a wild beggar. Face dirty, clothes torn and wings in need of grooming, she tried to make up for it with a proud stride and lifted chin.

The road to the city was clotted with travelers; it was early morning and the gates seemed to have just opened. Six guards stood at the entrance. At first, she wondered why there was a gate at all. Surely anyone could just fly over the wall.

Then she noticed more guards on the wall itself, carefully scanning the sky with crossbows in hand.

That ruled that idea out.

Looking up at the towers and buildings rising beyond the wall, she remembered the night she'd stolen the skystone . . . and the glimpse of a castle in the clouds. She'd never had the chance to ask the others whether they'd seen it too. But then, she hadn't really seen anything, had she? Castles didn't exist in the air. It had been a cloud, and her imagination had been running wild, what with gargols trying to kill her and all.

Shaking off the memory, she focused on the *actual* towers and walls before her. There was no denying the reality of Thelantis, at least.

People came and left through the gates, many with carts and wagons. She glanced around, wondering if she'd spot Nox, Gussie, and Twig, but they were nowhere to be seen. There'd been no sign of them at all since they'd flown off two days ago. She figured they must have some secret way of getting in and out of the city.

Clearly, many of these people were here for the Race. Groups of high clanners and their kids stood tall and proud above the humbler Finch, Robin, and other low clan farmers with their carts and livestock. They pushed their way in front, as if their size warranted them special privilege. The guards—both with black-and-white Shrike wings—waved the high clans in first.

Across a field to the right of the road, a ramshackle village flowed outward from the city wall, a conglomeration of canvas tents, stick huts, and shacks made of crates, barrels, and broken wagons. Perhaps it was some sort of market or slum.

Then she heard a tall Swan clanner muttering to his wife behind her. "They should have made the rotters gather *behind* the city, where we wouldn't have to smell their stench coming and going."

It was no market, Ellie realized.

This had to be Rottown.

Nox had told her about the village of wingrot sufferers, but she hadn't imagined anything so sprawling. There had to be more people there than in all of Linden and Mossy Dell combined. She could see them moving slowly, as if in pain, their faces downturned and their wings hidden beneath cloths.

All those people suffering, many dying, driven out of their own homes and away from their families. It was even worse than she'd thought.

Her stomach cold, Ellie turned back to the road. Her eyes kept returning to the town of the sick, and guilt chewed at her insides. The only thing she could do now was to keep walking. She thought again of the skystone, and inwardly cursed herself for letting Nox steal it back from her.

Finally, after nearly two hours, she was shooed through the gate and into the city, where she found an explosion of activity.

The buildings were taller than anything back home. Wide porches jutted out at all angles, providing easy landing pads, and protective ashmarks were drawn over every door. The sky over the city bustled with people, a flurry of wings. She wondered that so many could fly without crashing into one another. Soldiers atop high, slender towers patrolled the sky, blowing harsh whistles at anyone who flew too fast or recklessly. In an area cordoned off by ropes, a group of kids played skyball, kicking around leather balls in a frenzy while onlookers cheered.

Built on the footslopes of Mount Garond, the city rose gradually uphill. Standing at the lowest point as she was, all Ellie had to do was look up to see the whole of Thelantis rising above her like a swelling wave. At the city's highest point sat a white palace that had to be the seat of Garion and the Eagle clan. She marveled, trying to make herself believe she was really seeing all of this.

"Watch out!" yelled a voice, and Ellie turned to see a Hummingbird boy speeding toward her, his emerald wings buzzing. She stepped aside just in time to avoid being hit.

"Stay outta the messenger lane, dummy!" the boy yelled as he blazed past. He wore a pair of glass goggles, and a harness on his back supported the satchel that hung beneath his chest. He pulled a rolled-up paper out of it and expertly slung it into a letterbox hanging on the door of a nearby shop.

Ellie realized she had been standing atop a line of white bricks that curved away into the city. She stayed clear of them as another Hummingbird messenger buzzed past, tossing stone-weighted letters right and left.

Ellie turned away, her eyes snagging on a flash of white. She gasped as a dozen Goldwings strode by in full ceremonial uniforms—capes hemmed in gold, white leather vests and boots, golden wings embroidered across their proud chests. They walked in four rows of three, marching in unison, faces shining with noble purpose. Their spears glinted with every step, laid across their shoulders so that the Eagle feathers hanging from the shafts fluttered softly behind them.

Catching Ellie's stare, one of them—a man with obsidian skin and the brown-and-white-striped wings of the Hawk clan—smiled at her.

A sudden piercing whine followed by a loud pop pulled her attention away. She looked up to see streaking pods shot high into the sky, then bursting into explosions of colorful paper that fluttered down. Soon, the air was filled with the stuff. Children flew around, grabbing handfuls.

"What's happening?" she asked a small Nightingale boy.

"Race day!" he cried happily. "They're setting off the confetti bombs!"

Ellie's heart jolted. "What! Already?" Had she lost track of the days? Was she too late? For a moment, the world around her spun and she thought she might faint dead away.

"Nah," said the boy. "Tomorrow. They're just welcoming the racers to Thelantis."

Letting out a relieved breath, Ellie brushed paper from her shoulders. She started to ask the boy where racers were supposed to go to sign in, but he dashed away after another shower of confetti.

She found herself following the flow of the crowd, which took her into a busy marketplace. The street here was wide enough for ten wagons but instead was full of people and stalls and noise. She walked through in a state of shock, dizzied and overwhelmed, as vendors shouted at her to buy roasted fish, seashell jewelry, wing combs, flying goggles, rarest silks and coconuts from the far south, fur-lined capes, little plates with King Garion's silhouette painted on them, blown glass earrings, maps of Thelantis.

A change in the breeze brought a strong scent to her nose, one that stopped her dead in her tracks. For a moment, the crowd blurred around her as a heady rush of familiarity sent a splinter of shock through her frame. She inhaled deeply, unable to believe what she was smelling.

Home.

She smelled home.

Looking frantically around, she finally spotted it: a stall to her left, with a yellow awning and cheerful ribbon tassel.

Spread on its tables were jars and jars of sunflower oil.

SPARROW FARMS'S FINEST SUNFLOWER OIL read their labels. PUTS THE WIN IN WINGS!

All the lovely scents the Sparrow perfumers had concocted—lavender, strawberry, sage, lemon, and her favorite, apple blossom. The oils shone like golden honey. She'd doubtless picked and crushed the seeds for many of those very jars herself.

Watching the people of Thelantis jostle one another to get their hands on the jars of oil, buying it by the box, she felt a warm glow of pride race over her skin. But it was immediately followed by a sudden, powerful loneliness that sucked at her with all the force of a river's current. The oils were here, but there were no Sparrows in sight; the booth was run by a family of Orioles. It was just a reminder of how far from home she was.

Though Ellie had never been around so many people in all her life, she'd never felt so alone. Perhaps the city had opened its arms to welcome the racers, but it certainly didn't feel like it was welcoming *her*. A woman bumped into her, cursing her for getting in the way. Ellie mumbled an apology, stumbling back, only to collide with someone else, who shoved her and called her a rude name.

Gussie would know where I'm supposed to go, she thought. *Nox would know the quickest way of getting there. And Twig . . . he'd hate these crowds as much as I do.*

Ellie felt tears burn in her eyes. She knotted her fists and rubbed them away.

Feeling a sudden need for *space*, she launched upward, the down-draft from her wings knocking off hats. A chorus of curses and angry shouts rose from the crowd, but she ignored them and pumped her wings, lifting higher. The market dropped away. Confetti burst in the sky around her. She rose above it all, to the cool, wild breezes that combed the sky above Thelantis, crisp air carrying the scent of the cedars and pines from the forest outside the walls.

She hovered for a moment, studying the streets that webbed outward. Then she spotted a stream of high clanners about her age. They flew higher, toward the upper city. Judging by the kids following them and throwing confetti, they were here for the Race of Ascension too.

Ellie trailed after them.

A short flight later, the high clanners spiraled downward to land in an octagonal stone courtyard, in front of a wide building decorated with fluttering white pennants. Ellie landed softly in the back. A crowd was already gathered at the front doors of the building, which were shut firmly. On either side of the doors stood a Goldwing knight.

Ellie let out a breath of awe. This had to be Honorhall, the headquarters of the Goldwings. She clutched her hands to her stomach and stared.

"Hurry, Father!" a Hawk girl yelled. "They'll open the doors in two minutes! If I'm not at the front, I won't make it into the race!"

Her father grumbled as she sprinted over to the gathering crowd and tried to push her way in.

Ellie gasped.

All those people were here to enter as wild cards? There had to be a hundred of them—and there were only twenty spots. And of course, she noted with unease, she was the only low clanner in sight. She was a head and shoulders shorter than even the smallest of them. There was no way she'd be able to force her way through.

Backing away, she chewed her lip and thought. She had not come all this way just to fail now.

Then she remembered something Gussie had told her: *What you think of as weaknesses are actually your strengths. You've just got to use them right.*

Setting her jaw, Ellie got down on all fours and began to crawl. She was too small to push her way through the crowd—but she was definitely small enough to crawl between their legs, unnoticed.

Above, she heard the kids start shouting. A long groan told her the doors were beginning to peel open. She crawled faster, scrabbling around ankles, through legs, keeping her wings pulled tight to her back.

Then, at last, she popped up to her feet—at the very front of the throng. The doors swung open before her, and six tall Goldwing knights stepped out in full dress uniform, almost blindingly bright.

"Young warriors of the Clandoms," proclaimed the lead knight. "Welcome to the Race of Ascension's wild card draw. May the luck of skies be with you."

N ox had never been so glad to smell sewage.

Sure, it burned his nostrils and made him gag, but that stink meant he was back in Thelantis. He was home.

Or at least, nearly home. There was still at least a mile of sewer pipes to crawl through before they were safely inside the city walls.

"Have I said I am *not* okay with this plan?" Gussie called out.

"Twelve times," Nox grumbled.

"I just don't see why we can't go through the front gates like everybody else. It's not like the guards *know* we're thieves."

"I don't see why we have to go into the city at all," said Twig. "We could have been robbers in the woods, sleeping in trees, never taking baths . . ." He sighed wistfully, but avoided a dark puddle of mysterious, oozing goo on the floor. Even Twig had his limits. He'd miserably said goodbye to most of his little pets before they'd entered the sewer system, but Lirri was still curled in his pocket, her small horns peeking out.

When they came to an intersection of pipes, Nox looked around till he found the black arrow marking the correct path.

"Ugh." Gussie shook a glob of slime off her shoe. "This is *nasty*, Nox."

"We'll be home soon, and it'll all be over." He turned and smiled. "All of it, Gussie. The Talon will take care of everything. You'll get into that fancy school for geniuses. And Twig, you'll get your ship sailing south."

"To go see the elephants," said Twig, eyes shining.

"As many elephants as you want. All we have to do is get this stone to the Talon and our lives will change forever."

"You'll get your mother back," Gussie added.

Nox's heart squeezed. "Yes."

"Then what will you do? Keep thieving?"

"No way. I'm getting her as far from Thelantis as I can. Maybe we'll come with you to the jungle, Twig."

He hadn't let himself think much beyond this mission, but now he couldn't help it. He tried to imagine his mother's face, but it had been years since he'd seen her. Well, soon enough he'd set right all the terrible things that had happened to his family. They'd sail away and never look back.

The sewer tunnels took them beneath the streets of Thelantis. They passed under grates flickering with shadows of people walking above. The busy hubbub of voices felt like a relief to Nox after the quiet wilderness they'd traveled through. Not that he'd ever admit it aloud, but in the woods, he'd always felt a little bit lost. Now he was back in his element, in a world he knew upside down.

At last, they emerged through a loose grate beneath a bridge, not far from the den where they would meet the Talon. But the Lord of Thieves only conducted business at night, so they'd have to wait till then to turn over the skystone.

Stretching, Nox looked around and grinned. This was Knock Street, one of the main slums in Thelantis, and everyone here was either a thief, a con artist, a fraud, or a smuggler . . . In other words, they were Nox's kind of people. As the saying went, on Knock Street, rules were *optional*. No one blinked an eye to see three kids stumble out of the sewers.

They made their way to the Chivalrous Toad, the most notorious tavern in the city. The owner, Borge, waved when they came in.

"Oi!" Borge yelled. "It's Nox Hatcher! You three are still alive? Pay up, Winster."

He held out a meaty palm, and his partner, Winster—a skinny, one-eyed man—grumbled and handed over a coin.

"We're hungry, gentlemen," Nox said. "Haven't had a proper meal in weeks."

"Then sit yourselves down and be served," said Borge. Dropping his voice to a whisper, he added, "So . . . there's a rumor been going around about you three, and just what the Talon sent you to fetch for him. Is it true—"

"Now, Borge." Nox waved a hand. "You know what the Talon thinks about people discussing his business."

"Right, right." Borge backed off. He might've owned the Toad, but the Talon owned Borge. It was common knowledge that the Talon's gang operated out of the tavern, which was why Nox and his friends got free meals there. But some things were too secret even to share among fellow thieves.

As they ate rabbit stew—at least, Nox hoped it was rabbit—a few of the other patrons gave them hostile stares. He was careful not to touch the pocket where the skystone was hidden, which would be a dead giveaway that he had something worth keeping in there. And anything worth keeping was worth stealing.

Twig ignored his spoon and picked up his bowl, guzzling noisily while Lirri chewed a piece of meat in his pocket. Gussie stared at her stew, her hands in her lap.

"What's wrong?" Nox asked her. "You've never turned up your nose at Winster's Of-Course-It's-Rabbit-Meat-Stop-Asking-Questions Stew before."

"It's just . . ." Gussie sighed. "I've been thinking about what Ellie said. About the . . . you know."

Nox scowled. He'd spent the last two days carefully *not* thinking about the Sparrow. Or about how much her betrayal had hurt.

"Ellidee Meadows," he said slowly, chasing a chunk of slippery meat around his bowl with his spoon, "is a stuck-up, self-righteous know-it-all. I wouldn't think twice about *anything* she said."

"She wasn't that bad," Gussie argued. "She saved our skins a few times."

"The race is tomorrow," said Twig. "Do you think she'll win?"

Of course she'll win, Nox thought. *If she can't outfly them, she'll just out-stubborn them.*

"I don't care," he said. "I haven't even thought about her once since she left."

"Liar," said Gussie.

Nox slammed down his spoon and glared at her. "She *betrayed* us."

"Then why do I feel like the one betraying something? Nox . . . what if she was right? We could be helping so many people with the . . . you know . . . and instead we're only using it for ourselves."

Nox's stomach twisted. Inwardly, he cursed Gussie for voicing the very questions he'd been trying so hard to avoid asking himself. "It's like the Talon says. Listen to your wings, not your heart. Your heart'll get you killed." The way his father's heart had killed *him*, when he'd run into that fire. "Your wings help you survive."

She shook her head, still looking torn.

"Look," said Nox, "there's got to be other *you-know-whats* out there in the world. This can't be the only one. Someone else will figure out what they can do and use them to help people. Why do we have to be the ones who save the world? We're just thieves from Knock Street."

"Until tonight," she pointed out. "When we officially retire. Then what do we become?"

"Something new. Fresh start. Clean slate. Nothing that happened before will matter." Angrily, Nox slurped down the rest of his soup and then stood up. "I'm going to change clothes and catch a nap. Meet you tonight."

Nox had entered the tavern feeling hopeful and excited, but when he left, his stomach was in knots. He looked up to see confetti bombs bursting over the wealthier section of the city—no celebrations for Knock Street, of course.

"Stupid race," he growled. "Stupid Sparrow."

CHAPTER TWENTY-EIGHT
· ELLIE ·

"The wild card draw will now begin," announced the Goldwing captain, framed by the great front doors of Honorhall. "Please stay quiet and orderly. I know you're all excited, but remember, you must represent the best of the Clandoms."

Ellie nearly fell over in shock.

The knight who'd spoken, and who now surveyed the hopeful kids with a firm eye, was the same knight who had saved Ellie years ago. She'd never forget her face or her gleaming gold hair.

The captain indulged them with a tight smile. "I know you've all journeyed far for this opportunity to enter the Race of Ascension, but only twenty will be admitted."

A hundred kids cried out to be chosen, hands raised eagerly, some fluttering into the air in an effort to be seen.

Ellie stepped forward. "I wish to race."

The Goldwing looked down at her, eyebrows lifting in surprise. At first, Ellie thought the woman might recognize her too, but she only said, "You're far from home, Sparrow."

The other kids, noticing Ellie had the Goldwing's attention, began calling out angrily.

"She can't race! She's a flappin' *Sparrow*!"

"She's smaller than my dog back home!"

"This is ridiculous! Get out of the way, low clanner!"

The Goldwing put a hand on Ellie's shoulder. "All are permitted to enter the Race of Ascension," she said. "Go on in, child, and good luck."

The roar of protest from the crowd nearly knocked Ellie over. A red-faced Falcon man alighted hard on the steps, spitting with anger.

"My son is the strongest lad in our town!" he fumed. "How dare you let this—this *embarrassment* race instead of him?"

"Sir," said the Goldwing, her hand going to the short sword on her belt, "back up *now*."

The other Goldwings stepped threateningly toward him, and in a huff, the man flew off again.

Shaking, Ellie marched up the steps and into Honorhall, fists clenched.

But weariness dragged at her feet. She was tired of having to constantly prove herself worthy of things these high clanners *expected* to get, simply by virtue of birth. Raw determination had brought her this far, but when would she be allowed to rest? To take for granted what everyone else did? When would people stop saying *prove you can do it* and instead say *of course you can*?

Inside Honorhall, Ellie's spirits lifted when she saw the famous statues of Goldwings past. She knew all their names: Sir Rusviel, Sir Saryn, Sir Roth . . . Set into alcoves in the walls, they looked down fiercely as she strode past. Feeling dwarfed by their height, and by the cavernous ceiling arching above, she decided to spread her wings and fly instead.

She soared down the length of the hall and landed at last before another set of doors, these ones already open. Beyond them, a

Goldwing waited with an inkpot, quill, and open book. He had porcelain skin, a black warrior's topknot, and the unmistakable dark wings of the Eagle clan. He might even have been of royal blood. Ellie was too intimidated to ask.

He looked a little surprised to see a Sparrow standing before him, but he handed over the quill and told her to sign her name.

She did so, hand trembling slightly.

"And mark down your chosen weapon," he added, pointing at her staff.

"My weapon?"

"Everyone enters the race armed." He tilted his head, looking at her as if she had wandered in by mistake. "Did you not know? There's still time to back out."

"No way," Ellie said. She wrote down *lockstave* next to her name, then returned the quill.

"Congratulations," said the Eagle. "You're now an official contestant in the Race of Ascension. Skies be with you, little warrior."

Dizzy with euphoria and nervousness, Ellie let the Goldwings shuffle her through Honorhall to the barracks where all the contestants would sleep before the big race. It all passed in a blur—tapestries of battles between Goldwings and gargols, busts of Eagle kings and queens of the past, racks of fabled weapons, displays of Goldwing uniforms as they had changed over the generations, maps of the Clandoms and the lands beyond . . .

She told herself she didn't have to take it all in now. When she entered the Goldwing Academy, she'd train here every day. This would be her home, her family.

If she entered the academy.

She couldn't let herself get carried away just yet. She still had the hardest race of her life ahead of her, and as more contestants began to arrive—other wild cards as well as trial winners—her nervousness expanded until it felt like a great black shadow crouched behind her, its claws on her shoulders.

She sat on a narrow bed in the barracks, a round tower that reminded her of the seed silos back at Sparrow Farms. Circular platforms set into the walls added nearly twenty floors for beds, accommodating the four hundred or so racers.

Tucked onto a bed on the bottom floor of the tower, Ellie had a good view of all the contestants as they arrived. Many seemed to already know one another—they were clanmates, or had trained at high clan schools together. There was a lot of shouting, high fives, and comparing wingspans. No one seemed to notice Ellie at all. She preferred that to hearing their jibes and insults, so she tried to make her small self even smaller.

But then a group of contestants arrived from whom Ellie couldn't hide.

Zain, Tauna, and Laida strutted in with huge grins, carrying sheathed swords.

"Ellie Meadows?" Zain cried out.

He stared at her with a mixture of apprehension and amazement. Tauna and Laida looked shocked as well, but decidedly *not* pleased to see her.

"What in the skies is *she* doing here?" Tauna said.

Ellie bristled. "I have as much right to be here as anyone."

The girls rolled their eyes and fluttered to the higher platforms in search of bunks.

Zain sat on Ellie's bed, and she perched carefully beside him, her body rigid.

The awkward silence reminded Ellie of how much their friendship had changed in the last few weeks. She wondered if they could ever really be best friends again.

"Well," she said at last. "I did tell you I'd see you in Thelantis."

"What happened to you? You look like you got trampled by a bear."

She laughed. "Actually . . ."

"I just don't want you get hurt," he blurted. "You're one of the bravest people I know, for a Sparrow—"

"See?" Ellie said. "That's the problem right there. *For a Sparrow.* Why do high clans think they're the only ones who are brave and strong? I'm no braver than any other Sparrow. More stubborn, maybe. Definitely more reckless, as Mother Rosemarie always said. But *being a Sparrow* isn't something I have to leave behind or overcome, Zain. It's a part of me, and I'm proud to be what I am. And guess what? Being a Sparrow is exactly what's going to help me win tomorrow."

Zain raised his hands defensively. "I didn't mean—"

"And that's the *other* problem. You don't mean anything you say, do you?" All the things she'd wanted to say to Zain now came pouring out, a hundred pent-up speeches that had played out endlessly in her head. "I know you don't want me getting hurt; maybe that's true. But you also don't want me in the same sky as you, because you think that'll make you look weak. How embarrassing to see a Sparrow outfly a Hawk, huh? I'm allowed to be your friend, but only so long as I don't outshine you. Isn't that right?"

Zain's face turned red. He tried to stammer a response but clamped his teeth shut when Ellie laid her hand on his arm.

"You've been my best friend for years," Ellie said. "And I care about you. But I'm not giving up, no matter what you or anyone else says."

"If you lose," he said quietly, "they'll drag you to that terrible Moorly House and clip your wings. You won't fly again for *years*."

"I know." Ellie looked down at her hands. "That's why I cannot lose."

CHAPTER TWENTY-NINE
· NOX ·

The Lord of Thieves was a tall man, bald and paunchy, with one blue eye. There were many stories about how the Talon had lost the other eye, each one wilder than the last. Nox's favorite was that he'd lost it wrestling the same crocodile whose skin he now wore as an eye patch.

His wings marked him an Osprey, but Nox had heard he'd been formally expelled from his clan as a young man. So he'd built his own clan of misfits, reprobates, and criminals. The Talon had been the one to find Nox that awful day he'd run from the Goldwings.

The day of his father's execution.

"C'mere, kid," the one-eyed man had said. "I can keep you hidden from the big bad knights. Just do this one thing for me . . ."

That was the first time Nox had ever stolen something—an apple from a cart, to prove to the Talon that he could. Neither of them had their own clans, and Nox had always felt a kind of kinship with the man because of it. Not that he loved the Talon or saw him as a father—quite the opposite; Nox feared him as much as he respected him—but the Talon always upheld his deals. He repaid every deed fairly, whether it was coin for a job well done or a beating for a thief who dared cross him. Besides, he'd been there for Nox when no one else in the world had. The Talon's rules were the only ones Nox bothered to keep.

Now, as Nox approached the cellar beneath the Chivalrous Toad, he felt a twinge of sorrow. This would be his last job for the Lord of Thieves. Tomorrow, he and his mother would leave Thelantis behind forever.

"Nox Hatcher," said the Talon, reclined in his high wooden chair at the head of a long table. "My prized protégé, back at last. Come closer, lad."

His inner circle sat with him, the best of his thieves—or worst, as the Sparrow girl might say. They were all savage, ruthless individuals who eyed Nox like he was about to steal their wallets. Which, to be fair, he had done on one or two occasions.

"There are rumors of a certain angry general combing the countryside for a trio of thieves." The Talon grinned. "You pulled it off."

"We did," Nox said. "I've brought you the skystone."

He took the gem from his pocket and set it on the table before his master.

"Well done, my boy. Oh, well done, indeed!" The Talon picked up the stone, his eye shining. "Behold, friends, the rarest jewel in the world: the eye of a gargol. There are collectors who would sell their own mothers for it. Once I put it up for auction, prepare to become *disgustingly* rich."

The inner circle looked impressed. They leaned in, eyes greedy, but the Talon flicked his hand, and the stone vanished into one of his many hidden pockets.

"Right," he said. "You'll want to be paid, then. You, the feral one."

Twig stepped forward nervously, his hand clutching Lirri in his pocket.

"An Albatross ship sails for the south in two days," said the Talon.

"You'll have berth aboard it, as promised, with an ample allowance in your pocket besides."

Twig's eyes widened, and he nodded mutely.

"And for the brainy one," the Talon sighed, flicking a finger at Gussie, "it's a little more complicated, but by next week, you'll be admitted into Thelantis University."

"Thank you," Gussie whispered, looking dazed. "Thank you."

"And for my protégé." The Talon took a coin purse from his pocket and tossed it. The loud *thunk* it made when it landed elicited gasps from his inner circle, who looked at him as if he were crazy. "Ten thousand aquilas."

Silence.

It was a small fortune, more than anyone Nox knew had ever made from a single job. It could easily buy passage on a ship anywhere in the world, and then a house and land when he got there.

But he ignored the purse and looked into the Talon's glittering eye.

"That wasn't the deal," he said.

"Are you mad, boy?" burst out a brawny man seated to the Talon's right. "It's more than your sorry skin's worth. Take it and—"

"I said I'd deliver the skystone in exchange for a prisoner from the Crag," said Nox. "That was our deal, Talon."

The inner circle laughed.

"The Crag!" sputtered a woman with a blue-dyed mohawk. "The boy *is* mad. No one escapes the Crag."

The thief lord leaned forward, elbows resting on the table, hands laced beneath his chin. "I remember no such bargain, boy."

Nox blinked, struck speechless with confusion.

The Talon was *lying*?

He never lied to his crew, especially not about deals. If word got out he'd broken a deal with one of his own . . . But then Nox remembered the night they'd struck their bargain. They'd been alone, walking the rooftops, with no one to hear their conversation. It was his word against the Talon's. And against the Lord of Thieves, Nox's word was nothing.

"I don't want your money," he said, with a good deal less confidence. "I want what you promised me."

"As our lovely Melinde pointed out, no one escapes the Crag. Not even *I* have the power to pluck someone out of the king's prison."

"But . . ." Nox's throat thickened. His wings tightened as if bracing against a storm. "You promised. You *promised*. Everything I've done for you, everything I've risked and stolen and . . ."

"Take the money," said the Talon in a low, edged voice. "Take it, Crow, and tread lightly out of my presence while you still have your wings attached to your spine."

"C'mon, Nox," whispered Gussie, tugging his sleeve. "It's over, all right?"

Twig was already backing away, toward the door.

But an image flashed in Nox's mind: his mother's haggard frame trembling in chains, her face suddenly clearer in his memory than it had been in years. Her eyes dark like his, sunken into shadow, her lips murmuring his name as the Goldwings dragged her away.

Nox shook Gussie off and stepped forward. "You're a liar! You're a washed-up old crook, and I could steal the patch off your eye if I wanted."

In a flash, the Talon lunged out of his chair and grabbed Nox by the throat. Nox struggled to breathe as the man lifted him right off the ground. He spread his wings instinctively, but there was nowhere to fly.

"For that," grated the Talon, "you forfeit your pay *and* your friends'. You leave with *nothing*, Crow."

"The day you found me," Nox whispered, his voice hoarse under the Talon's grip, "you promised me one thing. That if I did whatever you told me to, and did it well, you'd pay me fairly what I was owed. You swore you'd never break a deal with me. I thought . . . I thought we were clan."

The words surprised even Nox. He'd never dared to think them, even to himself, until now. He felt weak and stupid in front of the only person he'd ever truly wanted to impress.

Shame burned on his skin.

"Then you're a worse fool than I thought. I'm not your father, boy. And this is no clan." He threw Nox onto the ground, then brushed off his hands. "Leave, the three of you, before I decide to have you thrown out of this city for good."

Gussie pulled Nox up and dragged him out of the room. The inner circle laughed as they slammed the door, shutting them in the cold corridor.

"That was stupid," Gussie said. "Stupid, stupid, *stupid*, Nox! Now Twig won't get his ship. I won't get my admission to university. And all because you had to—"

"He *promised* me, Gussie!" Nox looked at her, tears of fury in his eyes. "My mother will die in there!"

She bit her lip. "I . . . I'm sorry. Nox. I really am. But that was *stupid*."

He hung his head.

She was right, of course, but he didn't care.

All those times he'd accused Ellie Meadows of being naive, of trusting the wrong people, of *chasing moonmoths* . . . and here he stood, guilty of the same things. He had one goal he'd sacrificed everything for, one promise to keep, one person in the world depending on him . . .

And he had failed.

CHAPTER THIRTY
· ELLIE ·

Ellie closed her eyes and breathed in deeply, letting the chilled mountain air wash over her hammering heart. She stood on the rippling slopes of Mount Garond, with the city of Thelantis shining below. Flapping pennants anchored into the stone sported the colors of the Goldwings and the king.

All around her, the noise of the contestants and the crowd of spectators threatened to pull her apart. Taunts whispered in her ear: *"Stupid little Sparrow, you're going to get killed up there."* If she lost focus even a little, their words would wash her away entirely.

I am wind.

I am sky.

I am speed.

A hush fell over the crowd at last, as the royal envoy arrived.

Ellie turned to watch as trumpets rang out in fanfare. The reigning Eagles descended from the sky on dark gold wings—King Garion, Queen Corella, and the prince and princess, Corion and Diantha. Each of the royal family members wore the Eagle crest on their clothing, and they were flanked by a contingent of guards in blue-and-gold livery. Their wide wingspans cast flickering shadows over the hushed crowd.

With more grace than Ellie could ever muster in such heavy, fine clothing, the Eagles landed on a roped-off dais. Attendants rushed forward to drape fur-lined cloaks on their shoulders, and from a jeweled box, four crowns were taken and placed on their heads.

King Garion looked young for his age, with black oiled curls and piercing blue eyes. The queen and the royal children all had gleaming golden hair and brown eyes; they reminded Ellie of sunbathed statues, they looked so perfect. The crown prince, Corion, was Ellie's age, and he sighed as he looked at the contestants, as if wishing he could be one of them. His gaze briefly met Ellie's, and she saw his surprise at finding a Sparrow among the racers.

The king gave a speech about how being a Goldwing was the highest honor in the Clandoms, and how the contestants represented the finest of their clans, on and on. But the wind rushing over the mountainside made it hard for Ellie to hear much of it, and her attention wandered.

She matched gazes with Zain, who stood a short distance away, holding a tall spear. He gave her a weak smile. She returned it, hoping after all this they could still somehow remain friends.

Finally, the king's speech ended, and all eyes turned to the captain of the Goldwings—the woman who'd saved Ellie's life years ago. She'd since learned the knight's name was Aglassine.

Sir Aglassine shouted out the rules of the race: They could use their weapons but were to refrain from killing. The first fifty to reach the mountain's summit would find flags planted there. Bringing back a flag would mean securing one's place among the Goldwings. Other than that, there were no real rules. It would be a total free-for-all, nothing like the milder Trials most of the contestants had already won.

Ellie's hand tightened around her staff. She stared hard at the looming mountain, its shadow leaning on her as if to pin her to the ground.

Finally, Sir Aglassine called out, "Contestants, take your marks!"

As one, all five hundred of the fliers planted hands on the ground, ready to blast upward. Ellie's muscles quivered with anticipation.

"Wings out!" called the captain.

With a *whoomph* that echoed off the mountain, five hundred pairs of wings lifted and spread. Ellie was surrounded by a sea of feathers ranging from dark to light, flecked with black, gold, and gray, some striped, some spotted, some nearly as tawny red as her own. She stared at the ground, breathing in deeply through her nose and out again in short, strong breaths to loosen and expand her lungs in preparation.

Then a single trumpet rang out, and chaos exploded across the mountain slope.

Ellie shot upward, using her lighter body and quicker wings to her full advantage as she briefly rose head and shoulders above the rest. Then the swarm overtook her, and she flew like a bee in a hurricane, bouncing off the others, fighting to find space in the crowded air.

Hearing rasps of weaponry all around her, followed by wild cries of pain, she realized many of the racers were already skirmishing. A wounded Falcon screamed as he hurtled downward, and Ellie rolled to avoid being crushed beneath his fall. She saw with relief that the Goldwings were ready. They caught the boy in a net and carried him to the ground, his wing trailing blood. But no one stopped the race or yelled at them to play fair.

In the Race of Ascension, bloodshed *was* fair.

Ellie had never seen such savagery. It was as if the instant the trumpet sounded, kids who'd been friends all their lives suddenly turned into vicious enemies intent on winning at any cost. She flew in desperation, simply trying to avoid being hacked in two. Kids clashed in the air, swords clanging or spears cracking. They grabbed one another's wings and yanked out feathers. Screams of pain mingled with roars of rage. For the most part, the Goldwings hung back, only intervening to rescue the constants who fell.

Determined not to be one of them, Ellie ignored the battles raging across the sky and focused on one thing only: reaching the top of that mountain. Let the others fight, wasting time. It didn't matter who they knocked out of the sky if they didn't claim one of the flags at the summit.

But she wouldn't escape that easily.

Hearing a bellow to her left, Ellie turned to see a massive Eagle clanner hurtling toward her, swinging a sword. Ellie instinctively raised her lockstave to block his weapon.

The blade slammed into the staff with such force her entire body vibrated. She was surprised the blow didn't cleave the shaft in two. The Eagle boy struck again, and she blocked his blows desperately, her arms jarred by the impacts.

"Stupid little low clanner!" he hissed. "My father says you being here dishonors the race!"

"Honor?" echoed Ellie. "Look around you, musclehead. Do these kids look like they're fighting with *honor*?"

A Shrike girl fell by them, screaming, her wing broken.

"You won't make it to the top," the Eagle said. "Every kid here would rather die than lose to a *Sparrow*. Rule or no rule, you'll be dead before you reach the halfway point."

The Eagle kid pulled back, yanking his sword and swinging it again at Ellie's head. She gritted her teeth and once more blocked the blade. This time, instead of rebounding off the staff, it landed in the cross section of the smaller hook. Instinctively, Ellie twisted the staff, and the hook pulled the sword out of the boy's hand and sent it spinning downward.

"Watch out!" Ellie yelled, her stomach flipping as the sword hurtled to the ground, narrowly missing a Falcon girl below.

The Eagle boy gasped. "You—you cheat!"

He reached for her wing, but she swung her staff hard, rapping his ear. As he yowled and tumbled backward, Ellie shot upward, desperate to make up for the time he'd cost her.

The mountain seemed to rise forever. The higher she flew, the more the pack of racers thinned. The sounds of fighting faded below. Several fliers passed her, wordless, their eyes focused on the sky. Each would mean one fewer spot among the champions.

But those kinds of thoughts would only bring her down, and right now, Ellie needed to go *up*. Her wings clawed at the air until her shoulders screamed. She panted, finding it more difficult to breathe the higher she flew, as the air thinned and the temperature dropped. She had never been this high off the ground before. When she glanced down, she couldn't even see the crowd of spectators, only the gray slope of the mountain and the hazy blur of the city. Ellie had never been afraid of heights, but that view made her dizzy.

"Almost there," she panted. "Have to be . . . almost there . . . right?"

For several minutes, she flew without seeing anyone else. The distance between the racers had stretched so far, she didn't think anyone would even hear her if she screamed.

Then a Hawk boy fluttered up beside her.

"Zain!" Ellie noticed a red stain on his sleeve. "You're hurt!"

He smiled grimly. "The other guy's much worse, believe me."

"This race is . . ." Her voice trailed away.

He nodded. "When my dad warned me it wouldn't be like the Trial back home, I didn't believe him. He said the Race of Ascension is all about winnowing the weak. I guess they mean it literally."

"You're still here," Ellie pointed out.

"So are you."

"Surprised?"

Zain shook his head. "I don't think there's anything you could do, Ellie Meadows, that would surprise me now."

"Don't be so sure," said Ellie, and she swung her staff at him.

It wasn't meant to strike him, but it did force him to throw himself out of the way, buying her a few seconds. She put on an extra burst of speed, calling on reserves of strength she wasn't entirely sure she had.

"Nice one, Sparrow!" Zain called out below her.

"See you at the summit, Hawk!"

After a few minutes, Ellie's second wind began to flag. She found herself fighting for every wing beat, dragging every scrap of energy she could find from her exhausted body. Never had she felt this tired or beaten. Never had she had to fight against such powerful gusts of wind. They slammed into her, nearly throwing her into the mountain itself.

Her pace slowed to a near crawl. Flecks of ice and snow pelted her skin. Frost laced her eyelashes. When Zain finally overtook her, she saw he was struggling as much as she was, his lips blue, his breathing ragged. His wings flapped erratically.

She couldn't even spare the breath to speak to him. For a while, they flew close together, rolling when waves of wind rushed over them, fluttering to regain balance.

Then Zain gradually pulled away and disappeared into the hazy blue above.

Ellie flew into a cloud of snow and ice and wind, the cold overwhelming her senses. It was hard to see with ice shards pelting her face, blown off the frozen mountain. Muscles stiffening from the chill, she found herself fighting twice as hard for every thrust of her wings. The tips of her feathers turned white with frost.

And then, all at once, she shot into open sky, the mountain dropping away as she spun over the summit.

"Yes!" she cried out. Immediately, she dove toward the jagged pinnacle.

But where were the flags?

She flew in desperate circles, searching for any sign of them. Her stomach sank more with each passing second. Had they all been claimed already?

Zain was nowhere to be seen, nor were there any other contestants. Those who'd reached the summit must have already dived back toward the ground, prizes in hand, destinies sealed. Maybe Zain had reached the peak to find no flag either. Maybe they'd both lost.

Ellie flew to the flattest rock on the summit, landing softly in the snow. A clutter of footprints told her this must have been where the flags had been planted, but all that remained was a muddy mess. The sky around her was crystal clear, the view in all directions hazy and indistinct, a blur of brown, green, and gray.

She sank to her knees, heart thumping, lungs aching. *This is it. It's over.*

She'd be taken back to Linden. Her wings would be clipped and she'd be sent to Moorly House, where she'd only glimpse the sky through barred windows for years to come.

Ellie felt numb in a way that had nothing to do with the cold. Her entire future was like that sky around her—empty and bleak and fading into hazy uncertainty.

This was as high as she would ever fly.

Then she saw a glint of red in the snow.

It was as if someone had dropped a piece of jewelry. She crawled toward it, thinking perhaps she could return it to its owner.

But it wasn't jewelry. It was a shred of cloth. A torn sleeve, perhaps?

Ellie tugged it, and to her surprise, the cloth kept coming—and coming. A whole square of red silk had been buried in the snow, likely trampled down by a thoughtless contestant.

A flag.

The very last one.

Ellie's heart shot into the sky and burst like one of the confetti bombs. She gasped and forgot all about her shivering limbs and frosted feathers.

She had won.

CHAPTER THIRTY-ONE
· NOX ·

"Well, Nox?" asked Gussie. "How the sky am I supposed to get into university *now*? How's Twig supposed to see his elephants?"

Twig sniffed, his eyes red from crying. He held Lirri to his chest. The creature glared at Nox as if she knew this was his fault and was contemplating stabbing him with her horns.

"What's your plan here, Nox?" Gussie pressed. "To be thieves the rest of our lives? Because I did not leave home to—"

"I'm working on it!" Nox snapped. "If you'd just be quiet for three blasted minutes I could *think*!"

They were perched on the eaves of a schoolhouse they might have been attending had they been normal kids. It was Nox's hope that anyone looking for them would think they were students upon first glance.

"How long do you think the boss'll stay mad at us?" Twig asked.

Nox flinched at the mention of the Talon. He could still feel the man's hand on his throat and hear his own pathetic words echoing in his skull. *I thought we were clan.*

Skies, what a stupid weakling Nox must have sounded. Of course they weren't clan. They'd never been clan. That was the man's own blasted motto—*listen to your wings, not your heart*. He'd only ever cared about Nox until it might cost him something.

"Don't worry," snorted Gussie. "He'll think of a new job pretty quick. He can't stand for any of his twisted little clan to sit idle for long."

Nox scowled. "You're starting to sound like that Sparrow."

"What if I am? She was right about a lot of things, Nox. I'm sick of being a thief. I'm supposed to invent things, not steal them."

"Well, lucky for you, that won't be a problem anymore."

"What do you mean?"

"I mean . . ." His wings tensed as a shifty-looking Magpie boy flew by. The kid didn't look familiar, but that didn't mean he wasn't one of the Talon's many spies. He was always recruiting new wings. "I mean, the Talon isn't going to give us any more jobs."

"He didn't say we were kicked out," said Twig. "Anyhow, the Talon doesn't kick people out. He . . ."

"Disappears them," murmured Gussie.

The Talon couldn't risk angry ex-thieves turning on him. Instead, he made them take a big leap off a tall cliff . . . with their wings tied behind their backs. Gussie gave Nox a narrow look. "What do you mean the Talon isn't going to give us more jobs?"

He looked down at his hands, suddenly *very* interested in the small scar on his left thumb. It was a souvenir from the day he'd accidentally pickpocketed a bare knife from a merchant's pouch.

"*Nox.* Answer me."

Slowly, he raised his eyes to meet hers, knowing his guilt was written all over his face.

"Oh no." Gussie's voice deepened with dread. "What did you do?"

He spread his hands defensively. "Why do you assume it's something *I* did? Why is it never something anybody else did?"

"Because it's *always* you!"

He sighed and reached into his pocket . . . to pull out a familiar blue stone.

Gussie clapped her hand over her mouth, but not fast enough to stifle her shriek.

"It was only fair," he said stubbornly. "He refused to pay for it. Therefore, it's still ours."

"Nox! You've as good as killed us! You know what the Talon does to people who cross him!"

"That's why you've been jumpy all morning," Twig said in a horrified tone. "You knew the Talon's looking for us."

"He'll cut off our wings," whispered Gussie. "He'll nail them around Knock Street as a warning to others. He's done it before!"

Nox knew very well how much trouble they were in due to his impulsive decision. But he didn't regret it. The Talon had betrayed Nox, and Nox couldn't just let him get away with that.

"We'll sell the stone somewhere else," Nox said. "I'll use my money to bribe some guards at the Crag to smuggle my mother out. You two can use your shares to buy new lives. It'll all work out. Just trust me."

"Trust you?" cried Gussie. "Ellie *was* right, Nox! You're nothing but a selfish liar!"

She spread her wings.

"Where are you going?" Nox asked. "We need to lie low—"

"I'm leaving," she said coldly. "It's over. We're not selling the stone. We're not bringing any more attention to ourselves. I'm leaving Thelantis before it's too late. Maybe if I go home, my family will take me back. I'll be a . . ." She choked on the words. "I'll be what they want me to be. Maybe they were right. A Falcon has no business being an inventor."

"Gussie!"

With a flap of her long wings, she was gone, swooping into the city. Giving Nox an apologetic look, Twig also spread his feathers.

"Twig, wait—" Nox reached for the boy, but too slow. Twig swept away after Gussie, Lirri peeping out of the back of his collar.

Leaving Nox alone.

He crumpled his hands into fists. It was better this way, he decided. He'd always been strongest alone. People slowed him down, argued with his plans, looked down their noses at him . . .

People like Ellie Meadows.

You're nothing but a selfish liar.

"No," he muttered. "I'm more than that. You'll see! You'll all see!"

He just needed to save his mother, and then . . . Well, he'd figure it out.

He'd never been one for big, grandiose plans like Ellie or Gussie. The only thing he'd ever truly wanted was for the world to go back to the way it was before his family had been torn apart.

Though with the way things were looking right now, that seemed like the most impossible plan of all.

"Oi!" shouted a voice. Nox looked up to see a face hanging down from the roof—the Magpie kid he'd seen earlier. "The Talon's gonna rip you into pieces for stealing from him, traitor Crow!"

"Yeah?" said Nox. "Tell him he has to catch me first."

Nox pushed off the beam and let himself drop, wings spreading at the last minute to avoid slamming into the ground. Then he soared upward and winged over the city. Nobody knew Thelantis like Nox did. He wasn't going to let some snot-nosed new kid collect whatever bounty the Talon had promised for his capture. Nox Hatcher had a reputation to uphold, after all. It only took him seconds to lose the Mapgie.

But Nox wasn't safe yet. He had to find someplace to lie low, somewhere unexpected.

At once, he thought of just the spot.

Fifteen minutes later, Nox was feeling pretty pleased with his plan. There was no way the Talon would find him amid the throng gathered at the foot of Mount Garond. He was just one pair of wings among thousands.

He told himself that coming here had nothing to do with watching to see if Ellie Meadows won the Race of Ascension. But his eyes kept wandering upward anyway.

The sky teemed with battling contestants. A large group of wounded high clan kids was gathered beneath a canvas tent off to the side, nursing egos as injured as their bodies, no doubt, but he didn't see Ellie among them. She must have still been in the air.

Not that he cared.

A Robin clanner beside him was taking bets, grabbing fistfuls of coin and stuffing them into bags on his waist. Nox couldn't help himself. He nicked a few silver coins and let them slither into his inner pockets. Then he moved on, wriggling through the crowd.

A roaring cheer rose as a Hawk girl dove out of the sky, a red pennant flickering behind her. The first winner had returned. She landed in front of a raised dais where, Nox realized with a start, the king sat with his family. Nox's eyes wandered over the jewels and gold studding the royal family's attire.

After that, victors began landing in a steady stream, waving their red flags and turning acrobatic flips in the air, celebrating. Nox rolled his eyes.

High clanners. Always basking in attention.

Despite himself, he wandered closer to the winners' circle, pilfering the occasional coin out of pockets as he went.

Forty-seven winners had now claimed victory. Only three more would make it. He looked up, hating that his heart was beating faster, that his abdomen tightened in suspense.

Another victor swooped to land—a Hawk boy whooping in triumph as he held his flag over his head. A group of high clanners beside Nox burst into applause.

"Yes, Zain!" bellowed a broad-chested Hawk man. "That's my boy! My big, strong boy!"

Nox rolled his eyes and moved on. With the race nearly over, he needed to get away before the crowd dispersed and left him exposed. He'd have to find somewhere else to hide until he figured out what to do next.

But when he turned, it was directly into a bare blade. The tip of the dagger pressed against his neck, and Nox froze.

"Shh, shh, shh," murmured the Talon. "Quietly, my boy. Let's not make a fuss, hmm? Not here, anyway."

Nox swallowed. "How'd you find me?"

"Come, now," the Talon said. *"There's no better camouflage than a crowd*. I taught you that myself. And you always were my best student. I knew exactly where you'd go."

He put his hand on Nox's shoulder, the other shifting the dagger to Nox's ribs.

"Blasted stupid of you," the Talon said. "Thinking you could out-fly me."

He pushed Nox forward, and they slowly navigated through the crowd as another roar of cheers went up. Another victor had arrived, but Nox couldn't even turn his head to see who it was.

"I listened to my wings," Nox said quietly. "You can't blame me for that."

"I did teach you well," said the Talon, fishing the skystone from Nox's pocket and flicking it into his sleeve. "It's a shame I'll have to remove that clever head of yours, boy. A real shame."

"You could've just followed through on your promise," said Nox. His legs were shaking so much he could barely walk. Cold sweat soaked his clothes.

Though his eyes flickered around in desperation, he saw no avenue of escape. Instead, he saw more of the Talon's crew flanking them, moving through the crowd on every side. Even if he managed to tear himself away, a dozen more hands would grab him again. He'd have the Talon's dagger buried in his ribs in moments.

Still, the idea appealed. It would be an easier end than whatever the man had planned for him.

For a moment, he considered making that last, fatal move.

Then he heard another roar from the crowd as the final victor arrived. He couldn't turn his head to look, but the people around him began shouting angrily.

"What's with the Sparrow? Is this a joke?"

"Is she a servant?"

"She must have stolen that flag! This is outrageous!"

A tiny Dove girl atop her father's shoulders said, "Papa, Papa! If a Sparrow can become a knight, maybe I can too, one day!"

"Maybe, my love," her father said, sounding baffled. "I can't believe I'm saying it, but . . . skies, just maybe."

Nox laughed aloud, earning a jab from the Talon's knife that he knew must have drawn blood. But he didn't care.

Ellie had won.

Against all the odds, that little Sparrow had beaten hundreds of bigger, faster kids. And from the sound of the crowd, the high clans were not happy about it.

Nox's plan to self-destruct vanished like smoke in the breeze.

If a Sparrow could win the Race of Ascension, maybe a Crow could escape being murdered by the most dangerous man in Thelantis.

The chances were next to nothing.

But still . . . just *maybe.*

Exhausted and jubilant, Ellie landed before the royal family's dais amid the other forty-nine winners. Red victory flags fluttered from their hands, some tied around their shoulders like capes, some affixed to the shafts of their spears. Ellie saw Tauna among them, chin high and expression as firm and focused as ever, her red flag neatly folded in her hands.

Forty-nine high clan warriors and one small Sparrow.

Then another familiar face bounded toward her with a dopey smile.

"You did it!" Zain shouted. "You really did it, Ellie!"

"And . . . you're okay with that? After I nearly brained you up there?"

"Ellie." Zain looked her in the eye. "I'll be proud to fly beside you."

She grinned and hugged him, feeling almost dizzy with happiness.

"I'm sorry," he whispered. "I'm sorry I ever—"

"Not now," she said. "Let's just celebrate, okay?"

The king rose to give a speech, but angry cries began rising from the high clanners in the audience, interrupting him.

Ellie realized, with a jolt of dismay, that they were furious about *her*.

Fingers pointed, fists raised, everyone demanding to know why a Sparrow was in the race at all, insisting she must have cheated. Her eyes wandered to the Goldwing knights. They were glancing at her with expressions of shock and whispering.

Ellie's wings began to wilt.

But theirs weren't the only voices.

Soon a greater sound rose, a roar that drowned out even the loudest of the Hawks and Falcons. It took Ellie a moment to understand what it was.

The low clans!

From the back of the crowd came the sound of the Doves, Robins, Finches, and countless others, some fluttering into the air to make themselves heard. Gradually, their cries merged into one unified chant:

"Sparrow! Sparrow!"

They were *cheering*. And united, their voices echoed off the mountain. Parents lifted up children to give them a better view of Ellie, and their eyes widened when they spotted her. Hands lifted, wings spread, ribbons and handfuls of confetti were flung into the air—all in *her* honor.

Ellie glanced at the king on his dais, who stared at the noisy throng with narrow, thoughtful eyes. His guards gave up trying to silence them and exchanged helpless shrugs. Even the high clans were struck speechless, turning to stare in disbelief at the raucous spectators behind them. A few low clanners broke through to the front, waving to get Ellie's attention as they cheered.

Starting to smile, Ellie gave a small wave to the crowd and was met with a roar of approval.

"Sparrow! Sparrow!"

She brushed away the tears that gathered in her eyes. Warmth flushed her skin and burned in her chest, a feeling so unfamiliar and wonderful it left her breathless. Finally, her people weren't jeering and laughing. They weren't yelling at her to give up and go away.

They were *proud* of her.

It was like she'd touched the very stars. Heady happiness rushed through her veins, making her feel light as a sunbeam, on the verge of bursting. She grabbed hold of Zain's arm just to keep herself from floating away.

Eventually, the people did fall quiet, and the king continued his speech, but Ellie couldn't focus on him. Instead, she searched the crowd, looking for a certain pair of dark wings. But of course Nox wasn't there. She wished he had seen her prove him wrong. She wished she could look him in the eyes just one more time and see him nod in respect.

But why should the opinion of one thief matter to her?

She had to forget Nox and Gussie and Twig. She was about to become a knight, sworn to uphold the laws they broke every day. From now on, they'd be standing on opposite sides of a chasm no pair of wings could cross.

Pushing them out of her mind, Ellie held her head high as Sir Aglassine stepped forward to give instructions. The victors were to proceed to Honorhall to present their flags in a private initiation ceremony, where they would receive their Goldwing patches.

When she finished, a flutter of wings filled the air. The contestants took off in unison, whooping and cheering.

Zain looked at Ellie. "Together?"

Ellie nodded firmly. "Together."

As one, they shot into the air and turned on the tips of their wings.

The cheers of the low clans rose once more for her, and their voices were wind enough to lift Ellie right into the sky.

Minutes later, Ellie landed lightly on the steps of Honorhall, where the other winning contestants were filing inside one by one. A single Goldwing stood at the doors, a pile of red flags in her hands.

"You go," Ellie said to Zain. She wanted another minute to savor.

They touched fists, their old way of saying goodbye. He walked up the steps and gave his flag to the Goldwing, who waved him inside. Then the courtyard sat empty, with only Ellie left.

She closed her eyes, breathing in deeply, letting the city go still around her. She felt her heart thumping behind her ribs and the rush of air swirling in her lungs. She felt the breeze ruffle her wings. The cheers of the low clans still rang in her ears.

The moment engraved as deep into her memory as it could be, she finally walked up the steps, her soft leather shoes soundless on the marble. Raising the flag with both hands, she stopped before the Goldwing, unable to keep a grin from tugging her lips.

"I'm Ellidee Meadows of the Sparrow clan," she said. "And I won the Race of Ascension."

The Goldwing looked at her impassively. Then he said, "Wait here." Without taking her flag, he turned and disappeared into the hall.

Ellie opened her mouth, but no words came out.

Had she said the wrong thing? She was sure they were to only give their names and claim their victory in order to be admitted.

With no other choice, she stood on the steps and waited, her heart in her throat. Above Ellie, the white Goldwing banners hanging from the upper windows fluttered softly, fabric rustling against the stones.

Finally, she heard a shuffle of boots from inside, and three people stepped out to meet her. One was the man who'd taken the flags, but now his hands were empty. Another was not a Goldwing, but an old Eagle in fancy purple clothes. The last was Sir Aglassine.

Ellie's wings began to tremble.

"Ellidee Meadows," said Sir Aglassine. "We regret to inform you that your application to the Goldwing order has been rejected."

At first, Ellie thought she was dreaming. That her anxious mind had fabricated Sir Aglassine out of thin air, and that at any moment, the *real* captain would step out and welcome her inside.

So for a moment, she simply stood and blinked like a confused calf.

Then the truth of the captain's words struck her like a physical blow. She stepped back, gasping, and her foot slipped on the edge of the steps. Her wings shot out instinctively, fluttering hard to rebalance her.

"Wh-what?" she rasped out. "But—I won. I won fairly!"

"I am sure you flew nobly," said Sir Aglassine. "But the ruling stands."

"I don't understand. The rules say anyone can race."

"Indeed. However, it is the king who ultimately decides who enters the Goldwing knighthood, and in this case, he has declined to offer you a position."

"I . . ." Ellie's gaze moved to the other Goldwing, then to the fancy Eagle. "Are you sure?"

"As one of the king's advisors," the man said dryly, "I can guarantee you that we are *sure*. The king found your victory . . . amusing, but of course a Sparrow cannot be expected to perform at the same level as a high clan warrior. It's ridiculous. Admitting one into Honorhall would make a laughingstock of the entire order."

"Lord Gallus," said Sir Aglassine tartly, "I believe the point has been conveyed. Thank you for delivering His Majesty's ruling to us."

Sniffing, the Eagle turned and shuffled back into the hall.

"You don't remember me, do you?" Ellie whispered.

The captain merely gazed at her.

"Eight years ago, you saved me from a gargol," Ellie said. "You gave me *this*."

She pulled the tattered old Goldwing patch from her pocket, where she'd placed it that morning for luck. "You told me if I worked hard and followed the rules, I could be anything."

The captain's face softened only slightly. "You flew well, child, for a Sparrow."

For a Sparrow.

"I *flew* better than hundreds of other high clan kids!" Ellie said.

"There's no need for hysterics," said the other knight. "Now, I believe these are your folk here to collect you."

"My—" Ellie turned and sucked in a breath.

There stood Mother Rosemarie, Chief Donhal of the Sparrow clan, and Mayor Davina, all looking at her grimly. Where had *they* come from?

In Mother Rosemarie's hand was a pair of large scissors.

Ellie tried to breathe, but her lungs pinched shut.

It was a nightmare. She was dreaming. She *had* to be.

"No," whispered Ellie. "No, no, no, this can't be happening. I did everything right! I followed the rules!"

"The rules are designed for the good of all," returned Sir Aglassine. "And the king's rulings are incontrovertible."

Ellie had never even heard the word *incontrovertible*, but she had a good idea it meant *not going to budge an inch no matter how unfair it might be.*

"Ellie Meadows," said Mother Rosemarie in a tight voice, "come *here.*"

"Now, Ellie," said Chief Donhal. "We've been on the road for weeks, looking for you. Come with us, before you bring further shame on our good clan's name."

"No!" Ellie cried.

But when she tried to launch into the air, Sir Aglassine grabbed her arm. The Goldwing held her in a tight grip until Mother Rosemarie could shuffle forward.

Only Mayor Davina looked regretful about any of it. "For what it's worth," she whispered in Ellie's ear, "I thought you flew marvelously."

Ellie struggled, but there was no escape from Mother Rosemarie's practiced clutches. Would she try to clip Ellie's wings then and there, or would they drag her somewhere private? Clipping was a shameful thing; it would only double the humiliation to be maimed in the open.

Hot tears ran down Ellie's cheeks. Her head roared with anger and confusion until she could hardly think. Chief Donhal grabbed her other arm, and together he and Mother Rosemarie hauled Ellie down the steps of Honorhall.

"You've really gone and done it this time, Ellie," Mother Rosemarie said. "Moorly House is already expecting you, though I wonder if even their extreme methods can save you from yourself."

"Why do you hate me?" Ellie moaned.

"I don't hate you, child. But I have one job: ensuring you live to see adulthood. If this is the only way to prevent you from killing yourself over these foolish visions of grandeur, so be it. One day you will thank me."

"Never!" swore Ellie.

She struggled all the way across the courtyard. Glancing back, she saw the upper windows of Honorhall were open, and faces peered out curiously. The new initiates were watching—had probably been watching all this time. Even Zain was there, looking shocked. Ellie gave him a pleading look, but she knew there was nothing he could do.

Then, just as she thought things couldn't possibly get any worse, a voice called out, *"Stop!"*

Chief Donhal and Mother Rosemarie exchanged looks, then turned, Ellie still held tightly between them.

A man in a soldier's uniform gleaming with medals had landed in the courtyard. He lifted a hand, pointing directly at them. His face was familiar to Ellie, but it wasn't until he spoke that she recalled— with a stab of horror—who he was.

"That Sparrow girl," he said, "is wanted for robbery, assault of officers, and fleeing justice! Hand her over *immediately*!"

Ellie hung her head.

The Stoneslayer had finally caught up to her.

CHAPTER THIRTY-THREE
· ELLIE ·

"Tell him the truth," Mother Rosemarie had counseled Ellie as the Stoneslayer's soldiers escorted them to the king's palace. Ellie shivered the whole way, so dazed she'd barely even looked at the grand building. "It's the only hope you have, child."

Now Ellie stood alone before the king, on a great wide floor tiled with the crests of the many Clandoms, Sparrows included. Columns vaulted upward to brace a ceiling decorated in colorful mosaics of Eagle clanners in flight. Atop a dais velveted in red carpets, Garion sat on a throne inlaid with gold. To his right sat Prince Corion, who looked down at Ellie in bemusement, as if he couldn't quite believe the list of crimes laid against such a small Sparrow.

But they were all true, Ellie confessed. At least, they were *sort of* true.

She was still confused as to why she'd been brought to trial before the king. Surely he didn't handle all the cases of theft in the Clandoms. Compared to the big, important business of ruling the world, she was surprised her crimes rated as serious enough to merit a royal audience.

With Mother Rosemarie, Chief Donhal, and Mayor Davina standing behind her, she explained everything that had led up to the heist on the Stoneslayer's fortress, only leaving out the names of the three thieves who'd put her up to it.

"So you see, Your Majesty," she said, "I didn't *know* it was to be a robbery. I was as surprised as anyone when that skunk bomb went off."

"Skunk bomb?" laughed Prince Corion. "You've got to give them points for cleverness, Father."

"This isn't a joke, boy," said King Garion, while the Stoneslayer glowered at the prince.

It certainly wasn't. Ellie had never felt so ashamed in all her life. It was an effort to keep her eyes on the king and not her feet.

"I know what we did was wrong," she said. "If I'd known what would happen, I never would have gone along with it."

But even as she said the words, knowing they were true, a sour taste crept over her tongue. She kept seeing Nox, gently lifting Mally into his arms to carry her over the rapids.

"Ellideen," said Garion, and she had to bite her tongue to keep from correcting him, "it seems to me you are precisely what you say you are: an ordinary girl with a pure heart who was taken advantage of by miscreants."

She opened her mouth, but he stopped her with a raised finger. "I am prepared to absolve you of all guilt and declare you as much a victim as the good general here."

The Stoneslayer's eyes bulged. He made a groaning sound, as if he wanted to argue with the king but was barely holding back.

"Well," Ellie said carefully, "thank you, Your Majesty. I don't know if I'm quite as innocent as all that—"

"Ahem!" coughed Mother Rosemarie.

Ellie clamped her mouth shut.

"My mercy," said the king, "is of course dependent upon your cooperation, young Sparrow."

"I live to serve His Majesty," said Ellie, repeating one of the lines the heroes always said in her book.

He lifted one dark eyebrow, then continued. "Indeed. So go on, then. Tell us where we may find the skystone."

"The . . ." Ellie blinked. "I don't know."

The Stoneslayer growled. "She's lying, my king. The brat should be hanged!"

Ellie blanched.

"Silence, Torsten!" said the king, directing a stern look at the Stoneslayer. "Be grateful it isn't your head on the block, fool. You know the law: All skystones are to be turned over to the crown *immediately*."

"Sire, I had fully intended to—"

"I said *be silent!*" roared Garion, tilting himself to his feet and extending his glossy wings to their full sixteen-foot span. Cowed, the Stoneslayer dropped to his knee and bowed his head.

There *were* more skystones! Unable to stop herself, Ellie burst out, "Did you know skystones can heal wingrot, Your Majesty? If you have some already, perhaps then—"

"How dare you address the king out of turn!" snapped a guard, lowering his spear.

Ellie cringed, the words still itching on her tongue.

The king's eyes slid back to her, slits of burning gold. "Is this how the Sparrows raise their young? To speak to their king as if he were a commoner?"

"The child is no doubt overwhelmed, Your Majesty," said Chief Donhal, red faced. "Forgive her rashness, I beg you, sire."

Her stomach knotting, Ellie stared hard at the toes of her boots. As the king refolded his wings and sat down, the mood in the hall grew colder. Young Prince Corion, sitting more rigidly than before, had averted his eyes away from Ellie, as if he wished he were anywhere else.

"Do you know what skystones *are*, little girl?" said the king, as if he were trying very hard to keep his anger in check.

"Yes, Your Majesty. They're . . . eyes. Gargol eyes."

"Indeed. Not only eyes, but the very source of the gargols' power. How else could a creature of stone *fly*, unless it is by some dark magic? And as we know from the legend of our cursed predecessor, Aron the Fool, any power that could create the gargols is extremely dangerous and must therefore be destroyed."

"Destroyed!" Ellie gasped. "But—but that magic can also *save* people who have no other—"

"Enough!" roared the king. "Tell us the names of these thieves who used you, or face the full punishment for all *four* of you!"

Ellie felt the gazes of every person in the room leaning on her. She tried to speak, but her throat felt stuck. What did a quadruple sentence look like? Forty years in prison instead of ten? Or would they execute her four times? That didn't even make sense.

But *nothing* was making sense anymore.

She'd won the Race of Ascension, and still been rejected by the Goldwings.

She'd nearly been shipped off to Moorly House, wings clipped, but was instead arrested by the Stoneslayer.

Now she had the chance to buy her freedom, but it would mean turning in Nox, Gussie, and Twig. Who undoubtedly *were* thieves, but did they deserve prison . . . or worse? They weren't evil, or really all that dangerous. They just wanted better lives, chances the world had taken away from them.

While she stood mutely, King Garion waved over one of his guards and whispered in the man's ear.

Here it comes, thought Ellie. *They'll drag me away and chop off my head. Four times.*

The guard jogged away, and King Garion turned to Ellie.

"I can see you are at war with yourself," he said. "It has been a trying day. You flew to the summit of Mount Garond, for sky's sake!"

Ellie nodded uncertainly.

"Clearly this has all been a misunderstanding." The king's voice had turned soothing. Reasonable. As if he were talking to a friend, not a Sparrow so far beneath him she might as well be a toad. "Ellie, what is the highest virtue practiced by a Goldwing?"

"Honor," she said promptly.

He nodded. "And now is your chance to prove you possess that virtue. That you have, indeed, ascended the King's Ladder."

Ellie's jaw dropped as the doors behind her swung wide, admitting Sir Aglassine, followed by several more Goldwings and a bewildered-looking Zain. He was wearing a shining Goldwing uniform, looking like a true knight. When he saw Ellie, he gave her a questioning look. Ellie could only shrug.

Then she saw what Sir Aglassine was carrying.

She held in her hands a neatly folded Goldwing uniform, so white and crisp, Ellie knew it must have never been worn before. Glistening atop it was a golden patch.

"Ellie of the Sparrow Clan," said Sir Aglassine, looking at Ellie with her impassive gray eyes, "will you accept the office of Goldwing knight, a warrior ready to defend her people against all threats, both on land and above?"

Unable to summon words, but recognizing the ceremonial Goldwing oath on Sir Aglassine's lips, Ellie only stared.

"You have but to speak the names of the thieves," said King Garion. "And that uniform—and all that goes with it—will be yours. Upon my word as king. Three names, Ellie of the Sparrows, and you will be the first of your kind to wear the white and gold."

Mother Rosemarie gasped. Chief Donhal nodded encouragingly to Ellie. Mayor Davina smiled, her eyes glistening with tears. Ellie imagined she was already preparing a speech for Linden, explaining that the town had seen *three* of their own make it into the Goldwings—a new record. She pictured returning home with Zain in that uniform, amid a crowd of cheering Sparrows.

She imagined giving her old, tattered patch to another little Sparrow girl, whispering into her ear that she too could be anything if she worked hard and followed the rules.

Ellie licked her lips and tasted the salt from the tears running down her cheeks.

Everything she'd ever wanted could be hers.

It was that . . . or it was certain punishment. Her wings clipped, and more. Her life over.

It all balanced on the tip of her tongue: speak or don't speak.

Say the names or hold her silence.

"M-Majesty," she stammered. "Why did you reject me from the Goldwings in the first place?"

Groans sounded from the Lindeners.

King Garion's smile slipped. "What matters now is whether you can show me you have the honor of a Goldwing. Think of it as . . . one final test."

He hadn't answered her question.

Whatever his reasons, apparently they didn't compare to the importance of the skystone. Why else would he be reviewing her crimes himself? Why else would he be willing to walk back his own ruling and offer her a place among the Goldwings?

Garion wanted that stone.

He wanted it more than he *didn't* want a Sparrow for a Goldwing.

And yet, he either didn't know or didn't care that it could heal wingrot. So there had to be another reason he wanted it, one that had nothing to do with healing people.

"The skystone," said Ellie. "Will you use it to heal people with wingrot? Or at least test it, to see if it will work?"

Now King Garion's face darkened, and a shadow seemed to spread from him to cover the room. Ellie's skin broke out in goose pimples. No one spoke.

"My patience is wearing thin," he said through clenched teeth. "Will you give me the names or not?"

Maybe he would use it to heal people. Maybe he was just impatient and hurrying her along.

Or maybe . . .

Maybe Nox had been right.

Maybe the king could not be trusted.

Ellie swallowed. Her wings itched instinctively, urging her to fly away. But that wouldn't fix anything. She had to make her choice, and she had to make it now.

Just tell him their names, her own brain urged her. *You have everything to gain, and more to lose.*

How had everything become so complicated? Her plan had always been simple: Work hard. Follow the rules. Win the race. Become a Goldwing. Sure, it would be tough, but it was straightforward.

Until the day she'd met Nox Hatcher, and her world had become a great tangled mess of confusion. Now she didn't know what was right or wrong.

She didn't know who she was.

"Sparrow," said King Garion, "no more stalling. Do the honorable thing and tell me their *names!*"

Honor. That golden word, that final step in the King's Ladder of knightly virtues.

She thought of all the mornings she'd spent practicing those steps, engraving them in her mind and heart and bones. She thought of the rules she'd followed no matter the cost, even when it meant betraying her friends and ignoring the small voice inside her that whispered *this isn't right.*

She thought of Nox, sitting by a fire, asking what the point of a ladder was if you had wings.

She felt she was breaking in half.

If the rules are designed to break you, Ellie, that small voice whispered now, *you know what you have to do.*

She'd waited as long as she could. The king watched her intently. The room held its breath. Atop the knight's uniform in Aglassine's hands, the Goldwing patch glittered. Ellie could feel the weight of the entire Sparrow clan on her shoulders. She could feel her father's arms around her the moment before the gargol had ripped him away.

But most of all, she felt certainty deep in her soul. She knew the right, honorable, terrible thing she had to do.

"Tell me their names!" roared the king.

As a tear spilled from her eye, Ellie whispered, "No."

CHAPTER THIRTY-FOUR
· ELLIE ·

The worst thing about the royal dungeons was the lack of windows. No view of the sky, no breath of wind to stir the stale, damp air. Ellie sat instead against the iron bars of the cell door, trying to leech heat from the torch outside.

"Ellie," she whispered, "you've really screwed up this time."

Not that she would have changed her decision. She'd stood by it even when Mother Rosemarie had pleaded with her, even when the king angrily ordered her to be dragged away and locked up. No matter what he threatened, she couldn't betray Nox, Gussie, and Twig.

She'd cried after they left her in the cell, and when she ran out of tears, she went numb, unmoving and silent as the stone.

What would happen now? Would she wither away, to never see the sky again? Would anyone even tell her what would become of her?

If only you'd listened to me, she could practically hear Nox say.

Of everyone she knew, it had been the liar who'd told her the truth.

The Goldwings had never wanted her. Even when she proved herself to be as strong and fast as they were, the looks she'd been given and the whispers she'd heard had been proof that she would never be good enough in their eyes. And if the rules said she could be one of them, they'd just change the rules.

Anger simmered beneath her skin, hot and prickling. She was

angry at herself for naively trusting in empty promises, for ignoring the people who tried to tell her the real way of things.

For chasing moonmoths.

The problem was, if everything she thought was true turned out to be lies, what could she believe in now? Could she ever find something worth fighting for, the way she'd fought to become a Goldwing knight? Or was the future as bleak and empty as this dungeon cell?

Well, she supposed it didn't matter anyway, if she really was going to be locked in here the rest of her life. They hadn't even bothered to clip her wings. There was nowhere to fly.

Ellie didn't know how long she sat in the dark before she finally heard footsteps. As the person approached, she sat up, heart racing.

It was Zain, dressed in his Goldwing uniform. He stopped outside her barred door, eyes wide.

"Ellie." He sighed after taking it all in. "How did this happen?"

"I believe you were there," she said tonelessly.

"I mean, *why* did you let it happen? The king offered you *everything* you wanted. We were going to be Goldwings together. Instead . . ."

"Instead here I am," she said bitterly. "A prisoner. A criminal."

"But you're *not* a criminal, Ellie! C'mon, you're the most honest person I know. Remember when we found that gold coin in the fields, and you insisted we turn it over to the mayor so she could find its rightful owner? I wanted to keep it, but you said that was the honorable thing to do."

"I remember," she whispered.

"You always do the right thing, Ellie. So why not do it this time?"

"That's just it, Zain. I *did* do the right thing."

"You sacrificed yourself and everything you ever dreamed of for some low-life thieves!"

"They're not—you don't know them like I do. They're my friends."

"Then where are they now, huh? If they were your real friends, would they let you take all the heat? Why haven't they turned up to help you?"

"It's not just about them. You heard the king. He wants to destroy the skystone—*all* skystones. But that's a mistake. I've seen what it can do."

"You mean how it magically heals wingrot?" Zain sounded skeptical. "Ellie . . . wingrot's horrible, but there's no cure. Why do you even care so much about it?"

"Why *don't* you? You had to have seen all those people outside the city. They're dying, Zain, and that stone can help them."

As she spoke the words, a strange feeling crept over Ellie. Her scalp prickled. Her fingers tightened around the cell bars. The hole that had opened in the pit of her soul now began to glow, as something hot and fierce and new sparked to life there.

That something, she realized, was *purpose*.

The thing she'd lost the moment she'd turned down the king's offer.

And the thing about purpose was that it didn't let you sit around moping. It couldn't be contained by four walls and a lock.

It demanded action.

Ellie knew what she had to do.

She pulled in a deep breath of the dungeon's stale air. "Zain. I need you to go back up there and tell them . . . tell them I accept. I'll give them the names. Just take me to the king and I'll confess everything."

Zain stared at her. "You're . . . lying."

"No, I'm not!"

"I can hear it in your voice. You're a painfully bad liar, Ellie. You're just trying to escape, aren't you?"

"What if I am?" she shouted. "Won't you help me, Zain? There are people dying out there, and I know how to save them. The king doesn't even *care*."

"You've changed. I don't know you anymore. Those criminals did something to you, made you some kind of traitor."

"They showed me the world I believed in wasn't real. They showed me that when the rules are designed to break you, you have to break the rules." Ellie shook her head, feeling strangely pitying of Zain, that he couldn't see what she saw. "This world was created to love you, Zain. You can't see it, because you're surrounded by it always. But I grew up on the outside, a different world altogether. And even still, I thought I could earn my place in that golden, perfect world of *yours*. And I did earn it. I did everything right. I climbed the King's Ladder. I won the race. And they still shoved me right out again."

"But the king said he'd give you—"

"Everything I wanted, yes. I know. But maybe what I want has changed."

"Then what *do* you want, Ellie? To rot in here?"

"I want . . ." She gazed into the fire blazing on the torch. "I want a different world. One where kings care about their people, and where the rules are made to help people rise, not to keep them pressed down. I want a world where gargols don't hunt us and we can fly free in any skies. I want . . . something better."

"So, what?" Zain pulled at his hair, his voice rising with frustration. "Now you're going to declare war on the gargols?"

She sighed. Gussie had been right. High clanners really did think fighting could solve everything.

"My plan is to first get that skystone back. A person can make the world better in rags just as much as in gold and white." She stretched out a hand. "I'm sorry I'm not who you want me to be."

Hesitantly, he took her hand, and she pulled him in for a hug. "You're gonna be a great Goldwing," she whispered.

He sniffled, hugging her tight, then stepping back. "You're making such a huge mistake, Ellie."

"Then don't feel bad. You'll know you did everything you could to stop me."

He frowned. "Stop you?"

"From doing this," she replied.

She flipped the Goldwing dagger she'd stolen from his belt when he'd hugged her and popped it into the lock on the cell door. Before he could stop her, she shoved the door hard—right into Zain's face.

He crumpled, and Ellie gasped. She hadn't meant to hit him *that* hard. Kneeling by him, she felt for a pulse and was relieved to find one. He'd be okay, though he'd have a knot the size of his fist on his forehead later. But that was probably for the best. Everyone would know Ellie had escaped on her own, and that he hadn't helped her. He'd be reprimanded, but in a lot less trouble than if they thought he let her go.

"Can't believe you *still* fall for that," she sighed as she tucked his dagger in her belt.

Moving swiftly, she removed his jacket and cloak and pulled them on. The cloak, which hung to Zain's knees, swept the floor behind

Ellie, hiding her shabby leggings and shoes. The hood covered her tangled hair.

She really was a thief now.

"I'm sorry," she whispered. She bent low and kissed the top of Zain's head. "I hope you'll forgive me one day."

She'd crossed a final line. Her old life and her old dreams would be closed to her forever. There was no going back.

Ellie sprinted down the corridor, into the dark.

CHAPTER THIRTY-FIVE
· ELLIE ·

As she slipped through the king's palace, Ellie found the Goldwing cloak she'd stolen from Zain made her practically invisible. No one gave her a second glance—so long as whenever someone walked by, she bent over to fiddle with her shoe or sat with her face hidden in the hood, so they couldn't tell she was more than a little too short for a proper Goldwing.

Quite by accident, she'd found her lockstave and knapsack in a little room at the dungeons' entrance, with all her possessions still inside. After a tense twenty minutes with Ellie crouched behind a barrel, the guard on duty had finally taken a latrine break, and she'd darted in to grab them.

Now she searched for an open window, desperate to take flight as soon as possible. But all the ones she passed were locked. That, and the fact that the ceilings in this place were so low, made Ellie almost think the king didn't *want* people to fly. She worked her way deeper into the palace, and the farther she went, the busier the corridors got.

At last she came to a courtyard surrounded by columned walkways; the open blue sky glowed tantalizingly above. Ellie hid behind one of the columns and peered into the courtyard, where a group of Goldwings and soldiers stood around King Garion.

Her heart sank. She didn't dare try to escape that way.

But before she could slip off, she heard someone mention "the Sparrow girl."

"I could *make* her talk," the Stoneslayer said, stroking the dagger on his hip. Ellie's stomach twisted. "Just give me five minutes, my king, and the girl will tell us everything."

"Hmm." King Garion looked thoughtful. Then he said, "None of this would be a problem if you'd turned over the skystone to me in the first place."

The Stoneslayer blanched. "Majesty, I was merely waiting for the right time—"

"Do you have *any* idea how dangerous these stones are, you fool? They could undo the world as we know it."

Ellie frowned. Sure, the skystone was a gargol's eye and had magic that could cure wingrot, but it hadn't seemed *that* dangerous. What did the king mean?

She knew she should make her escape while she still had the chance—she didn't imagine Zain would stay out for long, or that her absence would go unnoticed—but her curiosity was too strong. Why did the king want the skystone destroyed so badly that he'd ignore thousands of dying people?

"Go question the Sparrow, General," the king said at last. "Use whatever methods you must."

The Stoneslayer nodded and hurried away, rushing right past Ellie. Tucked behind the column, she held her breath until he was out of sight. Now she *really* needed to move.

But then the king continued. "The rest of you go to Knock Street.

If these thieves are anywhere, they'll be there. Search every building, and if that fails, start burning the vermin out. That place is a filthy swamp, anyway. It's past time we cleaned it out."

The Goldwings nodded and took flight, launching out of the courtyard and into the sky.

The blood drained from Ellie's face.

She had to find Nox, Gussie, and Twig, had to warn them that the king was hunting them—and she had to get the skystone back. Likely Nox had already turned it over to his master, but she'd deal with that when the time came.

His meeting over, the king left down the opposite hallway, and Ellie took the chance to run into the vacant courtyard, wings unfurling as she leaped up. Below, she heard a sudden clang of bells and shouting.

Her escape had been discovered. She needed to fly faster, but her knapsack weighed heavily between her wings. Quickly, she reached a hand over her shoulder and opened it, and *The King's Ladder* slid into her palm.

She tore out the title page with her mother's inscription—*Watch the skies*—then let the book fall. It tumbled and hit the courtyard floor with a loud smack, the spine breaking.

There was no time now for stealth. Freed of the book's weight, Ellie looped high into the sky, then dove toward the city below.

CHAPTER THIRTY-SIX
· NOX ·

In the slums of Knock Street, bound to a hard wooden chair, Nox spat out a bloody tooth and laughed. "Thanks. You got the rotten one. Now I won't have to pull it out myself."

The Talon's henchman, a brutish Owl clanner who handled all the interrogations, stepped back to catch his breath. They'd been at this for three hours, and still Nox hadn't given them what they wanted.

"Where. Are. Your. Friends?" demanded the Owl. He was missing one wing—lost in a brawl years ago. Since he couldn't fly, he put all his attention into his arms. They were meaty, bulbous things, covered with thick hair.

"Hit him again, Pingo," said the Talon.

"Aw, boss. He's a kid."

"He *stole* from me."

Sighing, Pingo knotted his hand. Nox braced himself against the chair to which he was tied. If his cries had penetrated the attic walls of the Chivalrous Toad, no one heeded them. People were used to hearing screams coming from the tavern and knew better than to ask questions.

But before Pingo could follow through on what no doubt would have been another molar-ripper, the door creaked open and two more of the Talon's crew shuffled in, dragging a hissing, snarling figure between them.

"Boss!" shouted one. "We got the feral one!"

They pushed Twig into the room. He landed hard, his hands and ankles bound and his eyes wild.

"Twig!" Nox cried. "Are you all right?"

"Yeah," groaned Twig. Then he looked at Nox and gasped. "But *you're* not!"

"Just that brainy Falcon left, then," said the Talon, digging crud from beneath his nails with his dagger. "The city will soon see that *no one* crosses me."

"Let him go!" Nox said. "He didn't steal from you. *I* did it. Alone."

"Uh, boss?" Pingo had gone to the narrow window and was looking out. "Problem."

"Unless you see that Falcon girl out there, I don't care what—"

"They're burning things."

The Talon gave a long, dramatic sigh. "Who is burning *what* things, Pingo?"

"Goldwings," said Pingo. "They're burning *everything*."

Nox sniffed and caught a whiff of smoke on the air.

Then he heard the screams.

"Boss!" shouted Pingo, backing away from the window so the Talon could look. The Lord of Thieves peered out, then whirled.

"That coward king finally did it. He's ordered Knock Street razed to the ground." He cursed, kicking over a chair. "Alert the crew! Tell them to bag everything and regroup at the docks."

"What about them?" Pingo nodded at Nox and Twig.

"I'll deal with them. Go!"

The stench of smoke now clotted the room. Nox coughed, eyes watering. He had a terrible flashback of Granny Tam's cackling face.

"Why are they burning Knock Street?" he gasped out.

"They've been threatening to for decades," said the Talon, wiping his dagger on his shirt. "Never thought they'd actually do it. Wonder what set them off."

Nox eyed the dagger as the Talon approached him. "You're going to free us?"

"Ha! I'm going to leave you to the flames, you little rat. But your wings will carry my message to the rest of the city. *Nobody* crosses the Talon."

Nox struggled as the Talon seized the back of his neck and bent him over, exposing the narrow bases of his wings.

"No!" Twig yelled, trying to crawl toward them, despite his bound hands and ankles.

Nox clenched his teeth and shut his eyes, feeling the dagger press against his shoulder blades.

"I trusted you," he said. "After they took my parents, I trusted *you*."

The Talon sneered. "Did you learn nothing these last few years, Nox? You can't trust *anyone*."

The first cut bit like fire, and Nox cried out—just as the door burst open and a tornado of feathers swept into the room.

"GET OFF HIM!" roared a voice.

Nox looked up just in time to see something long and slender whistle through the air. It smacked the Talon's head with a loud *crack*, and the man crumpled to the floor.

"Ha!" said Ellie Meadows, thumping her lockstave on the floor. "Boy, am I glad I found you."

She was talking to her staff, Nox realized, not *him*, but he didn't care.

"Me too," he said. "What are you *doing* here?"

"They set fire to the Toad!" yelled another voice, and he looked up to see Gussie. "We have to get out *now*!"

"But—but—" Between the blows he'd taken and the smoke choking his lungs, Nox was having trouble making sense of anything. "Ellie—the race—you won!"

"It's complicated." In a trice, she'd cut through his bonds with a fancy golden dagger. Where had she found *that* shiny thing? He stumbled up, dizzy, realizing as he tried to walk that he was in much worse shape than he'd thought. He stared at the Talon, who was out cold on the floor.

Ellie asked him a question, but it went right through him. Coughing, he said, "Huh?"

"The *skystone*!" she repeated. "Where is it?"

"Uh . . ." He began digging through the Talon's pockets.

"Hurry, hurry," urged Ellie. "We've got to get out of—" She couldn't finish, because a fit of coughing overtook her. Flames leaped in the doorway. The building was so old and dry, it was going up like a haystack.

"We can't go out that way," said Gussie. "We're trapped."

The wall facing the street caught fire next, wood blackening, old paint curling and hissing. Nox could feel the heat coming through the floorboards in the soles of his shoes.

"Found it!" he said, yanking the skystone from the Talon's vest pocket.

Ellie ran to the window and smashed the glass with her staff, but the opening was too narrow to fit through. The only chance they had was . . .

"The wall," said Nox. "We have to knock through it."

Just like the nest at Granny Tam's, when he'd ripped open the fiery woven reeds.

"We can't!" said Ellie. She pointed to the flames now curling through the boards of the wall. "I can't get close enough to bash it!"

"Give me the staff," said Nox, holding out a hand.

"Nox, you'll go up in flames!" The wall was properly ablaze now. Getting close to it would mean stepping right into the fire itself.

I saw your death, Crow. Granny Tam's voice crept like a spider through his mind. *I saw your death in flames and ashes.*

"Ellie." Nox felt strangely calm. "Give me your staff. I can do it."

"What, *now* you're some kind of hero?" She had tears in her eyes. "I came here to warn you the king is looking for you. I messed up bigtime. He knows about the skystone and now he wants it. That's why he's burning down your neighborhood. I came to warn you but I was too late."

"Ellie." He put his hands on her shoulders and looked her in the eyes. "I know I'm a thief and a liar and the worst person you ever met, but right now, I need you to *trust* me."

"You'll die if you go into those flames," she whispered.

"You know why I'm terrified of fire?" he asked as his hands closed around her staff and gently pulled it away. "It's not because I'm scared it'll burn me."

"W-what?"

He turned to face the flames. "It's because I know it *won't*."

Before she could stop him, Nox charged at the blazing wall.

He didn't know if he was yelling or not—it felt like it—but the crackle of the fire and the roar of collapsing buildings was so loud it wouldn't have made a difference. He ran as fast as he could, intending to swing the staff, but he began choking so hard on the smoke he instead toppled into the wall himself—right into the worst of the blaze. Flames swarmed around him, lashed his skin, hissed in his ears—

And the wall collapsed.

Nox fell into the air amid a cascade of burning wood and debris. He would have fallen right into the street, but at the last moment, Ellie and Gussie caught him and pulled him into the sky. Twig followed, shouting for them to go faster. Goldwings below had seen them and were calling at them to stop.

The Talon was left behind. Hot tears blurred Nox's vision; the man had been a monster, but he'd been the only parent Nox had had for years. He wouldn't have left him to burn if there'd been any other choice. Looking back, he saw the Chivalrous Toad collapse in a great crash of sparks and smoke, people running in all directions from the destruction.

Knock Street was lost.

The Talon was dead.

Nox's entire world was gone.

And there was not a single burn on him.

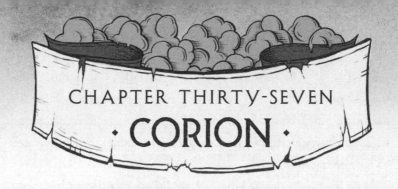

CHAPTER THIRTY-SEVEN
· CORION ·

Prince Corion of the Eagle Clan had never smelled such a stink. He'd always liked the smell of campfires, or the kitchen stoves in winter when the palace cooks whipped up some delicious cake for him. But this fire reeked of smoldering garbage and tepid, oily puddles. Abandoned buckets littered the ground where the citizens of Knock Street had made half-hearted attempts to put out the flames. Now they sat around staring emptily at the remains of their homes.

"Why did we have to burn it all down again?" he asked his father.

King Garion pressed a perfumed cloth to his nose, grimacing. "As I told you, it's for their own good. Now maybe they'll pursue honest lives, once they realize crime only leads to ruin."

Corion frowned. It didn't look like the woman sitting in the middle of the street, holding a screaming baby, had done much ruining. The Goldwings, on the other hand, hung out in groups, laughing and swapping stories of who'd set the biggest blaze, and how fast the houses had burned.

"Can we just go home?" he begged. "Why did you want me to come anyway?"

"You're my heir," his father said. "And old enough to start learning what it really takes to rule the kingdom."

"Clandoms," Corion corrected him, but under his breath so that his father couldn't hear. Corion's tutors had taught him that the Eagles reigned only by the consent of the clan chieftains, who, united, were the true ultimate authority in the land. According to tradition, if they deemed a monarch unfit, they could remove them from the throne by a majority vote. But Corion suspected his father didn't quite see things the traditional way.

"And besides," said the king, "I'm told there's a prisoner here with some interesting information for us."

Sighing, Corion followed his father down the ruined street, trying hard not to make eye contact with the gaunt people gathering to watch them. Their guards kept a protective circle around them at all times, but that didn't stop the stares.

They found a trio of Goldwing knights with a kneeling prisoner. He looked wretched, his clothes and hair singed. When he lifted his face, Corion nearly stopped in his tracks. The man had a hole where his right eye should have been.

"My king, we present to you the Talon," said one of the Goldwings, proudly sweeping an arm over the prisoner's head. "Congratulations on this capture, Your Majesty. Thelantis's own Lord of Thieves, collared by Garion of the Eagles."

Of course, the king had little to do with the man's capture, but Corion was used to seeing his father get credit for other people's work. He frowned at the man, who didn't look all that impressive, except for the missing eye.

"Hmm," said the king. "Hang him."

"Wait!" cried the man. He sat up straighter, his single eye widening. "I have information for you. Information worth my life!"

"I'll decide what your pathetic life is worth," grunted Garion. "So talk."

"A jewel," said the Lord of Thieves. "A jewel of unsurpassed beauty and value. I know where to find it! Or . . . I know who has it, anyway."

"I have a million such jewels," sniffed the king.

"Not like this one," said the Talon. "Not so beautiful it might have been pried from the stony face of a *gargol*."

Corion's eyes snapped to his father's face. The king stared at the man, color rising in his cheeks.

"Indeed? And who might have such a stone?"

Corion had long known his father obsessed over finding and destroying skystones, but he'd never really understood—or cared— why. Until now.

Until he saw his father burn down an entire neighborhood to find one.

"A boy," rasped the Talon. "A hateful, murdering boy. He goes by Nox Hatcher, but I happen to know his *real* name: Tannox Corvain, of the shattered Crow clan."

All at once, the king's hand darted out and grabbed hold of the grubby thief's chin. Corion gasped. He'd never seen his father *touch* a commoner before.

"Did you say *Corvain*?"

Looking confused by the king's reaction, the thief nodded. "Aye."

"And he's a Crow boy?"

". . . Aye?"

The king stepped back. "Hang him."

"No!" cried the thief. "I gave you valuable information!"

"Yes," said Garion. "More valuable than you could possibly know. Unfortunately, too valuable for *you* to know."

The Goldwings dragged the Talon off, the man screaming and struggling the whole way. Corion lowered his gaze, feeling ill.

"I don't understand," he said. "Who is this Corvain kid?"

"A ghost," murmured Garion. "One I thought I'd stamped out years ago." He beckoned one of this guards to him and said, "Tell all my generals and Sir Aglassine that the skystone is not important anymore. Tell them to search for a boy—a Crow—by the name of Nox Hatcher. Bring him to me at whatever cost. Use all our resources, every blasted soldier in the Clandoms if they must. Offer a dukedom and a castle to whoever brings him in. And tell them . . ."

He paused to look up at the sky, with a strange, cold expression Corion had never seen on his father's face before.

"Tell them I don't want him alive."

Ellie led the way out of Thelantis, winging over the stony foothills to the north.

She didn't know where they were going, only that they had to get there fast. The confusion surrounding the fire had helped them escape the city itself, but it was only a matter of time before the Goldwings realized their quarry had fled and took to the air in pursuit.

Where would they be safe?

The knights she'd looked to for protection, the ones she'd wanted to join herself, were now hunting *her*.

Everything had turned inside out in a matter of hours. She couldn't imagine it being any worse. At least they were alive, all four of them. Scraped, battered, and singed in places, but *alive*.

Which she was still trying to comprehend.

"What did you mean," she said to Nox, "when you said the fire couldn't burn you? Why didn't you die in a ball of flame?"

"Like I said," he replied wearily. "It doesn't burn me." The boy looked like he wished he'd never said anything.

"How can fire just *not* burn you?"

"Yeah," inserted Gussie. "And don't you think that woulda been an important thing to tell your *crew*? Like, *months* ago?"

"How did you two meet up, anyway?" Nox asked, clearly changing the subject. "And *why*? Or is rescuing me from murderers in burning buildings a new hobby of yours, Sparrow?"

"I heard her screaming for us all over the city," said Gussie. "She was extremely unsubtle about it. When she told me the king was hunting you and the skystone, I knew right where the Talon would be holding you."

"You were so sure he'd caught me?"

She only snorted in response.

"You're avoiding my question," said Ellie. "What's with the whole fireproof thing?"

Nox sighed. His left wing had to be hurting from the cut the Talon had made.

"I don't understand it myself," he said. "But all my life, I've been immune to fire. My father was too. That's how he came out of that blaze years ago without any burns. And that's why the Goldwings concluded he must have started the fire."

"Funny, how they go around executing people for starting fires," muttered Gussie. "Then burn down half the city themselves."

"But *how* are you immune to fire?" Ellie asked.

"I don't know, all right? It's . . . some kind of family trait. Apparently, my grandmother had it too. But my parents warned me never to talk about it. I suppose it has to do with the reason the Crows were shattered ages ago. People don't like the idea of us . . ." His voice trailed away.

"Being magic?" she finished.

"It's not magic."

"Well, what in the sky else would you call it?"

"Not magic!"

"Fine, fine." She shivered as a cold mountain wind washed over them. It was getting dark, the long shadows of the mountains slowly swallowing up the world, and the rocks below grew hazy.

"Let's just fly and not talk about it, please?" said Nox. "And I mean, really, *don't* talk about it. The last thing my mother said to me was that if anyone found out about my little . . . quirk . . . they'd execute me too."

"Why did you never tell us before?" asked Gussie. "Didn't you trust us?"

"I . . . guess I didn't really trust anyone at all. Until you three." He cleared his throat. "Now, Sparrow, are you going to tell us about the Race of Ascension or what?"

Ellie winced. She wasn't looking forward to hearing Nox say *I told you so.* "Right, about that. Um—"

"We've got trouble!" shouted Twig, who'd been watching their rear.

Ellie rolled and peered into the dimming sky behind them. It didn't take a Hawk's sharp eyes to make out the glints in the distance—light glancing off white armor.

"Goldwings," she muttered.

In the open air, four kids would be spotted in no time. Better to hide and wait, then take off again once they had the cover of darkness.

She banked hard, leading them toward the rocky cliffs of the mountains. There were a thousand crevices riddling the slopes. Choosing one at random, Ellie hovered while the others filed in, gripping her staff and watching the sky.

For the next two hours, they crouched in silence, muscles growing stiff and wings pulled tightly against their spines. Ellie heard the voices of the Goldwings ringing through the mountains; it was impossible to tell where they were, with their shouts echoing off every cliff. Once, just after sunset, she saw a flickering torch pass by, held by a grim-faced Sir Aglassine. Ellie held her breath, not daring to even blink until the Goldwing had vanished again.

"We have to get out of here," whispered Nox. "If they spot us, we're done for."

Ellie nodded, swallowing hard. Where could they go? How far would they have to fly to be beyond Garion's reach?

"I guess . . ." She paused, her eyes picking out a single spot of light in the darkness. Had the captain returned? But this light was white, not the fiery orange of a torch. "Hey, what is that?"

Twig clapped his hands. "Moonmoth!"

The small, glowing creature swooped toward their hiding spot, fine dust trickling from its wings. It drifted closer to Nox, then alighted on his shoulder.

The others stared, breaths held. Ellie saw the surprise on Nox's face as he tried to shoo it off.

"It's Twig you want, not me, bug," he said.

But the moth refused to budge, and instead shook its wings, sprinkling his shoulder with shining dust.

"It likes you," laughed Ellie.

Finally, the moth lifted away and fluttered ahead, where it soared in a lazy circle, as if waiting for them.

"Huh," said Nox. "You know that old saying?"

"Don't go chasing moonmoths?" said Ellie.

"Let's follow it," said Nox.

Ellie stared at him. "What?"

"Um, hello?" Gussie flicked a wing. "There's a *reason* you don't go chasing moonmoths, remember? No one knows where they go."

"Which means no one will know where to look for us," he pointed out.

"You've changed," Ellie said softly. "The Nox I know would never chase a magic moth through the night sky. What's different?"

"I don't know," he grumbled. "I guess I'm tired of listening to my wings and not my heart. And I have this feeling . . . Just follow it, okay, before I change my mind?"

Ellie chewed her lip a moment before replying. "Well . . . I guess *I am* tired of following the rules."

Nox grinned.

"Follow that moonmoth!" cried Twig.

"Shhhh!" the others all hissed.

He clapped his hands over his mouth, still smiling, and sped out of the crevice. The others followed one by one, dropping out of the rock and spreading their wings in silence.

Ellie thought this was beyond risky, but maybe Nox was right. The moonmoths had to go *somewhere*, and if no one knew where that somewhere was, it could well be the safest place in the world. Besides, she couldn't think of anyplace better.

And there *was* a certain thrill in breaking the old rules.

The fluttering moth led them higher and higher, like a dancing candle flame, away from the foothills and into the mountains themselves. They flew through silent air and pockets of whirling wind as the temperature dropped and snowflakes began melting on their skin and wings. Ellie couldn't believe that, just that morning, she'd been racing up the slopes of Mount Garond. The ache of the race was catching up to her, though. She couldn't fly much farther.

But they pressed one another on, chasing the little glowing moth as it flitted through the mountains. After an hour, Ellie began gasping for breath, sure she'd made a terrible mistake. Maybe there *was* a reason people said not to go chasing moonmoths—maybe they never actually went anywhere.

Then, just when she thought she couldn't fly another wing beat, she saw lights.

"More moths?" she wondered.

"No," said Gussie. "I smell smoke."

"There's . . . a *town*," said Twig.

Sure enough, a small cluster of buildings was hidden in the vale ahead, faintly visible against the pale stone cliffs. Yellow lanterns twinkled in their windows.

"I've never heard of anyone living this far off the map," said Gussie. "Are we sure we can trust them?"

"Do we have a choice?" snorted Twig. "My wings are about to fall off. We have to land. And eat." He patted his stomach sadly.

"It could be a safe haven," whispered Ellie. "Somewhere no one knows who we are."

"But for how long?" added Nox.

Ellie met his gaze for a moment, then said, "Long enough to make a plan, I hope."

"A plan?"

"This isn't over. As long as we carry that skystone, we have a responsibility to either use it to make a difference or find someone who can."

She waited for him to argue, to tell her it wasn't his job to save the world.

But then, with a grim expression, Nox nodded. "Lead the way, then, Ellie of the Sparrows."

With a grin, Ellie flicked her wings, putting on a burst of speed. She angled for the settlement in the mountains ahead, leading their battered little band through fog and wind, guided by the gentle, fluttering light of the moonmoth.

THE CLANS OF
SKYBORN

*The Clandoms and surrounding lands are home to many scores of clans, each with its own unique identity and heritage.
Here are a few found in* Sparrow Rising.

SPARROW CLAN

CLAN SEAT: Linden

CLAN TYPE: Low

WING DESCRIPTION: Elliptical; broad shape; brown, white, and copper feathers with dark flecks. Optimal for quick takeoffs, maneuverability. Less suited for distance and speed.

WINGSPAN: Short

TRADITIONAL OCCUPATIONS: Farmers, harvesters

KNOWN FOR: Making the most popular wing oil in the Clandoms

CROW CLAN

CLAN SEAT: None

CLAN TYPE: Shattered

WING DESCRIPTION: Broad, rounded shape; black iridescent feathers. Suited for fast flying over short distances or soaring.

WINGSPAN: Medium

TRADITIONAL OCCUPATIONS: Thieves, beggars, low-wage workers

KNOWN FOR: Rumors of dark magic and treachery in the past, resulting in their official shattering by the Eagle monarchs

FALCON CLAN

CLAN SEAT: Vestra

CLAN TYPE: High

WING DESCRIPTION: Long, thin, tapered, with dark and light stripes. Ideal for speed and maneuverability. Less suited for quick takeoffs and flight in tight areas like forests or cities.

WINGSPAN: Long

TRADITIONAL OCCUPATIONS: Soldiers, knights, nobles

KNOWN FOR: Strict upbringing and training, strength, and speed as warriors

HAWK CLAN

CLAN SEAT: Norivad

CLAN TYPE: High

WING DESCRIPTION: Long, broad, with dark and light stripes on the top and very pale undersides. Ideal for distance, diving, and speed.

WINGSPAN: Medium to long

TRADITIONAL OCCUPATION: Soldiers, knights, scouts, nobles

KNOWN FOR: Keen eyesight over long distances and in poor conditions, which makes them excellent scouts and trackers

EAGLE CLAN

CLAN SEAT: Thelantis

CLAN TYPE: High

WING DESCRIPTION: Long, broad shape with dark golden-gray tops and slightly lighter undersides. Ideal for speed, diving, soaring; less maneuverable.

WINGSPAN: Very long

TRADITIONAL OCCUPATIONS: Royals, knights, nobles

KNOWN FOR: Ruling the Clandoms in a centuries-old dynasty, being fierce warriors

MOCKINGBIRD CLAN

CLAN SEAT: Illris

CLAN TYPE: Low

WING DESCRIPTION: Gray with white patches

WINGSPAN: Short

TRADITIONAL OCCUPATIONS: Translators, actors

KNOWN FOR: Being highly skilled entertainers, often transient, traveling from town to town to perform. Gifted at languages, they're often employed by high clan diplomats as translators.

CRANE CLAN

CLAN SEAT: Silvermarsh

CLAN TYPE: Low

WING DESCRIPTION: Long; white with black tips. Slow and somewhat laborious fliers, they are more prone to walking than flying when possible.

WINGSPAN: Long

TRADITIONAL OCCUPATIONS: Fishers, trappers

KNOWN FOR: Being a somewhat reclusive clan who keeps to their marshes

DOVE CLAN

CLAN SEAT: Ashfield

CLAN TYPE: Low

WING DESCRIPTION: Light gray with two dark stripes, white underneath. Suitable for gliding.

WINGSPAN: Short to medium

TRADITIONAL OCCUPATIONS: Weavers, tailors, dyers

KNOWN FOR: Uncanny ability to find their way home, no matter how lost

ACKNOWLEDGMENTS

I am incredibly grateful to the team that has become part of the Skyborn clan. Thanks to you, what started as a doodle on my high school Spanish homework has grown into a world beyond anything I could have achieved alone. Your time, passion, and expertise are the reasons this book exists, and I could not ask for a better flock to launch Ellie, Nox, and the gang into the sky!

My editor, Zack Clark, has truly been the wind beneath Ellie's wings. Thank you for believing in this world and these characters as much as I do, and sometimes more!

I'm so thankful for the amazing Scholastic team that has gathered around this book. Thank you to David Levithan for continued enthusiasm and support and to Abby McAden for championing this story. My gratitude to Melissa Schirmer, Josh Berlowitz, Sydney Tillman, and Maeve Norton for all your hard and inspiring work in bringing this book to the next level and putting it into readers' hands. It still feels surreal that I get to work with such a talented crew of people!

I cannot seem to write a book without having to pour out my love and gratitude to Jessica Brody for her insight and support. Thank you, friend, for always being such an encouragement to me!

My agent, Lucy Carson, has been my constant true north for all these years, and I'll never be able to fully express my immense appreciation for her. Thank you, Lucy, for taking Ellie under your wing even when the odds seemed small. If Ellie has even half your determination and heart, she will overcome every obstacle in her path.

My family is a steady source of support and inspiration, and my love to you all for the time you spent looking after the kiddo whenever

I needed to spend a few hours or even days immersed in this story or hitting a deadline. Literally none of my books would exist without you. My sister LeslieAnn: When you were three years old, I promised I would write a book just for you; I just didn't know that it would take me fifteen years to fulfill that promise! But it had to be the right book, and this is it. To Ellie I gave your strength of spirit, your arrow-true heart, and your boundless talent and ambition. The sky is yours, my love. Just reach up and take it.

Always, my greatest love and gratitude to Ben and my girls, for being the reason I wake up and write every day. For believing, for loving, for supporting. Thank you for being my greatest story of all.

ABOUT THE AUTHOR

Jessica Khoury is the author of many books for young readers, including *Last of Her Name*, *The Mystwick School of Musicraft*, the Corpus Trilogy, and *The Forbidden Wish*. In addition to writing, she is an artistic mapmaker and spends far too much time scribbling tiny mountains and trees for fictional worlds. She lives in Greenville, South Carolina, with her husband, daughters, and sassy husky, Katara. Find her online at jessicakhoury.com.

A SNEAK PEEK AT

SKYBORN

• BOOK 2 •

CALL OF THE CROWN

CHAPTER ONE
· CORION ·

As crown prince of the Clandoms, Corion was used to keeping odd hours.

He never knew when his father, King Garion, might summon him before dawn in order to critique the changing of the guard. Sometimes he didn't make it to bed till well after three in the morning because his father wanted to drill him on the names of every Eagle ancestor who'd ever sat on the Aerie Throne. Being the royal heir meant being prepared for all sorts of strange tests, drills, and assignments.

But he certainly *wasn't* used to being woken in the middle of the night by a blade pressed against his throat.

Eyes wide, Corion lay very still, letting his eyes adjust to the darkness. His gaze flicked to the door, then all around his grand room, but he saw no sign of his guards. There was only the lean shadow of the man bending over him, his eyes hidden behind a mask of silk. The dark outlines of his wings blocked what moonlight might have trickled through the window; they were spread to their full length, stretching even wider than Corion's four-poster bed.

"Good evening, sweet princely pie," hissed the shadow. Corion saw the pale gleam of his teeth as his lips parted in a savage grin. "What a plump and perfect little pet you are! What must it be like, to be so pampered you can't tie your own boots?"

Every muscle in Corion's body drew taut as he muttered, "Actually, I *can* tie my own boots."

Was the man an assassin? A kidnapper? If so, he was a fool. Even if he cut Corion's throat this moment, he'd never escape the palace before a dozen Goldwing knights had buried their swords in his belly.

Still. How *had* the man gotten in here? How had he slipped past the twenty guards between Corion's room and the nearest palace entrance?

"What do you want?" Corion whispered. "Money? Remove your blade, and we can talk."

The shadow only chuckled.

Then, from the doorway, a deep voice said, "He is here to see me, Corion."

The prince swallowed, his throat touching the edge of the blade as he did. "Father."

"Put down the knife, Hunter," ordered King Garion, stepping into the room. He held a slim candle, its light barely strong enough to illuminate his regal features. "You've made your point."

"Have I?" said the shadow. "I once told you I could cut any throat in the kingdom, Your *Majesty*, and yet you have forgotten poor Hunter, let me languish in boredom for years. I want *work*."

"Why else do you think I've summoned you from your web, spider?" The king's voice simmered with disdain. "Back away from my son or be crushed beneath my heel as you should have been years ago."

With a hiss, the stranger withdrew the dagger. Corion let out a long, shaky breath and sat up.

"What's going on?" the prince demanded, eyeing the tall man who still loomed over his bed. Who was this creature who dared speak to the king of the Clandoms as if he were beneath him? Usually, Garion punished such insolence with a week in the stocks—or worse.

But now his father only walked closer, setting the candle on an iron table. Its light seemed to shrink, revealing nothing of the stranger's features.

"This man is called the Hunter," said King Garion, speaking to Corion but never taking his eyes off the intruder. "And he is here because I summoned him. But there was no need for these theatrics."

"What's the job?" said the Hunter. "A throat to be sliced? A hand to be diced? It's been so long, *too* long, oh King. You promised work, as much as I could want. But I'm *bored*. You've neglected your Hunter. My blades thirst."

"Yes, yes." Garion waved a hand dismissively. "You disgusting creature, you'll have your hunt."

"He's the assassin," whispered Corion, looking with new interest at the Hunter. "Is this him, Father? The secret assassin you always said you kept in your back pocket, for the hour of most desperate need?"

"I am in nobody's *pocket*!" protested the Hunter.

"Wrong," snapped Garion. "You are mine completely. Or have you forgotten what you swore to me the day I spared your life?" The king turned to Corion, the dark gold feathers of his wings shining in the light of the candle; they must have been freshly oiled to gleam like that. "Nearly a decade ago this beast set a building on fire—just to watch everyone inside burn. He's no man, but a killer, who feeds on death as a bee feeds upon flowers."

"You didn't execute him for it?" gasped Corion.

The Hunter snickered.

"As far as the public knows, I *did*." Garion gave him a smug grin. "Here is a lesson for you, son: Never let a bad dog go to waste. Leash it, train it to heel when you call, and the day will come when it will serve you well. My dog here is a secret weapon, capable of jobs even my Goldwings cannot carry out—or should not be *seen* to."

"Enough chatter!" howled the Hunter. "What's the job? Is it a duke? Is it a whole garrison of rebels?"

"A boy," said Garion. "It's a boy I want, by the name of Nox Hatcher, though he was once called Tannox Corvain. So far my knights have failed to bring him to me. We suspect he's fled to the mountains."

Corion withheld a sigh.

This again.

It'd been weeks since the Race of Ascension, which had started out in celebration and feasting, and had ended with his father burning down an entire neighborhood in an attempt to capture some low-life thief of a Crow clanner. Since then, his father had become obsessed. Every day he called for a report from his knights, and every day they brought the same news. Not so much as a feather had been found of the one called Nox Hatcher, nor of the three kids he'd been spotted with when he fled Thelantis: a piebald, with one brown wing and one white; a Falcon girl; and a Sparrow.

Corion recalled the Sparrow, for he'd seen her with his own eyes. *Ellie Meadows.* Now, there was a girl worth remembering. She'd won the Race of Ascension, something no low clanner had ever attempted, much less accomplished. Then she'd turned out to be a thief too, having burglarized a fortress and attacked the king's own soldiers. Now she was on the run with the Crow and two other criminals, with the entire force of Goldwing knights hunting them.

And, apparently, this Hunter too.

Corion shuddered. He'd only known the man a few minutes, but he was the most terrifying person the prince had ever met. Rubbing his throat, he eyed the dagger and hoped his father's so-called *leash* was as tight as he claimed. Even if the king did have the assassin under control, Corion wouldn't sleep easy for a while after this.

"A *boy*," sneered the Hunter. "Here I stand, more hearts stilled beneath my hands than all your paltry knights combined, and you send me after a *child*?"

"That's exactly what I'm doing," retorted the king. "Dispose of his cohorts and bring him to me alive, preferably, but if you can't manage it . . . Well, the important thing is, I want him out of the way. For good."

The Hunter cocked his head, as if considering the job—actually *considering*, not snapping to attention with a crisp "Yes, Your Majesty!" as any sane citizen would have done.

In the end, though, he nodded. "Very well. I'll consent to this child's play if only to stretch my wings a bit. But after this, oh high and mighty King, I want *real* work."

"You'll take what I give and be grateful," growled Garion. "Now get out of my palace. Your stench is fouling the air."

With a hiss, the Hunter flicked his wings and backed away. At first, Corion was confused—the door was on the other side of the room.

But then the man shrank into the tiny barred window, folding himself through the iron rods as lithely as if his bones were made of paper, and then he dropped away into the night. A moment later, he lifted away on broad, silent wings. *Vulture clan*, thought Corion, identifying the man's feathers at last.

"How . . . ?" Corion stared at the window. It was built to *prevent* intruders, its narrow slats barely large enough for a cat, much less a full-grown man.

"I believe he was a circus contortionist before he turned to murder," commented the king, scratching his stubbly chin.

"He put a *knife* to my throat!" cried Corion, slinging himself to his feet and facing his father. His hands were still shaking. "And you acted like it was nothing!"

"Bah." Garion flipped his hand. "He wouldn't dare harm you in truth. He knows I'm in control. With a word from me, he'd be due straight back to the gallows."

Corion was not soothed.

"At any rate," said Garion, "that's my little problem settled. The Crow boy will be mine within the week."

But as the king took his candle and left the room, Corion couldn't help thinking that his father had said much the same words back when he'd first dispatched the knights to find the Crow boy and his friends.

He'll be mine within the week!